A Day
In The Life
Of
Timothy Stone

Steve Herman

Gravier House Press
An Independent Publishing Company
New Orleans, Louisiana
2000

Library of Congress Publication Data:

Herman, Steve.

A Day in the Life of Timothy Stone / Steve Herman.

ISBN 978-1-7335181-8-5
(Original GHP Paperback ISBN 0-9671179-3-3)

Fiction.
Library of Congress Catalog Card Number: 00-90063.
© *Copyright by Stephen Herman, 1995.*

First Edition
April 2000

For Mom

March 20, 1989

...come on and get outta that car - you and little missy ridin around in your pretty little car - i am gonna rock your world - just throw him a bone rich - shut up dan - god dammit - look if you let me kill you now i promise i will kill myself later - okay - bam - good - now lets go we gotta get to that cliff and get to the hanging garden cuz jen really needs those poppies and bbbzzzzzzz what - jen needs those zzzzz god dammit i dont want to wake up now 9:48 price is right twelve minutes what was i dreaming shit i missed jane god dammit i wonder what she was wearing red blouse what hair what was i dreaming - julie lynn - it was her and we were on that cliff and i shot that guy god he was a pain in the ass - god that was really stupid - i could see her perfectly though i can remember her better in the dream than i can in real life

hey doggie - good morning - good morning doggie - twelve minutes to janice i gotta brush my teeth i hope they have her in a bathing suit today they always have diane in the bathing suit - i dont know why - janice probably doesnt do that stuff it probably gets cold or exploitive or something - i dont understand that exploitation stuff i mean they are getting something out of it - they get money they get power they get fame and all i get is the pleasure of looking at her for five seconds and then the pain of knowing i can never have her like julie marilyn monroe and all that stuff except with more respect except you probably wouldnt even get it - she would deserve it but they wouldnt give it to her - they never give it to you - i remembered her so well she is the most beautiful girl ever divine providence on earth that first day when she sat down next to me in the auditorium darby laughing the go between which is definitely the worst book i have ever read or tried to read or been told to read i dont think i even read the cliff notes - even - julie christie is hot in darling not in heaven can wait - i should have played miss celie right there and said im black im ugly im slow i caint draw and i caint sing but ise here and im gonna make the best of what i is and she gonna play miss shug and say well all right cuz if i had been with julie all this time damn i should give old julie a call i sound like holden caufield i should give old jane a call and we could have a couple of drinks and i dont have to be home until wednesday - i wish it was then and im that person and we are those people and the world is that place with that past present future and all of those things

i wonder what jane was wearing that red outfit - god i love her - i should call julie anyway - hello is julie there - this is she - hey this is tim - hows it going - i havent seen you in so long - i know - ive missed you - thanks - me too - so hows the north country - all right - how are you doing - fine - well you know it seems like we have always been the only ones in town at the end of these vacations and i thought i would give you a call and maybe we could go out somewhere together you know - that would be great "tim"

what

"you want some breakfast"

no

"sure"

yeah - some pancakes would be good nah i dont want all i will just get something when i come down maybe some chili or some tuna fish or something i should cook some chicken - anyway that would be so cool - is julie there - speaking - hey its tim - tim who - would she say that or would she know who it was she would probably know who it was nah she wouldnt know if she had a friend named tim at school or something that would suck if i called her and said hey its tim and she said tim who - o yeah tim stone - yeah the guy thats been in love with you for seven years - i havent seen you in so long - what have you been up to - same old thing different place that sounds so stupid i would say not much or something - what about you - not much - i thought maybe we could go out somewhere or something - that would be great - is tonight good - tonights fine tonights terrific tonight is excellent unsurmountable and superciliously sweet tonight is impossible - so what time should i pick you up - ten would be good - or do you want to drive - no thats all right - i just didnt know if you have become one of those new liberal women who wear black and drink coffee and smoke cigarettes and sometimes shave their legs and all they talk about is the c i a and abortion and rape that would suck - those people calling themselves liberals are so closeminded about everything that they are really conservative trying to tell everybody what words to use jumping in my freedom of speech freedom of architecture all that stuff about phallic symbols pretty soon they are gonna force us to build downward - dig out these great big oval trenches and stick some offices in there - plant some bushes around the perimeter but sheez not a liberated woman - she is a liberated woman but not a pseudolesbian - sheez one of those unfeminist feminists like annie who just want to be left alone - annie is really cool about stuff like that even though she did want to go out into the yuppy business world for some stupid reason i dont know why she didnt want to teach but you would be such a good teacher - thats such a horrible thing to say -

why is it a horrible thing to say - its chauvinistic - thinking that a woman should be a teacher - a woman should be a woman - whats that supposed to mean - i dont know - it means that some women would make better teachers than they would stock brokers and some women would make better stock brokers but those women are probably just stupid bitches anyway who dont know shit about people - just forget it

god i hate that when you wont let things get as hot as they can be just cut off that emotion all that energy - i dont want to fight about it - what could be better than a good fight - a lot of things - like what - a good picnic - ill do anything with you dont get me wrong im just a little stymied about a picnic - you got ants - ants get in the food - you got to eat on the ground - its better in front of the tv - ill do anything with you dont get me wrong - im just a little stymied about a picnic

yeah julies not one of those feminists - she doesnt want to paint everything red and hang pictures of naked women all over throw tampons and hardboiled eggs well damn them eggs and all the eggs there ever was - what was i thinking

okay - ill see you - i cant wait - hey - hey - how have you been - fine - how come youre not off in the bahamas or someplace - i just wanted to come home and spend some time with my family - thats nice - how are your sisters - theyre doing well - thats good - i think im going off to europe for a month this summer with some of my friends from school and maybe jennifer and steph might come so anyway i thought that i am going to be with them enough you know so i thought i just needed a break from all the hassle and stuff so now you know what a nerd i really am - a nerd - you are the most beautiful girl i have ever seen woman now its woman you are the most beautiful woman i have ever seen - thanks - you dont believe me - look i know that everyone is talking about how ive gained all this weight and how i look like shit - come on youre beautiful - whatever - she would never say that i would hope god i hate it when people dont look at the whole of a person and all they talk about is what parts are nice and what parts are ugly pieces parts like chicken mcnuggets god that pisses me off - oh she has a great rack - thats great what are you gonna do you gonna chop off her rack and marry it - jesus - you look at the woman and she is ugly or she is beautiful - thats a fine ass - well you can marry an ass but i want the whole woman - im not talking about the woman youre gonna marry im just talking about some chick - oh well then its okay

i want to marry an aura thats the most important thing the aura - do you believe in auras - sure - you do - not that there is an area around people but that you can know things about people feel things about people before you actually know them - or the area not really around them but the energy they emit - or the area not surrounding them but that - they consume - it has to do with motion - its like the difference between a static woman or a woman in motion - a woman is completely different in motion - the motion of her - thats the aura - god who cares if she is fat its only compared to the fact that she was perfect before besides it doesnt even matter there are a lot of girls who are skinny ugly girls and girls that are pretty and skinny but theyre not sexy theres nothing sexy about them you have to have a little weight to be sexy you have to have some meat on you you have to have some curves i mean look - if people are saying stuff like that its because those people looked at you but they never really looked at you - i mean its you that always made you so beautiful - me - yeah you - you were never afraid - afraid 9:57 three minutes to janice - what

oh yeah exactly i mean other girls were just as pretty - i mean i thought gayle was and jennifer and charmaine - but they were afraid and you never were - you were

never afraid - well gayle wasnt afraid thats not fair
gayle was really cool - not cool - special - gayle was
really special and courageous and you know she would
just be sitting and knitting and you would think she was
thinking about something stupid off quiet not paying
attention and then she would jump in there with this
little sarcastic twang and really let you have it - i loved
it when she got scott - yeah me too - california - what
was i saying

you were never afraid - you were never afraid of
talking to the wrong person or liking the wrong person
or being seen with the wrong person or wearing the
wrong clothes or the right ones - or the right ones
because feeling that you always have to wear tie dyes
and cutoff jeans is no more liberated than the person
who always wears duckheads and an oxford anyway
she wasnt you werent afraid of being yourself of saying
what you wanted i mean like when we were doing the
yearbook stuff at janes house and you and i were just
going off and everyone else was trying to be prudent i
mean that is the quintessential charmaine sitting in a
chair and trying to be prudent and then jennifer is the
other side who wasnt ever prudent but thats because she
was always trying to turn somebody on - but you were
just being - like you came into school as susans sister i
mean for two years you have been the little sister of
susan venus aphrodite i mean there was something so
godlike and classical about her beauty - she

there are some people who are beautiful and you call
them a goddess but theyre not really a goddess in the
way that you would envision a goddess - its just a form
of compliment - but susan lynn was a goddess in the
true sense of the word that she resembled aphrodite i
mean literally - and we had so many visions of her
unmolested and virgin in perfect beauty and now thats
all gone

anyway - what was i saying

oh yeah - you came in as susans little sister and within one week you were already julie - and - what else did she do

the divorce - and the way in which you handled your parents divorce at the jazz fest dancing off to the side while jennifer and steph were standing around trying to look so cool but you werent afraid to look a bit stupid i heard you took a piss on the floor in the cats meow is that true

that kinda bums me out

my love she speaks like silence

have you ever heard love minus zero no limit - i dont think so - my love she speaks like silence - without ideals or violence - she doesnt have to say sheez faithful yet sheez true like ice like fire - people carry roses matchsticks or is it matchsticks people carry matchsticks make promises by the hour people carry roses make promises by the hour - thats right - people carry roses - make promises by the hour - my love she laughs like the flower oh yeah thats right because roses goes with flower - my love she laughs like the flower valentines cant buy her - the cloak and dagger dangles - madams light the candles and candles go with matchsticks - thats right - the cloak and dagger dangles madams light the candles - in the ceremonies of the horsemen even a pawn must hold a grudge - statues made of matchsticks crumble into one another - my love winks she does not bother - she knows too much to argue or to judge

i wanna be your hero - mighty youngblood wishes he was famous - mister moses just wants someone to believe you believe in miracles - i believe in you if you believe in me

give me something to believe in timmy

on - up - yes - "come on down - jim hollis - come on down" EASTERN MICHIGAN where the hell is eastern michigan black river harbor no thats southern michigan western lansing is detroit in eastern "heather stansfield come on down youre the first contestants on the price is right - and now - here is the star of the price is right - bob barker" look at this guy this guy is such a bozo if you could count up all the times "here is the first item up for bids"

"its a new motor scooter from honda" aw its holly god dammit "scooter to the actual retail price" those are good dresses though - good hourglass people dont like hourglass anymore i like the top part of the hourglass like thirty six twenty four thirty thin hips but no big hips are good too it doesnt matter it just depends on the girl "what do you say heather" i dont know like nine hundred what did mopeds cost like five or six so this is probably nine if you buy it - eleven or twelve by price is right standards "eight seventy five" thats a good bid "jim" maybe low "seven ninety five" thats too low you gotta go higher "heather" heathers grim "nine fifty" 950 "grace youre it" eleven hundred "twelve hundred dollars" maybe too high "and the actual retail price of the motor scooter is eighteen hundred" jesus christ that is ridiculous who in their right mind would buy that piece of shit for two thousand bucks - you can get a car for that much - were there two was there a pair of them "right here next to me" get a kiss bob "hello grace" nah he doesnt kiss the black women you think he fucks them oh yeah - not janice janice would never do that - she was in playboy - she was a miss u s a - miss america - yeah miss america - whats miss u s a - its like our representative to the miss universe pageant - why dont we just use miss america - i dont know - i like missus americas - mom pies - yeah thats sexy those miss america people all look so fake theyre completely manufactured - theyre like barbie dolls - theyre pretty but to look at but theyre not sexy at all - but like missus america a married woman a mother thats like a real person she has a physical existence thats real and that is just so sexy - they can be sexy "behind those doors" a jukebox "a new refrigerator freezer and a lovely dinette set" oh god holly and diane where is janice i hope sheez not sick today or something "the kitchenaid twenty one cubic foot side by side refrigerator freezer with ice and water dispenser on the door - easy to clean glass shelves - preventing frost - and second this oak dinette group" what was i talking about julie lynn oh yeah julie she is so beautiful - what were we talking about bob dylan

love minus zero no limit - thats right - she knows too much to argue or to judge

thanks - i dont deserve it though - i wish i could sing or that i could at least make up my own lyrics so that i wouldnt have to be quoting people all the time - but once you get something in your head from a song or a poem you cant really start to make up another alternative in your own words i mean you start off with a few phrases and then you start to realize that you are making up a song which has already been - written whats the word for written

composed - and theres no way you can express that better - its so annoying i dont see how musicians write any songs at all its all been done - so anyway - julie - where do you want to go - ive never been to your place - my place whats that - bennys - oh okay - i thought she wanted to go to my place no cuz then it would be all over and they lived happily ever after living happily ever after and dying happily ever after is exactly the same

"grace - we have shell game for you to play - there is a ball under one of the these shells - you put a chip beside the shell that has the ball under it and you win those prizes" what was it a jukebox a refrigerator right and a dinette set piece of shit they dont even have janice out there "you know youve seen this" "yes" "whats the first prize" "an oak country wall telephone with country brass hardware and a light oak finish"

$100 a hundred dollars "now a hundred dollars is the wrong price" oh okay that makes sense "is the right price higher or lower" higher "higher" "you say higher and it is" HIGHER $140 "igher - so you get this chip"

"we would like to see another prize"

"all right - here we go - for deluxe instant photos of all your celebrations the polaroid two thousand has ten zone focus with built in autoflash and timer" eighty five dollars $65 "sixty five dollars is the wrong price - is the right price higher or lower" higher higher - higher "lower" no you stupid bitch that camera doesnt cost less than sixty five bucks HIGHER $105 "oh no - that was higher" oh god they are never gonna put janice on this thing

so what was i thinking we were going to eat no we were going to bennys - so you want to go to bennys - i thought you wanted to go to my place - no lets go to bennys - you guys used to go dancing there a lot - yeah - i dont know if she really liked it though - i think she just went there for me - low rider gonna get a little higher dum dum dum badum pah - low rider gonna get a little higher dum dum dum badum pah - this is war huh - yeah - they play a lot of blues and stuff like that - this place is so cool - yeah - it used to be just completely a neighborhood bar when robert found it and then he brought me here and we were like the only white people here and then all these tulane students came and now its just a bunch of yuppies but i guess thats just the way it goes - yeah but it goes the other way too - i heard bob dylan bought a house right around here on soniat i could easily imagine seeing him just hangin out in the back that loser dennis quaid used to play here all fucked up he plays the bass or something - bob dylan is proteus reinhart okay so we have bob dylan who is proteus reinhart who is like the bard or the minstrel and then we have hendrix who is like the blake and bigger thomas and and and - the other - where was i

- oh yeah - lets go in the back you can see well and they have a great drummer - you want something to drink - i want a black russian and a tom collins - i like a lot of grenadine - this drummer is awesome - yeah - professor longhair has all these drummers around cuz his beats were so messed up that anyone who had ever learned how to play drums in the classical style couldnt play because it wouldnt make sense so he just had to take these people completely from scratch and teach them how to play from scratch so now there are apparently these professor longhair drummers who cant play for anyone else - i dont know if its true but its a great story i hate people who disregard great stories because theyre not true - there is truth in any great lie story

i saw professor longhair at the jazz fest one time with my dad but i was too young to really remember him - he was just like sweeping up in a warehouse or something when he got old and doctor john found him in some warehouse and started getting him work again cuz before they would just like take him into the studio and have him cut a record and pay him like a hundred dollars or something and just send him right back onto the street - so who is this guy - thats j d - jefferson davis jammer no i dont know theyre called j d hill thats his name j d hill and they are called j d and the jammers the bar is owned by this guy benny hill but i dont think theyre related and z z hill the blues are alright is probably their uncle z z the blues are alright no down home blues z z down home blues hill oliver who shot the la la morgan jessie ooh pooh pah do hill - and so anyway i wonder if he is related to jesse ooh pooh pah do hill is probably a cousin of zz hill who has nothing to do with benny or j d - but so anyway i dont know if he even owns it its like a front for the neville brothers who grew up actually right there on valance and they wanted to have a neighborhood music bar with no admission so they started up this place and cyril used to

always play with these guys and deacon johns brother
charles moore who is the best bass player and they had
this awesome guitar player named george who
disappeared and cyril would play these bongos and
what the hell are they called tympanies no thats the
symphony reggae drums i dont know what theyre called
and sing and this guy would play drums james and j d
would play harmonica and sing backup and george
would play guitar and um charles moore would play
bass the uptown allstars cyril neville and the uptown
allstars and they were so good - they would play like
this mix of blues and reggae - it was good

you wanna dance - sure - take a little trip - take a
little trip - take a little trip with me - take a little trip -
take a little trip - take a little trip and see dum dum dum
dum badum pow - that was great - you wanna go to
preservation hall - sure - high reesa - high tim - this is
my friend julie this is reesa lombard - nice to meet you -
nice to meet you - is benjy here - no heez not here
tonight you guys wanna come in for a set - sure - come
on in - thanks - wont you come home bill bailey - wont
you come home - oh she cried the livelong night - she
said she would do the cooking and she would pay the
rent - oohhh you didnt have a cent - do you remember
that rainy night - she booted you out - nothin - but a
fine toothed comb - aint it a shame - you knew you
were to blame - bill bailey - wont you please come
home

thank you - bye tim - nice meeting you - nice
meeting you julie - tell benjy i came by - lets go
someplace where we can talk - okay - i know
someplace - here - out there over the levee theres this
bicycle slash jogging path i came here with tommy
once when we were in high school - it was all windy
and wet with the mist and we sat out here listening to
u2 and watching the waves come in on the steps and
you can see the lights going out over the causeway and

they would just fade away into nothing - it was the unforgettable fire - post holocaust - the stand - a brave new world - a clockwork orange and all that - with all the moonlight in the mist not really a clockwork orange with the moonlight and the mist all bubbled up and washed and crashing against the sand and stone where marking out the pitchforks and the razorblades with marksalot and washing dress machines all carried to the rows of blazing steel and ore

i was thinking about all those fish who are swimming away from us because they think we are coming for them with our nets

to gather them up for sunday dinner you see the fish are very wary of our paws so big and harry causing them to think that we are rather scary - at times - of course - why shouldnt they - we killed so many redfish god you could build a world trade center with the redfish those japs came over and stole those bastards - the greatest thrill is not to kill - i bet thats not true though its probably just a bunch of crap someone made up - it was probably some cajuns or something blew them up with dynamite like they did with all the fish in greece - but redfish does make good sushi though - yeah i hate sushi - anyway

the greatest thrill is not to kill - but to let live - but to let live - for when you look upon the sill and shining singing gold of dawn comes down and fawns the lampshade to the windy winding howl outside of geese and fowl abound and when you hear the sound of crickets moaning in the morning please dont scorn and give to every motion you can give - the greatest thrill is not to kill - but to let live - but to let live

so nothing ever happened with you guys - no - i think that there is a certain woman who is a girlfriend and a certain woman who is a wife - and i never really wanted a girlfriend i wanted a wife and i kinda skipped the girlfriend stage - whats the difference - well i think a wife is a bit more conservative and virginal and honest and mature and real and a girlfriend is more young and playful and sexy and i think that annie really wanted a boyfriend not a husband who would entertain her and play all of the games and all of that shit - i dont know - she wanted flowers and a movie and some funny conversation about do you know what adrienne did with sam the other night and can you believe whats going on on days with nick do you watch days - i love days - its really funny - i missed a whole term of classes cuz the class was at one oclock when days comes on - how did you do - not very well but it was just some stupid philosophy course or something - are you still premed - i think so - you know whats weird - what - i love physics - yeah me too - i hate the math but i love the actual physics - yeah i always had lab after days and i would get there after everyone else was leaving and do lab by myself which was pretty cool cuz i could fool around and stuff but there was no one to help me out except a couple of times there was this one girl that would come and she was really pretty she was sort of elizabethan - kinda yellow or orange - a bit red - from that part of the spectrum - very quiet - i got the impression that she really didnt want to be a doctor maybe a nurse but not one of those businesslike nurses but a kind of a nurse a spiritual nurse - maybe a gypsy or something a psychiatrist thats it she must have been trying to become a psychiatrist i never thought of it - maybe i will go to her and pour out my heart on her couch god i loved her i mean i didnt love her but i loved her - i could have loved her - thats great - but what about "oil of olay" sheez pretty "ill never go back to pasty dentures again" well neither will i that is so gross these people putting that plastic teeth in their mouth and glue it to their gums why dont you throw the food in a blender and mix it up i love those shakes with eggs and everything theyre thick and healthy i feel so sorry for old people it would be so hard and depressing when you lose your husband or your wife when people have been together for a long time and one of them dies the other one goes to pieces - yeah its sad "and our next contestant is" "sharon carlson - come on down" sharon has tits "the next contestant on the price is right" look at her oh sheez kinda fat no sheez pretty her face is really pretty "to this" she looks like the sensuous redhead with beautiful eyes and beautiful breasts "a new telescope" theres janice she looks good "the cambridge telescope fashioned in mahogany with adjustable brass mounted on an original brass tripod" pan left pan left "optical system" oh there she is "that guy looking through the telescope" yeah zoom in "is holding a beautiful puppy from the glendale society" are those nipples no its just the bra "cuz they need a home" look at sharon - sharon wants that puppy oh those are nipples "now sharon what do you bid on the telescope" dont listen to these assholes they dont know anything "eight hundred" "and heather" heathers grim "eight twenty five" thats good trump her EASTERN MICHIGAN 550 oh jim come on you gotta be dry humpin me blind "and dawn" dawns got tits "one thousand" yeah sheez gonna win "and the actual retail price is one thousand five hundred and fifty dollars" fifteen hundred dollars good christ look at those tits she is young - thats not sexy thats disgusting she is really young

"now dawn - you have a very nice smile" sheez got the kappa alpha theta tooth problem "a lot in contestants row - but i bet you will be smiling a lot more" a new car "if you win this" a new car "a new car" i knew it is it janice no it wont be janice she did the intro "a ford probe" back back oh its holly shit i hate holly - holly is trying to get ahead with acting diane is trying to get ahead with sex janice is already married and sheez happy with her job and she doesnt want anything so she just does whatever they tell her not

whatever they tell her but she just takes the leading role
sheez classy - do you think she doesnt do the bathing
suit cuz you dont have to do that anymore cuz you pay
your dues and do the bathing suit when you start and
then after a while you dont have to do that anymore - or
do you think that they wont let her cuz sheez too old
and they want the young chicks in the bathing suit - i
dont know - its probably sheez offended or insulted that
she doesnt do it any more - but at the same time she
doesnt want to do it cuz its degrading - degrading she
was in playboy - yeah but that was a long time ago -
they didnt even show bush back then - really - no - they
didnt show bush until like nineteen seventy five - when
was she in - may seventy one - you know the issue - of
course - its blue with a scuba outfit on the front - is that
janice in the scuba outfit - no

she was young she was innocent she was just - sheez
a whore - she was miss u s a and then she did playboy
and then she probably fucked bob barker a few times
and now she holds up cards in front of prizes - yeah but
people do a lot of jobs that are more offensive than that
- i mean in the scale of all the things you can do to
make money being on some game show is relatively
inoffensive - i bet he fucks diane - oh yeah definitely -
he definitely fucks diane sheez a slut - sheez fat - i bet
he fucked janice when she first came on the show and -
but not any more - but anyway so there are five women
- the sister the lover the girlfriend the wife and the
friend - janice is the wife and annie c julie is the
girlfriend there is something else - what else is there -
sister girlfriend lover girlfriend already said that lover
girlfriend wife friend - sister lover girlfriend friend wife
friend - what - camera subject thats it subject but you
are the girlfriend

you are the girlfriend you are the quintessential
girlfriend - me - actually c is the quintessential
girlfriend - who is - c sheez very sexual very blue in

constitution very blue and sexual you are an art history major right - yeah - well you know that renoir the boating party where they are eating lunch with the sailboats in the background and they have the girl up in front to the left who is kissing the dog - yeah - well c is that girl who is kissing the dog - sheez ava gardner in night of the iguanas - she must be very beautiful - she has these piercing eyes you can see them from a mile away you can see them in the dark theyre so cool - sheez been around since the beginning of time and so have you - me - sure you were in troy rome - i was - sure - helen cleopatra do you believe in reincarnation - elizabeth taylor sheez a little but elizabeth taylor but mostly ava gardner since the beginning of time - sure - i used to be a rock - and you will be a rock and the sun and the sea and the air we are never born and we never die its the second rule of thermodynamics that the sum of matter and energy is a constant and nothing is ever lost we are never born and we never die we are just changing forms

so anyway tell me why i should be your girlfriend - not just my girlfriend but the girlfriend - and i guess all the others - what others - theres the girlfriend and the wife and the sister and the lover and the subject and the friend - the sister is like the woman with whom you love and youre close to but youre not intimate theres nothing sexual and you cant really tell them any secrets which is the main difference between a sister and a friend you love your sister more but you would tell a friend a secret or share something especially if you were drunk that you wouldnt tell your sister - why - because you have to put on airs for your sisters you have to look good in front of them you have to try to impress them so you cant really let your guard down let down the walls - especially in your case because you pretty much had to be a parent - yeah i guess so - thats probably part of it - you would have been a good sister

to have cuz you would have always brought hot girls
over to the house which would have been nice - shut up
- then theres the lover and thats the person who has no
identity its like dark and secretive and ethereal you dont
really hate her but you dont like her theres a little bit of
hatred and its like transgression and maybe almost rape
the devil not the devil but she evokes the devil in you -
and you dont want to know her or talk to her or
anything about her like in the graduate its just pure lust
just nameless faceless dark secret adulterous lust judy
judy hamilton michael hamiltons mom she is so sexual
she is the most sexual woman sheez not even that pretty
sheez kind of ugly but she is so sexual i love her i mean
i dont love her but i lust her she is so sexual she is the
quintessential lover - and the subject is like the same
thing but on the other side its not sexual its completely
visual and spiritual and its just a photograph like you
just want to look at her and watch her and appreciate
her beauty from a distance with no violation no
conversation no revelation no interaction and its not
sexual its aesthetic - thats what a lot of girls dont
understand about playboy - a lot of them are sexual and
base and disgusting and all of that but a lot of them are
not really sexual at all - theyre just aesthetic - its just
like in art you have these nudes which arent sexual -
they dont turn you on - they appeal to your intellect and
your eye not to your bowels or your genitals - thats the
difference
        girlfriend wife sister lover subject whats the other
one
        friend - oh friend - yeah the friend is just someone
that you like but theres nothing sexual but theres
something intimate because theres nothing sexual so
you can let your guard down and not be afraid to share
something but she likes you thats always the problem
its always that one just wants to be a friend and the
other wants something more and then you realize that

so then you put the guard back up because you dont want her or him to fall in love with you and then youll have to hurt them which sucks men and women cant be friends sex always gets in the way - i remember you said that men and women cant be friends - thats right they cant - well what if the girl is ugly - eh you pretty much wanna nail them too - so what happened to you and dave - when he went off to school i realized that i had really been in kind of a bubble there for all of those years with all of these feelings for other guys that i had been sublimating all of the time and then i kinda knew that he was fooling around with other people at school and then everything just kinda dissolved it was really bad for a while but i mean i still care about him a lot - we still talk and stuff - when we broke up i felt like there was this great freedom that had been lifted from over me but at the same time i was sad because i always thought that we were going to get married and have this beautiful perfect life together and live happily ever after - and that whole - myth was gone - but living happily ever after and dying happily ever after is practically the same thing - i mean i dont want to be missus brady or june cleaver - i love that show - the brady bunch - leave it to beaver - wallie was so cute - you think so - when i was young i had a crush on him and then i saw him in one of those shows that they are doing now and he is such a geek - oh my god - and the beaver is fat - thats so funny that he got fat and june looks exactly the same - id still fuck her - thats nice

   this guy is such a ted - whats a ted - a nerd a loser a fag a geek a ted - i think it was derived originally from ted knight on the mary tyler moore show - i dont think that anyone is ever a nerd until someone calls him a nerd - thats a good quote like if there is a fly i dont kill the fly because i hate the fly i kill it because i hate the annoyance - do you think that god does not know that he is being worshipped in the pictures and images do

you not think if a worshipper makes a mistake god will
not know his intentions - what the father said in the
garden by cutting the poppies the son understood but
the messenger did not hamann thats how you know if
youre successful if you only have one name plato
shakespeare milton faulkner melville hamann stone
who the heck is hamann where is that fear and
trembling thats the epigram for fear and trembling
kirkegaard nietzsche kant darwin einstein fraud
shakespeare milton coleridge byron blake joyce
faulkner de vinci michelangelo stone what was i
thinking

so what is this sisters theory - if a guy has a sister
then he is more he has more he thinks of women more
in the virgin great whore dichotomy - he has one set of
women who he sees as on this pedestal and virginal and
good and pure and true and he loves them spiritually
and aesthetically but not sexually supersexually - but
not sexually - and then there is the great whore for
whom he has no respect but he wants to fuck and has
lust - and he puts women in one or the other category -
where guys who dont have sisters just kind of think of
girls all the same - they just like them more or less but
if they are pretty they want to have sex with them and if
not then no but its along a continuum they dont see
women as quantifiably different - but guys who have
sisters they see women in an entirely different way - so
theyre more respectful - to some - they are more
respectful of the ones they respect but they are less
respectful of and more hostile and belligerent and
degrading or whatever to the ones they dont have
respect for the great whore dichotomy virgin great
whore because everyone thinks its mothers but its not -
its sisters the sound and the fury - like in the sound and
the fury with dalton ames its did you ever have a sister -
did you - its caddy that drives him crazy not his mom -
its a freudian book but faulkner was smarter than freud

because its sisters and the original catholic - whoever it was that created the virgin great whore dichotomy - saint paul - he had a sister i guarantee it - and so anyway - but what was i thinking

judy hamilton - an affair is a sad thing i mean i always feel like crying when i think about a woman having an affair - i mean it would be great and i would love it and it would be exciting but it just seems so sad and lonely there is nothing lonelier than a married woman having an affair - i mean when its the man having the affair its different because heez like some asshole who is going out on some conquest with some secretary bimbo who is just some stupid whore and its just kind of dirty and bad but its not sad - but with a woman who is married having an affair it seems like it would come out of this emptiness like this empty lake desert like a mirage thats what it is its like a mirage there would be this oasis which would be great but not the beauty of the oasis but like the transparency of it all but if there is going to be an affair it might as well be between me and judy hamilton or aunt grace but she would never love me julie would never love me they always love those assholes like david they want a challenge c wants a challenge they dont want to be comfortable they dont want someone to make them happy people are so afraid i am the real challenge they dont want a challenge but im so ugly god i wish i werent ugly i wanna be jim rogers - jim rogers is ugly - yeah but

how can you talk to people who can have anyone that they want - why would they want me - i mean i would want me - im the balls - i would treat her better than anyone else but how would she know that unless she wanted me enough in the first place to find out and i dont want some ugly girl so why should they see through to the inner me if i wont see through to the inner them but its really the outer them the aura and

caroline is ugly but i had a crush on her - but you
thought she was pretty - but no one else did - thats why
i need gayle im going to have to marry gayle she is the
only person who ever wanted me except jennifer i hate
jennifer i mean i guess i hate her maybe i love her
maybe she is the most beautiful girl in the world thats a
scary thought no we have to say the sexiest but c is the
most sexual but jennifer is the sexiest and annie is the
loveliest and julie is the most beautiful and susan is the
most godlike and judy hamilton is the most ethereal or
is it ethereal is the sky like ether no earth eartherial
doesnt sound right whats the opposite of ethereal
material no

celestine olympic cathonic apollonian dionysian
etherial material mystical metaphysical base thats what
it really is base

but how would everything sexual is so unsexual i
mean we make it so unsexual that it becomes more and
more sexual like a hand covering the breast please let it
down but when she drops her hand its not as sexual
anymore its weird - dont you think thats weird - lets go
get something to eat - whats open - we could go down
to the quarter and get some coffee and doughnuts - all
right - god i wonder if a girl knows what goes on in a
guys mind i wonder if she knows that every guy that
sees her says i want to fuck her he looks at her for one
second and says i want to fuck her - god thats offensive
- god that pisses me off - thats so lifes so complicated -
so what do you really want to know - i want to know
how it feels when wherever you go you look around
you and you see all of these guys and you know that
they immediately just want to fuck you or in some cases
make love to you my aim is true love you make love to
you but most just want to fuck you and that knowledge
is so powerful - you know - i mean are you flattered or
are you offended or bothered by it or what - well first of
all not every guy looks at me and wants to sleep with

me - thats what you think yes they do - i dont think so - anyway it mostly depends on the guy i mean if he is gorgeous and i notice him looking at me then i am flattered but if its just some cheezy guy then its annoying and sometimes i get scared - what do you mean - well - uh - one night i was at this party at this house - i was a sophomore - and i was between guys - just dancing and stuff - trying to have fun - without getting too serious or anything - and there is this guy there - who i have seen around and i dont really know who he is but ive seen him around - and he is okay - not really handsome or anything - and he asks me to dance - and im like okay why not - and so we are dancing and all of the sudden one of his friends is coming by with this huge plastic mug and spills beer all over me - i mean all over me - i mean you always get a little beer spilled on you at a party and its no big deal but i was soaked - and im really cold and its a long way back to the dorm and so the guy asks me and im not even sure if he didnt set the whole thing up i mean he could have like told his friends to spill it on me i dont know - but anyway he asks me if i want to go up and put on one of his tshirts - and i know what he is thinking - but i figure i will just put it on and dodge him tell him i want to dance some more you know - i mean to be honest i might have fooled around with him a little if he ended up being cool and i was a little drunk and everything but - but

you dont have to talk about this if you dont want to - no i want to - i mean i think i should talk about it - okay let me pull over - thanks - so he gets me his shirt and he like turns his back like he isnt gonna look - and so i - you know - i turned my back to him and took my shirt off - and really quick put the other shirt on - and then all of the sudden he wraps his arms and i can feel his arms around my stomach - and i spun around trying to push him off - and then he reaches out with one of his arms and turns on the stereo really really loud so that no one can hear and it was this really bad classical stuff like an opera and i started reaching for the stereo and yelling get offa me you fuckin bastard and he was like ripping my bra off and then he threw me on the bed and i punched him in the face pretty hard i didnt think i could hit him that hard and he grabbed his nose and called me a bitch and i lunged at him but he just grabbed me and he was pretty big that he could hold me down and his nose was bleeding and it was dripping down on me it was so gross and i spit at him and i spit in his hair and then i grabbed it with my teeth but it just fell through and he started to pull down my jeans and i really wanted to hurt him i was trying to hurt him but i couldnt and i screamed but no one could hear me and i would get my hands loose a few times but then he would just fall on me with his body and knock all of the wind out of me and i was trying to catch my breath and coughing and then

it hurt so much which i dont really understand because usually its fun so it must be psychological it must be really psychological because it hurt so much and it seemed like it lasted forever - it couldnt have been more than a minute or so but it seemed like it lasted forever - here - thanks - and and and so i just felt so dirty you know and so cold so dirty and cold so he got up and said to me he said you tell anyone and youre dead and then he said by the way youre all right like its supposed to be some sort of compliment or something - and i just started to cry because i never hated anyone before not like i hated him and i have never felt so empty and alone he left the room and i was just lying there not even crying anymore and i was so cold i couldnt move and i just laid there for like an hour or i dont even know how long but it seemed like hours and i could hear the music coming through the floor and the hall from downstairs and everybody laughing and

talking and i just felt so empty and cold and alone with
all this stuff in my mind because it was unreal like a
dream and you cant believe that it actually happened or
that its actually true and its like when youre about to
fall asleep and all of these myriad thoughts come
rushing into your mind at tangents and you have all of
these thoughts that dont even make any sense which
you are thinking and then you have what you are
hearing and then what you are seeing and ill never
forget the ceiling of that room - the white cold tiles -
and then i got up and it took me like ten minutes to get
up and i was so weak i just stood there wiping my eyes
and the blood off my face and chest onto his shirt but i
just didnt have any energy i just didnt care i didnt care
about anything i just wanted to go to sleep for like
twenty years and then wake up all married and safe in a
big white house with kids and a dog and then i put my
bra back on and i had pulled up my jeans but my
panties were ripped so i started to go though his clothes
to get some of his boxers but then when i thought about
him standing inside the boxers i started to get sick and i
ripped them off and then i opened up his desk drawer
and i found some scissors and i cut the boxers i guess it
was pretty stupid but i cut his boxers into nothing and
then i see all of his fucking posters on the wall his
fucking swimsuit calendars and christie brinkley posters
and budweiser with these fucking blonde whores in
bathing suits half naked and cut them all up and ripped
them and i wanted to smash things but i knew it would
make noise and i didnt want him to come back because
i would have taken those scissors and stabbed him or
something because i was just so sad and ashamed and
alone you dont know what its like just like so alone and
so i cut all of his wires to his computer and his stereo
and i found his wallet and i cut up his i d and all of his
credit cards and there was like sixty dollars and i took it
and cut it up into little pieces so then i walked home but

it wasnt like i was walking it was like i was crawling only on my feet and when i got home i went into the bathroom and turned on the shower and took off my clothes and sat down under the shower for like an hour i sat down on the floor with the water running all over me and it was wet leaves falling all over me these dark green leafy leaves and they stuck to my skin and they would start to drip down into those little rivers that go down you - you know - but there would must be more not a storm just this soft drizzling but like it would never stop night and not dusk either or clouds of like purple or orange but just night and i dont even know where the light is coming from that shone from the leaves a streetlamp and there is a streetlamp and the leaves and the water and the black and i think i might have fallen asleep - i did - i fell asleep in there and i was dreaming about this soccer game that i played in once when we were younger and i was wearing these pink longjohns and then i woke up and i got up and i just walked to my room and i never dried off or put on my clothes - i just didnt have the energy - i didnt care - and i climbed onto my bed and i cried for a while and then i went to sleep - did you report it - yeah i woke up the next day and went to my counselor and talked to her and i just sat there for like an hour and i couldnt say anything because it was like in a dream and i couldnt still believe that it had happened but i knew that once i said it out loud then it would become real

shit i wonder if she really did get raped - i hope not - did i hear that somewhere she got date raped at school - no "im doing okay this year - whats my average - its about"

"its sixty three"

"its higher than sixty three"

"its higher than sixty three"

"well im going to make this one right here" this guy is such an asshole - he gets to sit around and watch janice all day and all he does it putt some golfball into a hole and be a dick to these old people who cant even hear what the hell he is saying - he is such a ronald reagan wannabe - he should definitely be the next president - heez stupid heez an actor heez old heez an asshole conservative old gray fuck from orange county john wayne airport probably voted for goldwater in sixty four i was goldwater in sixty four and all that - just stopped dying his hair i should definitely call "well jim - you get another chance - you know why" why bob "because we are playing hole in one - or two" oh my god this is stupid - i hope nothing happened to her she is such a good person - that is so rare - i mean when do you ever find a genuinely nice person - its so hard to find rare is such a good word - rare - things are so rare theres been an accident son - beth - lynn - come here please - this is probably the worst thing youll ever hear - its the worst thing ive ever had to say - kids - im very sorry - theres been an accident - your parents are dead

"okay - everyone is trying to convince heather that she has the possibility of getting up on stage" and we go - lassie go - and we all go together - in the wild mountain time - all around the blooming heather - come on dah dah dah tatatatatata bom bom bom tatatatatata bom bom bom whats a lassie lassie the dog i hate lassie a young girl in ireland a virgin a lassie no a virgin is not a lassie a lassie is open for business - she does - "what are you grinning about sharon - youve been down here a long time yourself" sharon is a lassie the rose of sharon sad eyed lady of the low land barbara ellen she looks like the sensuous redhead with beautiful eyes and beautiful breasts "whos next"

"none other than cruz cortez" cortez what are those crackers cortez they look like dogfood constantinos conquistadors thats right they look like dog food what is this woman doing sheez lost - sheez fuckin lost - she doesnt know what sheez doing "cruz cortez who is down here with all of these beautiful young ladies with blue and white shirts" its like a fucking bowling team "volunteers from bakersfield - i hope you get around that hospital better than you get around this studio" ha - bob - he kills me "we are worried about the patients - are there any of you volunteers left up there to take care of the patients"

"yes" the patients are better off without them come on janice "what is the next item up for bids please"

"attache" what the hell is an attache "all weather wicker" thats a fuckin bakers rack "durability for indoor or outdoor living designed to grace any home from lloyd flanders" that things worth about a hundred bucks a hundred and ten dollars my mom bought iron and glass bakers racks and we painted them in the apartment with spraypaint for about sixty bucks each and they are nicer than those things "goes a supply of scot tussin" what is that "sugar free alcohol free sodium free servitall free" yeah janice knows she knows everything just ask the axis why the hell does that go with a bakers rack and cough medicine - heres a lamp - and a sailboat oh that would be great if they had a sailboat and they put her in a bathing suit theyre not gonna put janice in a bathing suit theyll put diane they always put diane - sheez fat - but sheez got big tits and sheez very sexual - sheez not really sexual sheez kinda grim but everyone knows that she wants it and you got some old man sitting at home in his wheelchair fantasizing about her thats what old people think its not whether she is pretty its whether she has the airs of being pretty they dont really understand the concept of good from far but far from good its kinda just like looks good to me - but to those people bob barker probably looks good - you put him in a dress and slap a wig on him and lipstick "ive forgotten your name" what a loser look at this senile old fuck heez just like ronald reagan there is no difference between this guy and ronald reagan - why do you hate old people so much - i dont hate old people i just dont like them in charge - they have all these ideas that come out of the fifties that just dont work anymore and they think that they are so wise and smart and if we could just go back and you cannot go back time only moves in one direction - what was true in nineteen forty isnt true today - no matter how much you say how much you want it to be youre on the other side get out of the old road if you cant lend a hand - get yourself a rocking chair old man and get outta my way - get out on the golf course get out on the freeway go sailing and swimming and scuba diving and hiking and exploring take pictures and play music and visit your grandkids - but dont put the noose around my fucking neck an albatross around my neck our future - youre not even gonna be here why do you care - why do you care so much - why is it so important to you to cling to these antiquated notions of government and religion and bad comedy don rickles and bob hope and twelve angry men - its just leave it alone - watch the reruns go to the beach play with your fuckin poodles and ill do the same when i get to be old age sticks - you dont understand - your grandkids are going to be saying the same thing to you - old age sticks - i know and theyll be right

"six fifty one" oh jesus 651 if that thing is worth six hundred and fifty one dollars "actual retail price twelve hundred and thirty nine dollars" oh my god that is amazing did i miss something was there something else

"im gonna take you back here where we have the pricing game all ready for you - before you go back to bakersfield i want you to win this"

"a new snowmobile" look at those legs "the arctic cap of puma state of the art snowmobile - whether youre just setting into the art of snowmobiling or are a seasoned enthusiast - the puma deluxe" look at her legs she is so pretty "on the snow" "cruz is saying theres no snow in bakersfield but she can go to the pahatachfee mountains and play with her snowmobile" look at those legs oh yes yes you little snow bunny playboy bunny god i wish she didnt do that i mean that is just so - how can you face your kids - thats such a bad thing to do to your kids - they come home with some friends all teenagers and all of your sons friends are getting these old copies of playboy and spanking about your mom - theyve seen your mom naked - thats so wrong - that is so wrong how do you be with friends - you are with another couple and your husband and the man in the other couple has seen you naked your best friends husband has seen you naked - that is so wrong - i just dont understand that at all - these people just - california its california they just have a completely different set of everything there is nothing real in california theres no respect for everything is plastic and fake so its understandable - who can respect things that are plastic and fake but you still have kids you still have a wife and children - they all get divorced

but she was young she was innocent she didnt know what she was doing she didnt realize that she was gonna have kids - she wasnt thinking about it - she might have known that she was gonna get married and have kids but she wasnt thinking about it - its like having sex now in college or in high school - you know that you are gonna get married and when you do youll wish that you were a virgin and that you only had sex with your wife but you dont think about it now - you realize - but its not real enough to you to make you alter your actions - its not concrete enough

but theres still a distinction between janice and diane - i mean if diane did a layout in playboy it would be completely sexual - it would not be innocent at all - it will be provocative and demur not demur the opposite of demur the opposite of discreet what does demur mean the opposite of mysterious and sensual - itll be base thats what itll be itll be base - but janice on the other hand has a certain class - she doesnt have class she is just some bimbo that advertises prizes on a stupid daytime television game show host sheez not even the host - sheez an ornament - but class - is a quality - class doesnt have anything to do with what you do - it has to do with who you are - you cant take that away from her - like wolves - like wolves like a pack of wild birds picking at everything and tearing it up and tearing it down like vultures and pulling it apart you cant just appreciate things and let them be you have to tear them down martin luther king you have to talk about his affairs you just couldnt let him be - but you want to tear down idols that you dont like - you wanna tear down reagan you wanna tear down elvis and bob barker and bob hope and jerry lewis and john wayne not jerry lewis why did i say jerry lewis - but because you disagree with them politically - you dont care if they cheat on their wives or beat their kids or say nigger but you will tear them down for those things because of the real things about them that you dont like - its just like gary hart - no one gave a shit that he had affairs - republicans just picked on him for that just because they dont like his politics or reagan with iran contra no one really gives a shit if he broke the law or if he lied you just wanna tear him down on that because of his policies in other reasons - you know what i heard - what - i heard that iran contra really began before the nineteen eighty election because reagan was scared that the hostages were going to get released right before the election and jimmy carter would be a hero all of the sudden and thats the only way that reagan could lose - so he sent some people in his cabinet campaign at that point sent some people in his campaign to paris to meet with representatives of the iranian government and reagan paid them like three million dollars to keep the hostages until after the election - and it was at that point that iran said okay fine we will do it but if you get elected we want you to sell us some weapons which reagan was happy to do because they told him that they were afraid that russia might invade iran and take over the oil fields so they had like a coalition of these old military secret c i a fucks and drug dealers and arms dealers that did all this black market shit in vietnam and cambodia and then they were the same people that were behind the coup in chile with pinochet and then they moved to central america with the contras and ran drugs and arms and money back and forth and kept a bunch for themselves and probably funneled it into reagans campaign who knows - really - who knows - but anyway - but i dont hate reagan cuz heez conservative i respect people who are conservative and intelligent like bone i just hate reagan because he bumbles into everything because it is stupid because it is accidental because no one knows what the fuck is going on - you cant argue with well - you can argue with george will or bob novack or bone but you cant argue with well

but i think that having an affair is important - its more important i have more respect for someone that is - honest - that is faithful to his wife and keeps his word even in the simplest way than some fucker who goes out and sets the world on fire and does all of these things and cant even keep his word to his wife - whom he loves - god i wish he didnt do it - why did he throw it all away - for that - for something so petty and worthless he was so great why

if there could just be one person from childhood

i wish i was that person among those people living in that world with that past present and future and those things

"sheez still smiling - and we will be back with the showcase showdown right after this" good - showdown "ever notice how when youre comfortable everything feels right" June Allyson who the hell is june allyson "well your friends at depends have been working on comfort - your comfort" oh god "introducing new depends undergarments with a clothwrite outer cover - look" CONSULT YOUR DOCTOR ABOUT BLADDER CONTROL PROBLEMS why the hell do you have to consult your doctor - theres some danger if you wrap it too tight or some chemical like toxic shock syndrome thats tampons "depends - cuz youve got a lot of living to do" thats true - thats good that they have that - that would suck if you couldnt control going to the bathroom anymore - when i get that old just turn off the machine - no way - im gonna fight my last fucking minutes outta here - they aint gettin me without a struggle - cuz once youre gone thats it

"because practice always lasts just a few more minutes"

"introducing minute recipes"

"recipes you make in thirty minutes or less"

"delicious meals like stir fry pepper steak" they have steak in rice or is it powdered flavoring that would be grim "back in the hot"

"minute recipes - for the time you have"

$ the price is right "we are talking over here folks - and kevin from the university of michigan" eastern michigan no thats jim - this is the real michigan "mark from san diego is gonna spin second - and cruz from bakersville is going to spin the wheel last" no but milton thought - what did milton think - milton was a puritan who believed in the virgin i have no trouble with the church - i have no trouble with priests i think there is something so cool about saying that you are married to god consecrated in thy service my will be lost in thine - its like samson and the nazarites separate unto god jesus was a nazarite not from nazareth he was from bethlehem but a nazarite - cant drink cant do something and cant cut your hair - separate unto god "has a dime - i bet you wanna spin again" yeah "yes" "he does indeed - he got a dime in his first spin - this is his second spin and whatever he gets will be added to a dime - lets hope its ninety cents - here it comes - here it comes" no its going too slow "oohhh - kevin from michigan has fifteen cents - over here mark - you think you can beat that" how can you not beat that ten i guess you can get two fives thats the only way you can not beat fifteen "eighty five cents" what did he get "eighty five cents and mark is in the lead" come on cruz you got it baby - ninety ninety five a dollar no she wont get a dollar sheez gonna get ninety - come on cruz - santa cruz - vera cruz - vera on cheers "baltimore maryland - cruz is trying to beat" 95 "what did that start on" eighty five "did that go around once" i dont know it looked pretty dismal "you win" yeah cruz "and we will be back with the fabulous showcase of prizes right after these messages"

"when i get a yeast infection" what exactly is a yeast infection beer in the vagina "the monostat seven combination package gives me a cure - i can start at bedtime - and a cream i can use for fast relief anytime" MONOSTAT 7 "monostat - the number one choice of women and the number one recommendation of doctors" okay if you say so "todays woman wants to keep it simple - thats why todays advance home pregnancy test introduces one easy step advance - one step is all it takes to get lab reliable results" *Not Pregnant* "new advanced - one simple step to lab reliable results" there is just no respect for human life - you piss on a piece of plastic to find out if youre pregnant - newer cheaper faster - most of the people using the test are probably gonna use it to find theyre pregnant so they can turn around and get an abortion theres just no respect you would think that liberals are for against abortion and that conservatives would be for it so that they can get rid of all these babies before they grow up and just become a drain on society - you would

think they would want to encourage abortion - thats
what i think - you got too many people too much
population growth we should want as few new kids as
possible - and the liberal should be saying no you have
to have faith in life you have to have faith in hope you
have to let things live and grow and have faith that
everything will turn out all right because people are
beautiful and you want to let them be all that they can
be - but then you get the chicks thrown in because they
dont want anyone telling them what they can do with
their body which really doesnt have to do with anything
- i cant murder with my body i cant rape with my body i
cant steal with my body but why if some woman wants
to have an abortion why wouldnt you let her - its fine
with me - you certainly cant not let people do things
just cuz the bible says so - or the bible doesnt even say
so the bible doesnt say anything about abortion i can
promise you that its just some fucker like falwell or pat
robertson or billy graham and who the hell is gonna
listen to them - you gonna run your government based
on what jimmy swaggart says or jim bakker - good
christ "volunteer cruz" lets get ready to
ruummmmmbbbblllllle "and if you are less than one
hundred dollars away without going over we will give
you both showcases - grace since you are our top
winner you can bid on the first showcase or you can
pass that showcase to cruz and bid on the second" pass
the second one is always better - not anymore - the
second one was always better but now theyve started to
mix it up a little if they give you a car thats the good
one if not pass "the first showcase is about time - and
we think its about time the bells ring at the notre dame
cathedral in beautiful paris" god dammit there she is but
she looks pretty "victor hugo" les miserables whats that
other thing the miserab the mystery the missus bridge
misanthrope thats it the misanthrope moliere and
tartuffe those sucked - i would love to go to paris with

her not paris venice venice would be nice and not with
her with julie or annie or c c would be fun in venice
kendall she lived in florence "time you kept track of the
time at home with your new grandfather clock" holly
actually thats nice i wonder if it is really good like an
antique or if it is just some fake thing that looks nice
not an antique but new but something that will become
an antique how do you know massproduced is not
limited edition it has to be limited in some way i guess
if its handmade it will but if its machinemade its not
"clock from saran furniture" well ive never heard of
saran i dont know who makes clocks tiffanys makes
nice clocks but not grandfather clocks i dont think north
carolina is where they have all those nice furniture
stores i bet theyre there "now isnt it about time you kept
time in your new clock in this new sportscar" what is it
a mazda no its american god that was stupid new time
in your new clock inside the sportscar what the fuck is
that EAT DINER tin men god this is stupid one of those
people was from baltimore "a ford probe" thats about
fourteen the clocks about two thats sixteen the trips one
thats seventeen or seventeen five - say seventeen five
"why are you listening to them" exactly "what do they
know that you dont" nothing - exactly - just say
seventeen five "eighteen thousand" wow good bid "teen
thousand is your bid - cruz this showcase is for you"
  "cruz your showcase begins with this terrific game
room" why dont you give her a real pool table i hate
those little things "tint from beta east - tommy the
pinball wizard" theres got to be a twist the pinball
wizards got such a supple wrist "enjoy some of your
favorite games on your unique game table" thats such a
piece of crap - why do they put all those bumpers in the
middle i would rather have a good championship pool
table and forget about the other two - i guess a lot of
people dont have room for them in their homes "quality
craftsmanship - unique design - from beach billiards -

and for a real challenge" its a trailer theyre gonna stick
her with a trailer i bet a thousand bucks "and why not
have some of the outdoors" see a trailer i knew it "with
a new sport boat" bathing suit its diane god dammit i
knew it she is such a whore look at her in that fuckin
bikini god dammit "incredibly fast hunter with a
durable thirty horsepower hatsu outboard motor with
galvanized custom trailer - and this showcase could be
yours if the price is right" god dammit fourteen who
cares "cruz what do you bid" fourteen "six thousand"
six thousand "six thousand dollars" well the first one
was sure a hell of a lot better this time "graces bid is
eighteen thousand dollars - grace - the actual retail price
of your showcase is twenty four thousand one nineteen"
jesus christ "a difference of" 6119 "nineteen - cruz you
bid six thousand dollars on your showcase - and the
actual retail price of your showcase is fourteen
thousand eight" i said fourteen thousand i said fourteen
thousand "a difference of eight thousand" the other
chick wins grace wins good i like grace - she doesnt
look happy "you are the winner grace - bob barker -
reminding you to help control the pet population - have
your pet spade or neutered - goodbye now" bye look at
her she is so pretty i would never have my dog castrated
that is so cruel we dont have the right to do that that is
so wrong wardrobe bye - bye look at diane trying to
stick her tits in the shot

i gotta get up i gotta take a shower and brush my
teeth and then ill watch days and then go deposit the
check and go see if sound warehouse has another side
of bob dylan and then ill make a tape of it and then ill
pack dinner tv bed freelance pallbearers the freelance
pallbearers i used to think it was paul bearers i buried
paul hey doggie hello little doggie - you stay here and
im gonna go take a shower - bye doggie i wanna be
your hero - mighty youngblood wishes he was famous -
mister moses just wants someone to believe - you

believe in miracles - i believe in you if you believe in
me POWER PLAY one two three i was livin down laid
"i was livin down laid up with her next to me with her
makeup running down the edges of her face - she was
playing her" blue "maroon guitar" why does he say
maroon it should be blue guitar "looking at the tv star
and wishing that she could do the same - mister moses
in the corner with his bottle and his peanuts crushed
beneath the weight of all that gold and stone - drowning
his own tears in alcohol and made up fears until the
barmaid closes up and takes him home - i wanna be
your hero - mighty youngblood wishes he was famous -
mister moses just wants someone to believe - you
believe in miracles - i believe in you if you believe in
me - on the other side the young ones watch the dancers
full of pride and kid themselves knowing theyll go
home alone - and on the streets outside where vampires
mete the crosses wedged beneath the pompanos - the
young man with his painting brush a masterpiece a
pickup truck a stream of dirty water flows and flows -
in that great mirage of harmful hopes and songs the
wise man knows its best to give you less that he can
give - but in the small and bashful shadow children
running live with all that they can live - i wanna be your
hero - mighty youngblood wishes he was famous -
mister moses just wants someone to believe - you
believe in miracles - i believe in you if you believe in
me" gold and rose the color of a dream i had why does
he say maroon guitar he must have consciously not
wanted to do blue guitar because it would have been too
cliche - this way i guess its both because you think one
and hear the other i wonder if he knew that it would be
both - or if its just an accident - or if its just me - and
rose the colour of a dream i saw - not too long long ago
- misty blue and the lilac too - never to grow old -
where have all the flowers gone and write me thats

what i should do write her a letter - what should i write her

dear julie should i say dear julie or just julie - dear julie i know that people have been saying that you are fat but i still think youre beautiful - julie - dont ever make the mistake of ever thinking that youre not beautiful yeah thats good im sorry we didnt get to know each other when we had the chance does that sound sexual good no not sexual i im glad sorry im sorry i didnt get to know you when i had the chance i wish you all the best tim should i condition my hair no "tim" what yeah what "where are you"

in the shower

"well come downstairs when youre done"

okay did you walk the dog did you walk the dog no "no" of course not "beth is supposed to" sheez not here you lazy bitch would you please walk him god dammit "okay" good christ - where have all the flowers gone the girls have picked them every one oh when will they ever learn oh when will they ever learn

and the sad bells of rhymney what will you give me oh the sad bells of rhymney why sister why sang the silver bells of wyeth oh and what will you give me said the sad bells of rhymney and who killed the miner "im going to walk the dog" okay okay good christ where do you wanna go for dinner

"um - i dont know - you wanna go to china orchid" roasted pork okay roasted pork wanton soup fried wanton moo shoo pork "you sure" yes yeah thats fine good chinese food "okay ill see you later" bye "bye" what was i thinking

the letter cuz im gonna write me a letter need some paper and a pen okay **Julie,** i thought i was in love with annie but maybe all of this no there were a lot of things in high school some things there were some things there were a few things some some some things in high school that i thought i was doing them for annie but now it seems as maybe if i was were subjective were no was is it subjective not it happened was doing them for you yeah thats good there were a lot of things some no there were some things start over

Julie,

There were some things I did in high school that I thought I was doing them for Annie - but now it seems as if no **that maybe I was doing them for you.** i know that things have changed **I know that** things some things a lot of things **a lot of things have changed,** but **;** but

the really important things dont ever change but **the really important things - they don't ever change.** what now - thanks for - what um um what am i gonna write now about the double date **One night, we were still freshmen and I had just got my license, and Robert and I decided that we were gonna go out on a double date together. We had been going out with Bob Young and Melanie and Jennifer all the time, so I thought that we would ask Melanie, (who Robert kinda liked at the time). And we would ask you. We were careful to pick a Friday night – that way David would be playing basketball and you would be free. "Who's gonna call her?" Neither of us could amass the necessary courage. Finally Robert said "I'll call her." Two seconds later the phone rings and Robert tells me that Susan answered – she was home on Thanksgiving break – and said you weren't home. "Bullshit," I said. "You never called her. I'll call." So I called. And Susan answered the phone – she was home on Thanksgiving break – and said you weren't home. So we ended up calling Charmaine.** okay anyway - i wish i had gotten to know you when i had the chance

Anyway, I wish I had gotten to know you when I had the chance. no matter what anyone says no something first marilyn you have to watch the marilyn film festival she is exactly like julie lynn - no sheez not - she doesnt look anything like julie lynn - just watch you have to watch her mannerisms goodbye norma jean though i never knew you at all madonna aunt grace i was in love with this woman once continuum of beauty there is this continuum of beauty which flows from marilyn to aunt grace to madonna to someone to you so what am i talking about - if man could see the past the present and the future all on one instant then he would see life as it truly is the honey flower blooms in desert with the bumble bee - so what was i thinking

i was once in love with this woman - i always thought that you would grow up to be her - still do thats good i was **I was once in love with this woman. I always thought that you would grow up to be her. I still do.** now **No matter what anyone may tell you, do not ever make the mistake of** thinking believing thinking that youre not beautiful believing that youre not beautiful too formal **thinking that you're not beautiful.** good luck at yale no good luck at yale - i hope that you and yale agree with each other one another no each other no one another

I hope that you and Yale have agreed with one another. love take care or love too much - no take care take care

Take care,
Tim

there now i just need an envelope third drawer here and a stamp and address the newman directory "tim" what yeah

"im leaving - you have to walk the dog again around three"

okay - have fun

i have to find her address Apfel Davidson Herman
Kossover Labadie Lake Lynn here it is Julie Lynn julie
lynn **Julie Lynn** Yale University yale university
YaleUniversoty 1823 Welman Ave. one eight three
two or two 1823 one eight two three one eight two three
Welman Ave. one eight two three welman avenue **1823
Welman Avenue** New Haven, Connecticut new haven
New Haven, Connecticut 09884 o nine eight eight
four **09884** there now ive got to find a stamp – okay

Julie,
There were some things I did in high school that I
thought I was doing them for Annie, but now it
seems as if maybe I was doing them for you. I know
that a lot of things have changed; but the really
important things, they don't ever change.
One night, we were still freshmen and I had just
got my license, and Robert and I decided that we
were gonna go out on a double date together. We
had been going out with Bob Young and Melanie
and Jennifer all the time, so I thought that we would
ask Melanie, (who Robert kinda liked at the time).
And we would ask you. We were careful to pick a
Friday night – that way David would be playing
basketball and you would be free. "Who's gonna call
her?" Neither of us could amass the necessary
courage. Finally Robert said "I'll call her." Two
seconds later the phone rings and Robert tells me
that Susan answered – she was home on
Thanksgiving break – and said you weren't home.
"Bullshit," I said. "You never called her. I'll call."
So I called. And Susan answered the phone – she
was home on Thanksgiving break – and said you
weren't home. So we ended up calling Charmaine.
Anyway, I wish I had gotten to know you when I
had the chance.

I was once in love with this woman. I always thought that you would grow up to be her. I still do. No matter what anyone may tell you, do not ever make the mistake of thinking that you're not beautiful.

I hope that you and Yale have agreed with one another.

Take care,

Tim

thats good now what was i looking for shoes ties makeup oh yeah a stamp top left drawer paper clip no pens here they are twenty five cents is it still twenty five or did it go up to twenty seven 25 no its still twenty five ill put this in the mailbox and then ill watch days i hope jen is on today hey doggie hello doggie whatcha up to no you cant go outside ill be right back ill be right back just goin to mail the letter and then ill be right back in anger she smiles there do i have the right address

Julie Lynn

Yale University

1823 Welman Ave.

New Haven, Connecticut

09884

yeah i think thats right i wonder if she will write me back towering in shiny metallic purple armor my yellow in the case is not so mellow in fact im tryin to say aw fuck did i lock the door no good what time is it 11:44 sixteen minutes - okay - good should i go to domilises or make chili or chicken or maybe tuna fish would be nice nothing seems so nice as tuna fish on ice and mixed thrice and diced with a pinch of lime with lice on ice mice thrice already used that should i mail this im not gonna mail this its tedly but its not for you its for her - its not for her - how do you tell someone why they are special and why would you to make them

feel good - but its never that simple theres always
motives to consider strings attached and all that if you
could just do one thing purely altruistic i took my hat
off to you cuz i know the difference the heisenberg
principle you cant get around the heisenberg principle -
im not mailing this - how would you tell her anyway its
not sexual - its - treasuring something that is rare like a
religion appreciation the virgin mary what is good what
is noble what is true - you know what you said one time
and ill never forget it - you said i dont think anyone is
ever a nerd until someone calls them a nerd i dont kill
the fly because i hate the fly i kill the fly because i hate
the annoyance - she is a goddess if susan is aphrodite
then julie is athena no c is athena julie is diana artemis
softer better kinder juno no juno is not kind who is kind
aphrodite thats susan i dont know im not mailing this
thirteen minutes to days

ever since my parents died i have tried to imagine
that they were watching god was watching you were
watching someone was watching - ever since my
parents died i sometimes imagine that when i am doing
things sometimes you are watching - because and annie
when i had a crush on her and alexandra and c because -
i try to do things no live i try to live to act to be in a
way with the integrity - coolness - or poise or grace as
if you were watching me

theres been an accident son - beth - lynn - come here
please - this is probably the worst thing youll ever hear
- its the worst thing ive ever had to say - kids - im very
sorry - theres been an accident - your parents are dead

thats what i should write no its tedly im not going to
send her anything

because its not for her thats the problem you delude
yourself into thinking that its for them that you are
doing something nice for them because they will feel
uplifted and appreciated and special but you are really
burdening them with an awkward and uncomfortable

thing that they have to deal with - its really pretty selfish which is why the shallow murmur the deep are dumb if you really love some one you will do it from afar and not change like the heisenberg principle the thing you love

on up up up 06 goodbye norma jean - though i never knew you at all you had the grace to hold yourself while those around you crawled - and it seemed to me you lived your life like a candle in the wind - never knowing who to cling to when the rain set in - bum bum bum bum - hooblee dooblee doo "one - this woman has a merit badge in swearing - two - this woman has never been a boy scout - three - this woman used liquid tide with bleach" this woman shoved it right up her ass

i wish i was that person and it was then and i was that person among those people with that past present future and those things and the world was that place with marilyn and network and spartacus and faye dunnaway

hooblee dooblee doo and fames the price you paid - they put you on a treadmill - with the press still hounding you all the papers had to say no - and even when you died - all the press still hounding you - all the papers had to say - was that marilyn - was found in the nude "thousands of heavily armed chinese troops poured into lhasa to enforce what have become the most oppressive security measures in china since the end of the cultural revolution in nineteen seventy six" yeah baby truth is on the march and nothing can stop it "soldiers checked identity cards and demanded special permits from residents who ventured" your old road is rapidly aging - please get out of the new one if you cant lend a hand - for the times they are a changing "the regions monasteries and buddhist devotees have yet to recover fully from the decade long cultural revolution when hundreds of monasteries were closed and tibetan monks were sent to labor camps by the thousands" the line it is drawn - the curse it is cast "traditional buddhist culture as a dangerous source of rebellion" rebellion i thought they just sat around with their legs folded and meditated - what kind of rebellion is that "if the chinese people continue as they are - warned steve marshall - a frequent traveler to tibet - in ten or twenty years the tibetan culture will be something you can only read about in the library" yeah well shit happens - you cant stop truth - you cant stop culture - just because people dont put out their little relics you think they dont believe - you cant change whats in somebodys mind just because you take away their toys - for the times they are a changing oh the time will come up when the winds will stop and the breeze will cease to be breathing - like the stillness in the wind before the hurricane begins the hour that the ship comes in - and the sands will roll out a carpet of gold for your weary toes to be a touchin - whats that other verse and the fishes will laugh and the fishes will laugh as they swim out of the path and the seagulls theyll be a smiling - and theyll pinch themselves and squeal and theyll know that its for real the hour that the ship comes in - the fish dont know dont pinch themselves the foes do the foes will rise and the sleep with the sleep - god dammit - oh the foes will rise with their sleep still in their eyes and theyll pinch themselves and think theyre dreaming thats it and theyll pinch themselves and squeal and theyll know that its for real the hour that the ship comes in - and theyll raise their hands say we will meet all your demands and we will shout from the bow your days are numbered - and like pharaohs tribe theyll be drownded in the tide - and like goliath - theyll be conquered

"this what life is" never "never" never "stand still" stand still this is what life is this is the most annoying commercial "hi - im jane pauley" oh jane jane god i love you what is she wearing "are the japanese really buying up america" yep "tomorrow on today" god i love you what is she wearing that no thats what she was wearing today when she did the spot she wont be wearing that i hope that red thing or the beige thing little boobies

i dont buy into that shit at all buying up all of our stuff cuz why do i give a fuck if sony or some american company owns the skyscraper next to me - its not me - why they hell do i care fuckin donald trump has more property than the japs and heez much more of an asshole plus japan sucks who the hell wants to live in japan all they got over there is suicide and plastic and little electronic gizmos all overpopulated and theres no aesthetic what ever happened to the aesthetic over there in japan they aint got no jane pauley ill tell you that i have never been turned on by any oriental girl in my life i think theyre pretty in an aesthetic way sometimes but theyre just not sexual at all - oh i love orientals - really - i have never been turned on by an oriental - i mean theyre pretty theyre just not sexy - blacks like em - black men love oriental girls you ever notice that - youre no supposed to say oriental - youre supposed to say asian - oriental is a vase or a rug asian is a person from the continent of asia - thats bullshit - somebody made that up - thats just a test because theyre both american words an asian is a person from asia and an oriental is a person from the orient which is asia its just a test its like african american is just a test to see are you one of us if are you in the group - are you willing to make the effort - but there is nothing especially inoffensive about african american theres nothing offensive about black - theyre not gonna call me hebrew american or jewish american youre gonna call me a filthy jew you spike lee farakan mother fucker - you call me white and theres nothing offensive about that so what is offensive about black - its just a test - and when african american gets widely accepted then they will think of why thats offensive and they will make up something else - to see if youre in the group - its stupid - i mean white people said nigger which was derogatory and offensive so then it became colored or negro no it became negro and then when that became widely accepted it became inappropriate and then it became colored and that became unacceptable and so it became black - well i think thats enough and im not gonna say african american and im sure as hell not gonna say asian - but why would you consciously make the choice to offend someone if you know that youre gonna offend someone why would you just not say what they want - because i resent them putting me in the position i resent them judging me its got nothing to do with how i feel about black people or about orientals as people as human beings economically socially politically whether i respect them whether i believe in them whether i love them - but im not gonna play all these fuckin games and have to take a test - if you appreciate people you can show that in different ways better ways than proving it by just using some words which dont really mean anything anyway - yeah but - but - what was i thinking

aesthetic yeah theres no aesthetic over there in japan i mean all you get are these pressures and shit and school like twenty four hours a day and they never enjoy their lives suicide and pollution thats all it adds up to plus all their shit comes from us all their ideas come from us they are smarter than us no doubt about it but they just dont have any vision and i mean that is real intelligence is vision theyre smarter but you can get a fuckin calculator to figure out math problems - my dad thinks that orientals are smarter than jews who are smarter than regular whites who are smarter than blacks - thats terrible - yeah heez really into genetics - yeah but how do you ever know i mean how can you compare some black motherfucker born in the projects his mother is some illiterate doesnt even have a father

goes to these shitty schools where they just basically
babysit you to keep you off of the streets and then
youve got some jap over in china who goes to school
for like sixteen hours a day from the time they are like
four years old - how can you compare that and say that
its genetic - i mean im sure some of it is but i aint ever
seen any fuckin jap who could speak like martin luther
king ive never even seen a white person who could
speak like martin luther king and wynton marsalis and
ralph ellison and thurgood marshall and ken carter and
millions of others that come up from nothing out of the
projects in the face of poverty and bigotry and
everything in the world is against them - and then - i
didnt say i believed it i just said my dad did - yeah who
knows that chicks got nice tits

suicide and death - pollution - thats all this
reaganism shit we are replacing all of our aestheticism
with economics cds computers airplanes rockets clocks
and all down into death the assembly line we are too
efficient but that isnt gonna last mark my words the
antichrist is coming - would you shut up about the
goddamn antichrist - heez coming mark my words - the
year two thousand - hitler was the antichrist - hitler
wasnt the antichrist the antichrist is against christ
against order against rationality dionysian and chaos
and physical pleasure hitler was just masked in christ he
was the ultimate in order and rationality he was just a
false prophet the antichrist is someone more like caesar
or alexander hitler was just fuckin hitler probably didnt
even know what he was doing like reagan i mean
reagan is sucks but heez not the antichrist heez the
opposite heez for law and order and caste and but theres
just no rationality behind it theres just no vision to it its
just a false prophecy but its not a dionysian prophecy -
thats the same thing as hitler he was a false prophet but
he wasnt a dionysian prophet he was an apollonian false
prophet - he thinks heez serving god heez just wrong -

if the right eye causes you to sin pluck it out or your right arm cut it off for it is better that one of your members perish than the whole body go down into eternal flame but thats not what he was talking about he was just wrong but satan knows that heez rebelling against god - he knows that heez rebelling against christ he knows that heez rebelling against order - hitler and reagan and all of these other guys think that they are christian and they use christian tools and they speak the word of god they think they are doing what god wants but theyre wrong - but hitler killed millions and millions of people and jesus was an extreme pacifist - yeah well heez a pacifist for now but when he comes down heez gonna throw everyone into hell who isnt his kind which is exactly what hitler did - he threw everyone into hell who wasnt his kind - he was assuming the role of god not the role of satan he was just saying look if youre not christian youre going to the concentration camps which is exactly what god says if youre not christian youre going to hell and thats exactly what fundamentalists are saying today if youre a fag youre gonna get aids and youre gonna die if you get an abortion god is gonna get even - its your fault - its an inquisition

i am a christian and i dont think that christ would throw anybody into hell - he would forgive them - which makes me more of a christian than you - i have more faith in christ than you know because i know that god is good and god is not vengeful - you think god cares - you think god cares if some guy fucks some guy in the ass - you think god cares if people get abortions - you think god cares if people wear rubbers - god just wants people to love each other and have a little bit of respect for each other and appreciation for what is precious and what is godlike and what is holy god doesnt care - dont you think that god knows that he is being worshipped in the pictures and the images - if a worshipper makes a mistake dont you think that god will forgive him - god "lenscrafters took exactly one hour to prepare my glasses" yeah i bet they did a great job too there it is again economics and convenience everything falls to economics and convenience beauty respect virtue love its all going down its all falling down im guilty of it too but jesus christ lets not get ridiculous lets not all become robots shall we "today marks the one hundred and twentieth murder in washington d c - washington d c whose economic vitality is based on tourism - but now people are afraid to travel there" here too "im here with local bar own marvin guerry - how is the rampant crime in this city affecting business" its cutting down on business al "what people dont understand is that the crime is isolated to a few poor neighborhoods and that all the murders are black on black drug related incidents i mean its not the tourists that are getting killed but nevertheless it deters people from coming"

"washington hotel owner jim dunn"

"i started this bar ten years ago and then i decided to buy the whole building - run the hotel - if i miss one payment im dead"

"and the tourism has decreased"

"oh yeah" well who the fuck cares about your hotel thats the whole fucking problem because everyone is worried about the tourism and the fuckin hotel owners and the fuckin bar owners when they should be worried about the people that are getting killed - and the people that are doing the killing - thats who you should be talking to the mothers and the sisters and the daughters they dont even have a fuckin name you put jim dunn the hotel owner up on the screen to personalize him what about randall washington or tonika jones and then all of those fuckin people saying they dont have respect for human life - how are they supposed to have respect for human life when you just treat them like statistics - good christ

"some activists feel that because of the way that weapons are glorified in movies" oh my god "such as rambo and tv" on my god "shows such as miami vice that audiences particularly children" fuck off "will tend to underestimate" fuck off "the grave and dangerous effects of these weapons and are more likely to use them in a controversial situation" fuck right off you bitch why dont you ban the weapons themselves instead of banning their appearance people have to have some fantasy jesus fuckin christ on a popsicle stick "up next - bob with the weather and jim with sports" we gotta shake these fuckers up you better get yourself a rockin chair old man and get outta my way "any woman who takes a laxative is very much a lady in waiting" oh my god a lady in waiting why dont you just strap a depends around your waist and dont worry about it "have your cake and eat it too" the cosby show what a farce i mean you got missus cosby sheez a mom pie fine may we all have wives as beautiful as missus cosby but other than that come on that little fuckin bitch i hate that they dont want to take the time to write something thats actually funny or good so they just stick her up - oh sheez so cute - fuck you come on probably gonna be doin heroin before her eighteenth birthday its not like she is ever gonna act again once she isnt so adorable anymore i mean one day bill is in the junkyard with fat albert and the next day heez livin on fifth avenue with his doctors office and his wife is a lawyer and five beautiful kids who wouldnt even think of doing drugs or getting drunk no vanessa got drunk that one time chug a lug god that was so tedly - i mean maybe its good to have those role models black people this is the way it should be but lets not take all of the blackness away from them movin on up yeah but what happened to sanford and son and good times theyre still sitting in the fuckin ghetto and no one even cares about them anymore thats why reagan thinks there arent any poor people anymore cuz he doesnt see them on tv - only in reruns "partly cloudy with some scattered showers" only reason that show is big is cuz white people watch it aint no black people watchin that show just white people saying why cant they all be like that - why dont you put on spike lee in that spot and see how long that lasts because he is a good safe model of our safe little understanding unexciting world what happened when ajax died oh i dont care if they are doctors and lawyers just dont let them take anything away from us the civil rights movement didnt cost them anything but now we are asking for a piece of the pie and that is going to be a much more difficult struggle - i think he was wrong about that - the civil rights struggle cost them more - its harder to break the psychology and once its broken theyll let you into the market they might not hand over forty acres and a cow but theyll let you play i mean theyre not going to take money out of their own pocket and hand it to you but theyll let you earn it once the psychology is broken - thats what happened when ajax died and the world got a little less exciting - but they will let you be doctors and lawyers they can have their little culture as long as its white as long as rex is the parade they can have their little zulu and bo diddly can write all of the songs as long as elvis makes the money and all of the songs they are good role models the cosbys he doesnt even use bad words why dont they put a fuckin richard pryor show on thursday night lineup thats what i would like to see "saints leading receiver eric martin reportedly signed a new three year contract today - martin who is on track to break danny abramowitzs all time receiving record has caught passes in eighty seven straight games - the deal is reportedly worth two point one million dollars plus bonuses and incentives" i wanna be your hero - mighty youngblood wishes he was famous - mister moses just wants someone to believe you believe in miracles - i believe in you if you believe in me "spring training is underway in what is now officially known as baseball city florida where tom gordon of the kansas city royals hopes to improve on last years" when the hell is days coming on 11:58 good "you can get road maps and game schedules from the baseball commissioners office at two one two three seven one seventy eight hundred - thats two one two three seven one seventy eight hundred" god i hate - if they spent as much time telling us about things that were interesting as they do about things that they feel are necessary thats the problem you have all these shows that are supposed to be news shows that are doing all of these bullshit stories so that they can compete with the hard copies and the extras and the current affairs if you wanna see entertainment tonight if you wanna see those shows you can watch them but for the news there should be news - i guess thats right but i dont know i just wanna see days "later this afternoon - and that will do it for today - have a nice afternoon" lynn ganser youre all right - sheez grim - if thats the prettiest woman they can get she just looks like - makeup - well theyre not supposed to be beautiful theyre supposed to say the news - yeah but anybody can say the news it doesnt really require any skill you look at the teleprompter and you read it its not that hard - yeah but you gotta keep control and things get fed in and you have to get your timing down cuz youre feeding into stories and commercials and then when you have to do live reports i bet theres a lot to it - i would still get the prettiest person i mean people are not watching the today show for that theyre watching it for jane pauley - diane sawyer was miss america too and people think that sheez pretty - i mean you have qualified people on who are pretty and qualified people on who arent pretty you might as well put someone on who is pretty - see thats the thing i agree with broadcast news that thats the way things work and albert brooks deserves to do the news and he gets fucked but i completely understand having william hurt do the news because heez qualified to do that i mean he can read the shit so its probably the way it should work that albert brooks does all the substantive stuff and then tom gruniger reads it and it sucks that he gets the credit but it makes sense - but sam donaldson is on - thats why broadcast news isnt really accurate because for men its completely different - thats the problem - yeah but if you put warren beatty on channel six no one is gonna watch sam donaldson no woman is and if they put on someone who is a bigger pie than jane pauley then no one is gonna watch her anymore no but sheez not really a pie i mean sheez cute and stuff but i bet she has the cutest little vagina - shaved - no of course not that is so disrespectful she wouldnt do that plus she doesnt have to shave - i hate shaved - its so unnatural its better natural but i bet jane pauleys is nice and pretty and cute - no but she has that professionalism she has that respectability she seems very smart and sharp youve got to have that too you cant just put some bimbo up there even men will get bored - thats why those women are so desirable because you would actually want to spend time with them you would actually want to marry them bimbos are a dime a dozen if you want to watch bimbos you can just watch baywatch but people are watching the news - they might be watching jane pauley because she is pretty but theyre listening to her because sheez smart

"its a meal i hate to miss - kibbles and bits and bits and bits - variety i cant resist - kibbles and bits and bits and bits" come here doggie come here doggie hey hello how are you hey hey hey im gonna take you out in just a little while okay ill watch days and then go to the bank and sound warehouse and try to get another side of bob dylan i once loved a girl her skin it was bronze

and then ill take you out okay we can go for a long
walk okay okay freelance pallbearers and tv and bed i
hope i can fall asleep tonight "hi" hi jen "whats up"

"april was here - and then i went into this conference
- and when i came out she was gone"

"what are you so down about"

"emilio - i think"

"whats" jen on days is the hottest girl ever i mean
annie is the most beautiful but jen is the hottest is julie
the most beautiful maybe susan lynn is maybe c is
alexandra give me something to believe in "well since i
am alone youre alone" she looks like someone there i
think its the hair who is it "well we could go to
shenanigans and then" thats maia "the fish market" god
dammit thats maia "for a little sister youre not so bad"
she is the hottest girl ever youre just sorry you cant
have her thats maia come here doggie yes yes god is
doggie god is dog from the other side i wish i just loved
her i wish i could go back and she would just be the one
and i would love her and she would love me from the
very beginning with no other loves or lusts or
temptations or sex and she is the only one i have ever
been with for my whole life and she and i am the only
one she has ever been with god i wish i could go back

thats all i want tim theres been an accident son beth
lynn come here please this is probably the worst thing
youll ever hear its the worst thing ive ever had to say
kids im very sorry theres been an accident your parents
are dead

god im hungry "days of our lives" ba dumpa dumpa
dee da dum Melissa Brennan   Jenifer Horton do i want
soup tuna fish maybe tuna fish chicken parsley herring
Mary Beth Evans   Kayla Brady Johnson is that sheez
not the girl in terminator who shows boob sandra
connor no thats the character thats - thats - she looks
just like her what was i thinking

lets see i could have some soup or some shit we dont have any soup maybe ill have some tuna yeah where is the tuna fish why is the tuna fish called breast of chicken we dont call breast of chicken tuna im having breast of filet thats like a swordfish steak is like a hamburger made out of ham no its made out of beef and there isnt anything better on beef than a l we need some onion and some green onion and some olive oil and some pepper and some garlic and some mayonnaise so give me something to believe in dum badum ba dah lord above give me something to believe in dum badum ba dah lord arise - well my best friend died a simple man - he was the king of the vietnam vets - he fought a boring war on a foreign shore and his country didnt want him back - he said forgive me for what i done there cuz i never meant the things i did

and give me something to believe in - oh lord above - so give me something to believe in - oh lord arise so give me something to be you take the high road and ill take the low road give me something to be you take the high road and ill take the low road dum badum ba dah dubba dabba

no but what you have is kind of a democratization like matthew arnold dover beach is born to run and thunder road - but can you really put poison in the same vein - no but its still the inarticulate poets of the masses masked eloquence but maybe its accidental - its not accidental but its not what he thinks it is - thats what makes it ironic and funny even though its give me something to believe in - i thought he said boring shore - no foreign shore losing war he fought a losing war on a foreign shore - whats that other verse - i dont know - honey mustard no i dont want that i need some toast yellow mustard ill put a dab of yellow mustard just a dab theres no celery shit where have all the flowers gone "bbbzzzzzz" theres the toast someone needs to figure out a way to make a knife that can spread the

mayonnaise on one side and the mustard on the other
"ding" what the fuck is that come on jens on
 what the hell does this guy want
 hello
 "you need your car washed" shit
 no thanks - thanks anyway
 "okay" shit i should have said yes should i have said
yes
 god dammit
 is that jen no "i heard the harp is the most sexual
instrument" thats cuz you got those big beautiful lips
"how come" lips "maybe it has something to do with
the lips" see i fuckin knew it im a fuckin prophet im
fuckin nostrafuckindamus "start blowin" oh god kayla
oh god with those lips she would be so good oh that
would be great we should take a road trip down to new
york to see the shooting of days and then we can go
down for the morton downey show do a whole circuit
letterman and morton downey and days second avenue
deli they have the best cole slaw
 fuckin geraldo - i hate that fuckin guy - heez a
lawyer - he aint no fuckin lawyer - he says his first case
was a rape case and he had to defend this guy he knew
was guilty and it made him sick so he quit - thats a
bunch of bullshit and if its not bullshit then heez a
pussy i mean he spends three years in law school and it
never occurs to him that if youre gonna be a defense
attorney you have to defend people that are guilty and
then so what does he do fuck barbara walters and get
into street fights with fifteen year old ku klux klansmen
i mean look at his fuckin shows heez got male strippers
and shit and heez worried about defending a rapist thats
a bunch of crap go fuckin climb into al capones vault
and spank yourself to death you piece of shit
 "im going to tell you the same thing my mom told
me" suck it up kid it wont be the last "do you douche"
jesus christ she just pops in there do you douche -

usually they ease into it - walking down the beach with the mom - mom can i ask you a question - sure sweetheart - but here it is just bam do you douche there it is aint no two ways about that thats okay all the kids are off at school - im not worried about the kids im worried about the husbands they dont want to know about that stuff god damn tampax back to back its like feminine hygiene hour its the hour power of womens discomfort with the tampon from tampax and the depends commercial and the home pregnancy test now you got the disposable vinegar and water douche im sittin here trying to eat my tuna fish sandwich and your talking to me about a vinegar and water douche now that isnt very appetizing why the hell do they even use vinegar and water who ever thought of putting vinegar up there - its probably the only thing that kills the smell - come on some diluted apple juice thats probably been sittin out in the sun since civil war days robert e lee probably drank some of that stuff you use to wash out your vaginas with that - that is disgusting - what if they had commercials for spanking what brand of kleenex do you use to masturbate - i use kleenex brand kleenex - thats kind of an oxymoron its like a hoover except its more like a hoover cuz a hoover is a vacuum cleaner but kleenex is kleenex its like a xerox machine a xerox machine can be a cannon xerox machine but its still a xerox machine and puffs is kleenex - what was i thinking

rubbers what a ridiculous idea i mean you are out on the farm playing tag with a few friends and some guy drives up salesman trying to sell you rubbers - whats that - well its this new invention you put this piece of plastic over your thing while youre having sex - thats a good idea - the guy would get tarred and feathered and run out of town and we just accept them as every day common practice we just accept that tuna fish is breast of chicken we just accept breasts i mean thats okay and all of these laws and conventions what is important life freedom self the person death god alone i mean you cant kill you cant steal you cant rape you cant kidnap and kidnap in any way imprison we should tear down all the cages in the zoos and let all of those animals free the condor in the five foot cage and all the birds and elephants because when its our freedom its so important but when its someone elses freedom then its just not that important to us - and you cant kill you cant steal actually can steal some things like food and stuff that just depends on the circumstances what you cannot steal is me you cannot steal something that is a part of me or rape or kidnap but all of the other laws we have arent really anything essential or inherent or anything they are just all convention and institution you cannot fuck your aunt - well why not - its not really wrong - well it would be awkward when she came over to dinner well society would just run a lot better if no one did but if everyone did no one would care know one would think about it there wouldnt be any strain - bullshit there would always be strain you cant get rid of the psychology you cant get rid of jealousy just by making it conventional if everyone cheated on everyone so that there was no cheating and you didnt even take the vow people would still get jealous - people would still treasure the virginal - and the unadulterated and the faithful even if they werent faithful themselves and people would still kill each other and hate and covet

what about the speed limit - thats a perfect example i mean fifty five is arbitrary its just convention why cant it be seventy - well you might get into an accident - society would just run a lot smoother if everyone went fifty five but if you go seventy thats not wrong its like smoking and gambling and drinking and taking drugs prostitution just a bunch of crap to make things work better just a lot of shit for the rulemakers to give them power so they have something to enforce but its not

anything transcendent or anything if we just had like
five laws - no rape no murder no theft no rape what else
is there no bad tv no no - um - beating - and then
whatever other damage you cause you can pay for - but
no littering no graffiti vandalism you have to have
destruction of property i guess drinking and driving
could be a crime

but not all this morals shit not all this religious shit
not all this things could run a lot smoother i wish no
harm nor put fault on any man who lives in a vault but
its alright ma if i cant please him - thats actually a good
credo if there is one thing that i think governs kants
catagorical imperative two rules that i think govern its
kants second categorical imperative do not do unto
others that which you would not have them do unto you
and i wish no harm nor put fault on any man that lives
in a vault - but its alright ma if i cant please him

never treat a person as a means to an end but always
as an end in and of himself - or herself - yeah thats a
good one too

so no murder no theft no rape no destruction of
property and no battery if you just had those five laws
honor thy father and thy mother what if you dont have a
father and a mother that cant be transcendent that cant
be integral keep the sabbath holy kosher big fat rush
limbaugh doesnt keep kosher he is always talking about
eating lobster and how morals come form god from
religion from the ten commandments well where the
fuck do you think kosher comes from fat man - the
same book of the torah as the ten commandments - well
you dont keep kosher - thats not the point though the
point is that he uses the argument that laws and morals
come from the bible and that we cant controvert that
and makes all of these religious arguments that the
bible is not just a collection of words but the divine
inspiration of god and therefore we cannot in our legal
systems controvert what is in the bible but then he picks

and chooses quoting the ten commandments which are
in the exact same book in the old testament as hundreds
of other laws which according to him are mandates of
god and yet he completely ignores them - you know
what i dont like about rush limbaugh - what - i mean he
is entertaining and funny and he has a good radio voice
and the political stuff doesnt really bother me cuz
people are always yelling bullshit back and forth about
politics but you know what i think is truly dangerous -
what - and wrong - is when he starts talking about the
environment he is so full of shit because he says that all
the tests and studies he doesnt like to hear are full of
crap but then he will get behind if a test comes out the
way he likes it like on the ozone layer if they say the
ozone layer is being depleted he will say those
seventeen tests by the commie liberals are all a farce
and you cant put faith into any tests but you should put
faith in this one test that says that the ozone layer is
perfect - dont listen to tests you cant trust tests and to
prove that those fifty tests are wrong - but - this one test
the true test is right - because people are so lazy and
they are just looking for one excuse one little thing to
lay their hat on - it takes them fifty million times to get
people to recycle or not use fluoride or conserve or
whatever and then just one little piece of crap from rush
about how everything is okay and its like the straw that
broke the camels back no house of cards there goes the
whole house of cards

its hard to cure problems like pollution because only
its accumulative effects are noticeable

why cant you do drugs - well it hurts society - how
does it hurt society - it hurts you - and thats your
decision the reason is that its a drain on the economics
you are not contributing to the economics youre not
contributing to our institution you are a waste but there
isnt really a reason its just that things would run a lot
smoother run better if no one took drugs but you can

still take them - all of those laws based on conventions can be broken - if you hurt someone then its civil damages but you cant make things criminal unless they are really criminal rape murder theft murder theft destruction of property destruction of property doesnt even need to be a crime that can be handled by civil court too and - what else - whatever that last one was - and its just that we are measured by how we serve the institutions that is so wrong - we should be measuring the institutions by how well they serve us - we are the ends we are the essence we are inherent economics has no value it just has value in what it brings to us we are not here for the economic system the economic system is here for us - the government is here for us the church is here for us not just people but the sea and winds and the waters and the waves and the grasses and the mountains and the birds - we subjugate ourselves to machines and calculators and and all of those things are just "no - i dont want to" and if you think that abortion is killing then you have to be against birth control if no because the sperm is wholly different from the conceived shell "go to your room" thats - thats - what was i thinking

   its not a person because its life depends upon the egg without the egg it isnt life i mean if i never have sex my sperm left to their natural course of action will never amount to anything never be anything theyre life but theyre not life individual individual life separate and apart from what it was before - conception has to be the beginning of life because its the only point at which it is something different than it was before irrevocably it is the only point you can point to look at its the only point you can look at and say this person is irrevocably separate and apart from these people before it and the same as everything afterwards not the same but not irrevocably different distinguishably its like the difference between a two year old and a six year old - is like saying that a helium atom is the same as two hydrogen atoms the materials may be the same but the essence of the chemical is very different - it has different properties its completely different - and you can add more and more helium and it can float around the universe but its still helium you havent changed the essence of that being whose life as it began in its recognizable form began at that one point of fusion - sure it was life before that but it was not the life of helium it was the life of hydrogen and that particular life of helium began when they fused and became helium - so youre saying that its murder - yeah its murder but who cares - thats the question everyone has the wrong question its like art when people say its art the question is not whether its art but whether its good - thats the question and with abortion the question is not where life begins - the questions where do you care - where is it worthwhile - where is it criminal - not a threat to society its never criminal you only put people in jail if they are a threat to society where you can say this person is a criminal and if we dont put him in jail he might hurt someone tomorrow not do drugs but murder real crime murder rape theft maybe drinking and driving drinking and driving i dont know thats a close one

but they have that quote about i knew you before you were even born or conceived no i think it was born i knew you before you were born and that guy who spilled his seamen on the floor and god struck him down with lightning thats why they think its against birth control thats why theyre against it but if i never have sex then my sperm will just die its all contingent upon the egg its like a bomb a bomb physically isnt an explosion - of course it is an explosion - explosion is the end of the bomb the essence of the bomb but explosion is not the essence of plutonium or nitrogen the plutoniums explosion is contingent upon the nitrogen or the t n t or whatever you know its like saying that you should destroy all the plutonium in the world you know it is a very different statement than saying we should disassemble all of the bombs than it is to say that we should destroy all of the plutonium - so basically you are just saying that life begins at conception - no life begins before conception but a life a single particular life begins at conception - life begins at the beginning before conception and ends beyond death it never stops - i mean when you die you will be part of the plants and the dirt and the oceans and the winds but you wont be alive as you youll be alive as something else there is a psychology and an essence both physical and emotional and spiritual that one essence which is judy hamilton you are at the same time a baby and an old woman and a mother and a daughter and a child if you could see life in just that one instant in just that one grain of sand rintrah roars and clouds swag on the deep in deserts bloom the flower bumble bee and honey comb and all the doors of perception would open and you would see the whole world as infinite as it truly is - infinite - holy and infinite the past present and future all in one second the riddle of the sphinx old man walks in water on three legs when he is older and two legs four legs thats it four legs in the morning when he crawls two legs in the evening when he is older and three legs at night with a cane who figured out the riddle of the sphinx oedipus alexander no alexander cut the gordian knot did he figure out the riddle of the sphinx too no i think it was oedipus jason or jason it might have been no i think it was oedipus ozymandis was ozymandis the sphinx or some other statue that was the only good poem shelly ever wrote that and ode to the west wind ode to the west wind wasnt even that good

it begins when the parts fuse in together one part which says me "weekdays at five here on channel six"

oh i love you at five thats when you come on if i have a
wife i want her to look like you you are such a mom pie
youre not mom on seaver sheez the best but youre
sexier sheez not really that sexy sheez pretty michael j
fox must have had so many fantasies about you i bet he
spanked about you every night - michael gross too that
loser hey doggie hey doggie little doggie yes yes come
here doggie i wish i had the power to give people
thoughts too if she that would be great i wish it was
then and i was that person and we were those people
and the world was that place with more land more water
more fresh water more oil more granite more marble
more iron more soil more oil more oxygen and nitrogen
less carbon dioxide more ozone more produce more
plankton more algae more grasses more forest more
rain forest more produce more livestock healthier
livestock healthier produce seafood endangered species
with no pollution and the mississippi river and destin
and lake pontchartrain and we were those people and
we had that music that art that literature that
photography that tv film computer clothes sports stuff
toys   games   collectors   items   miscellaneous
paraphernalia and mom and dad and uncle g and
bernard and robert and beth and lynn and life health
wealth welfare success with susan and julie and judy
and c and aunt grace and i wish no i wish there were
just one woman just one person who i loved and who
loved me from the very beginning with that beauty and
that reverence and respect and appreciation and love
and likeness and lust no not lust just that supersexual
feeling that spiritual symbiotic sensual not sexual
supersexual and sensual and appreciation and trust and
faith and she would be only with me and i would be
only with her but someone real

   i wish i had an affair with judy hamilton but no one
would find out and but then you would get married and
it would always be there i wish i could just exorcize

yourself of the feelings to begin with that would be great if you had no lust if you had no temptation no desire just love for one person and you have these fantasies but if they were actualized like her husband and her kids that would suck - they are good as fantasies but just as fantasies its like a paradox lamia and typee with the tattoo and you cant go back - rapaccinis daughter - ive gotta go deposit that check ill go deposit the check on prytania and then ill go see if they have another side and then ill make a tape should i stay and watch days no i cant just sit around here any more kayla looks good yeah but i dont like kayla that much its not even worth it even if they have jen sheez not that sexual you cant fantasize about jen sheez just a girlfriend sheez the quintessential girlfriend you really wouldnt want to marry her and sheez not that sexual not at all not that sexual at all sheez just like julie actually you cant marry her you just want to take her to the prom - would you have i dont even think i would have sex with her nah not at all - i dont understand you stone - you are so fuckin weird - i just dont there is no way you cant say that some chick is pretty or beautiful or love her and not want to have sex with her - if sheez a pie you want to fuck her if sheez a grimbo you dont - thats completely wrong thats completely false if you love i mean if a girl is pretty that is completely an independent factor from sexy its like entertaining and good - people think that if a movie is entertaining or a book or tv then its good but good is a separate quality there is no correlation you might have something that is good but boring or good and entertaining or bad and entertaining or bad and boring - you can have things that are good and also entertaining but thats just a coincidence - and so with women it is the same thing you can have a woman who is both pretty and sexy but that is just accidental there is no correlation between the two they have ugly girls who are sexual judy hamilton and beautiful girls who are not sexual jen all the barbie dolls blonde haired blue eyed skinny girls with fake boobs are not sexy theyre not sexual - theyre striking - you notice them you look at them but you cant theyre not sexual sexual girls are brunettes and redheads that kinda have something weird or interesting about them with some roundness to them and something sexual like marilyn monroe is not sexual she is beautiful and kind of wonderful in this great mysterious way but she isnt really sexual like ava gardner ava gardner in night of the iguanas is sexual or patricia neal in hud - and thats whats - what is that song is the end of bold as love maybe its the end of rainy wish or

so he encompasses the fire with all of the if six was nine im gonna live my own life and i aint gonna follow you and the violence with all the smashing and the burning and the violence and the fire so much energy "you got me floatin - round" oh this was the end of if six was nine the violence of purple haze and then the vision and inspiration and childlike song of rose and gold the colors of a dream i had not so long long ago misty blue and the lilac too lock the doors cant rose the color of a dream i had **WELCOME TO EXPRESS BANQUE** four o five one 4051 withdraw cash shit cancel TRANSACTION CANCELLED AT YOUR REQUEST god dammit WELCOME TO EXPRESS BANQUE okay 4051 deposit to checking "on sunday" god i hate smoking two o o point o o IF CORRECT 200.00 okay correct all these fucking people who dont even have money to buy clothes or food spending their last pennies on cigarettes and then what the fuck does it do for them they die early and it pisses everyone around them off and all those bitches dressed up with their lipstick and their martinis who you just want to fuck holding them away from their faces and blowin all the smoke at you while youre trying to eat - god that pisses me off - those fuckin cigarette companies feed all these

people shit and get them hooked and then dont pay for a
damn cent when all these old pathetic fuckers get
cancer and insomnia not insomnia what the hell to they
get ensemnia emphysema thats right what the hell is
emphysema - i dont know - neither do i but they get it
and then we have to pay all our tax dollars for their
wheelchairs and oxygen tanks and electronic voice
boxes like stephen hawking smoking out of the
blowhole while those bastards just count their fuckin
money and laugh themselves all the way to the bank
and "you got a bag for me" what the fuck is this lady
doin gold and rose the color of a dream i had - heres a
nickel babe knock yourself out

shit - im sorry - god dammit - ill give her a dollar

her ya go

"thank you" but what the hell are you supposed to do
i mean they just more and more all of these these
problems just cant do anything its like throwing a
bucket onto a forest fire

"gold and rose" here it is "the color of a dream i had
- not too long ago - misty blue and the lilac too - never
to grow old" there i was "there you were" there you
were thats right "under a tree of song sleeping so
peacefully - and your hand a flower played - waiting
there for me - i have never laid eyes on you not before
this timeless day - but you woke and you smiled my
name - and you stole my heart away - stole my heart
away" its your stop sign bitch "gold and rose the color
of a dream i had - not to long" long "ago - misty blue
and the lilac too" never to grow old

if they dont have it im just gonna leave im not
buying anything else i wish i could buy that billie
holiday collection one hundred bucks damn i wish i had
all those collections the miles davis on prestige
thelonius monk on riverside or its it charlie parker on
riverside the louis armstrong collection muddy waters
jimi hendrix ten of swords thats what i really want

Crosby Stills & Nash Neil Diamond Bob Dylan here
we go BEFORE THE FLOOD another side of another
side of BEFORE THE FLOOD BEFORE THE FLOOD
greatest hits bringin   THE NICE PRICE it all back
home or highway sixty one revisited highway sixty one
revisited Blood On The Tracks 6.99 Blood On The
Tracks maybe i should get another blood on the tracks
album i love that album - thats when you know you
love an album you know you have it at home but every
time you go into the store you have the urge to buy it
again maybe ill have to get a cd no that girl is hot is that
no she didnt go to newman who is that The Doors Bob
Dylan here BIOGRAPH BIOGRAPH dylan and the
dead dylan and the dead should i get that no i want
another side of BEFORE THE FLOOD i wanna get an
album i dont want a c d greatest hits volume two
basement tapes before the flood before the flood
freewheelin freewheelin where the fuck is another side
of i once loved a girl her skin it was bronze **Nashville
Skyline** BLONDE ON BLONDE 17.95 i think i paid
twenty at school did i pay twenty no no it was thirteen
highway sixty one revisited maybe i should get another
highway sixty one revisited its kinda scratched on
desolation row no im sure its at school highway sixty
one revisited and BLONDE ON BLONDE god damn
where the hell is another side of that girl is a pie maybe
ill get that james booker no ive spent too much money
already THE BEST OF oh here it is they dont have the
picture thats weird should i buy it no ill wait and get it
from robert no im not stealing any records bitch have
you seen the new album cover - no - do you like it - no
- i know c b s dicked us you know they have the rights
to all of our recordings so they just went ahead and did
it they didnt ask us if it was okay or make a new cover
thats why theres no picture - oh yeah - thats what he
told me cuz you need five albums to make a box set and
they want a box set so they needed to make another

album is that no theres no north carolina sticker didnt she go to north carolina so the brady bunch was struck an earthshattering blow little jan in the hospital for bulimia anorexia i think it was just anorexia you know jan was a dyke really - yeah - eve plumb - did she get it on with marcia - no cindy - was she like an alcoholic or drug addict or something - no that was drew berrymore oh yeah thats right - greg and mom on brady what was her name the louisiana chicken oil lady carol yeah carol brady and greg had an affair when he was like fifteen on the show - really - yeah thats great that would be so cool im sure that michael j fox fucked merideth baxter bearney or at least wanted to and mike on seaver with joanna kerns no she would never do that sheez not like that sheez more like "anger" he smiles "he smiles towering in shiny metallic purple armor - queen jealousy envy waits behind him - her fiery green gown sneers at the grassy ground - blue are the lifegiving waters taken for granted - we quietly understand - and once happy turquoise armies lay opposite ready waiting but wonder why the fight is on - and theyre all bold as love" let me tell you now "theyre all bold as love" come on baby now "theyre all bold as love - just ask the axis" he knows everything "my red is so confident he flashes trophies of war and ribbons of euphoria - orange is young full of daring but very unsteady for the first go round - my yellow in this case is not so mellow - in fact im trying to say its frightened like me - and all these emotions of mine keeps holdin me from giving my life to a rainbow like you but im bold as love - im bold bold as love - let me tell you now - im bold as love - just ask the axis" he knows ev "he knows everything" yeah yeah   bam   bam   badda   da   dum   dum dabbadabbadabbadabba da doodle do doo MY CHILD IS AN HONOR STUDENT well she must get it from her father bitch cuz you sure as hell cant drive is that jennifers car no baby let me follow you down well i do

anything in this god almighty world if you just let me
follow you down thats a salesman you know salesman a
mile away just by the tie he has - what kind - light blue
or grey with horizontal stripes willie loman my yellow
in this case is not so mellow in fact im trying to say -
come on - lets go - im frightened like you
HANDICAPPED yeah you are handicapped ill vouch
for you but im bold bold as love let me tell ya now im
bold bold as love let me tell you now im bold as love
just ask the axis he knows everything

hello doggie hello whatcha up to now huh doggie
whatcha up to where is that book suitcase come on -
come on doggie so ill read it and then eat dinner and
watch tv and pack and im all set where is it okay here it
is

After The Fall
A Streetcar Named Desire
THE FREELANCE PALL-BEARERS
here it is i should read it here or downstairs im
gonna read it downstairs come on doggie we are gonna
break into tom mccanns and then theres gonna be some
worldshakin luke we gonna send you a postcard what is
that an ant a priestking on the window i wonder where
george is - george has changed - really - yeah we are
like come on george lets go out and he is like i think im
gonna curl up with a good book - well he always had
that side you just didnt know him gor what a beautiful
child i think we will name him gore can i pet the rabbits
george sure lenny and george says i get to pet the
rabbits george says i get to take care of the rabbits and i
will love him and pet him and romp her and stomp her
an terrorize her for the rest of her natural life - say man
we cant work out on the yard we gonna work out on
your head - shut up you mexican cracker jack - now im
mexican too so what you gonna do you gonna jump in
the face of mexican blood - fuck you you rat faced

nigger - now im one of them nigger types too - so what you gon do - this is not a political situation - this is a pocket situation - your pocket - hey man we cant work out on the yard we gonna work out on your head

dreams - expectations - theyre the worst kind - the worst - never happen man - nothing ever happens - yeah - yeah - settle down - get off the main line - get off the main line - oh yeah well i need things mistah - you run until you cant walk - then you walk until you cant talk - then you zone out like a glue sniffer until the next day when you do the whole thing again - naw mister murphy you dont need no one - no how - no way - you gotta be the luckiest man alive - you dont have to do no kind of desperate stuff - oh oh are you tellin me youre not gonna be around cuz without me bein around without captain midnight fillin your souls with funky inspiration there aint no way you gonna be champeen - right - right - cuz it is laid out - it is laid on - i am gonna win the gold medal - in the olympics - right - right - and instead of given them your hand over your heart - or the black power sign - you can give the whole world the jailhouse salute - dreams - expectations - they never happen man - they the worst kind - the worst - nothing ever happens

THE FREE-LANCE PALLBEARERS An irreverent novel irrelevant no irreverent because its the language by Ishmael Reed call me ishmael ishmael is the outsider the muslim the arab han Dedicated to My Daughter TIMOTHY BRETT ashley REED Da Hoodoo Is Put in Bukka Doopeyduck we gonna break into tom mccanns and steal all the shoes - reed must be his real last name he must have changed his first name to ishmael holy thats what it means holy no it was his son it was him and han and isaac and then he went out crying in the wilderness like john the baptist a voice crying out in the wilderness vox clamantis in deserto and han was the arab or he was the arab and han was the african the oriental what else is there but does it mean holy i don know

The excrement, which is all that remains of all this holy no wealthy no it doesnt mean wealthy it means hear me shma no that would be shma it means holy blood guilt. that sounds like faulkner blood guilt jason benjy if he only had a mother By it we know that we have murdered. It is the compressed sum of all evidence against us. blood - no excrement It is our daily and continuing sin outlaw thats what it means outlaw not holy how we isolate ourselves in it. In special rooms, set aside for the purpose we get rid of it; it should be the reason we get rid of it not the purpose we get rid of it our most private moment is when we withdraw there; we are alone with our excrement. a man and his shit we are ashamed of it. It is the age-old seal of the power of process of digestion which ishmael in moby dick is not really an outlaw heez on the outside looking in telling the story heez really on the inside looking out to those outer spheres i would strike out at the sun if i thought it offended me the age-old seal of that power-process of digestion which is enacted in darkness heart of darkness and which, without this, would remain hidden forever.

- Elias Canetti, *Crowds and Power* i guess that is like a history book that gets checked out every five years when some poor sod gets stuck writing this piece of shit term paper one of those things professors write to get tenure that no one ever reads its just all this self perpetuating bullshit which only serves the purpose of sustaining itself so stupid and the book is only in the library no one actually owns a copy just elias canetti and the library and his mom now what was i thinking

but ishmael and ishmael in moby dick is the story of the man who is trying to conquer leviathan and imagination and fantasy and sexual desire and sin and hell and the book is saying that he who is trying to capture him and conquer him and kill him is not only insane but tragic tragic and insane insane is sane dreamlife waking reality poetry is truth and if you try to conquer them you will end up like ahab tied to the whale tragic and insane - great so he is ishmael teller of this war and so anyway - We felt so dirty after seeing it that we felt compelled to eat at Senor Picos, senor picos what the hell am i reading We felt so dirty after seeing it that we felt compelled to go to Senor Picos, a popular Mexican restaurant. We ordered the spiciest food they had just to burn ourselves out, inside.

- Shirley Temple, after seeing *Night Games* night games what the hell is night games shirley temple i hate that fuckin little self righteous bitch lollipop ill pop you shirley temple drake raped PART I *Da Hoodoo Is Put on Bukka Doopeyduk* I live in HARRY SAM. sambo niggerville browntown HARRY SAM is something else. yeah what is harry sam again - not sambo something else uncle sam maybe uncle sam A big not-to-be-believed out-of-sight - sometimes referred to as O-BOP-SHE-BANG   or   KLANG-A-LANG-A-DIG-DONG. SAM has not been seen since the day thirty years ago a christ figure is it thirty or thirty three its both when he disappeared into the John the baptist into the wilderness with a weird ravaging illness.

The John bathroom outhouse is located within an immense motel not outhouse which stands on Sam's Island just off HARRY SAM. uncle sam A self-made Pole and former used car salesman, SAM's father was busted for injecting hypos into the under-bellies of bantam roosters. giving them smallpox thats right rooster crow the crow indians who gave them the blankets The ol man rigged many an underground cockfight. chicken george SAM's mother was a low-down, filthy hobo infected with hoof-and-mouth disease harry s yeah thats right its harry sam truman cuz he killed all the japanese with the atom bomb and sent

the blankets with the smallpox to kill all the indians A
five-o'clock-shadowed junkie who dies of diphtheria
and an overdose of pheno-barb what is phenobarb the
stuff in brave new world phe no thats somnia soma no
soma soma i wonder if harry trumans mom died of
diphtheria or maybe rutherford b hayes thats who sent
the blankets because he was reconstruction and
everyone thought he was this great black savior and he
sent all of the blankets to the indians with smallpox and
they died Laid out dead in an abandoned alley in thirty-
degree-below snow coke is snow is coke - maybe his
mom was a fuckin drug addict dead in the snow it
sounds like edgar allen poe

An evil lean snake with blue, blue lips and white
tonsils. Dead as a doornail she died, mean and hard;
cussing out her connection until the last yellow flame
whisped from her wretched mouth. But SAM's mother
taught him everything he knows. "Looka heah, SAM,"
his mother said before they lifted her into the basket
and pulled the sheet over her empty pupils. "It's a cruel,
cruel world and you gots to be swift. Your father is a
big fat stupid kabalsa who is doin one to five in Sing
Sing for foolin around with them blasted chickens.
father is the rutherford b hayes from which he inherits
the white house hadn't been for those chickens little
pills, I would have gone out of my rat mind a long time
ago. I have paid a lot of dues, son, and now I'm gonna
pop off. But before I croak, I want to give you a little
advice. i love this this is the best part "Always be at the
top of the heap. If you can't whip um with your fists,
keek um. If you cant keek um, butt um. If you cant butt
um, bite um and if you cant bite um, then gum the
mothafukas to death. or drop a bomb on their heads lips
with a ragged sleeve and if you cant bite em gum the
motherfuckers to death i love that the graveyard is full
of peoples what talks too much so dont ever let them
know what youre thinkin that is just like native son He

became top dog in Harry Sam Motel and master of
HIMSELF because god knows he doesnt take care of
anyone else but his own kind which he sees through
binoculars he is blind the invisible man he cant see
black people like ronald reagan with the white house
and the blind binoculars he inherited from harry sam
and rutherford b hayes and harry sam across the bay.
san francisco bay yeah oakland yeah yeah he lives in
oakland and teaches at berkeley he used to teach at
dartmouth heez friends with professor cook the hudson
hornet Visitors to his sprawling motel because they are
like visitors like tourists who come to america brought
to america on slave ships and they just pay rent like a
motel but they dont own it corridors and passageways
descending to the very bowels of the earth. the labyrinth
the abyss she was an abyssinian maid and on her
dulcimer she played singing of mount albora

High-pitched screams and when they came to find
her there those sunny domes those caves of ice and all
who came beware beware for they on honey dew hath
fed and drank the milk of paradise - okay

High-pitched screams and cries going up-tempo are i
wonder if they actually think about that stuff - i bet they
are trying to do the right thing - they are just wrong
ignorant they are just ignorant it pisses me off i mean if
people would just look at things i mean if you ask
someone what his five biggest problems are heez not
gonna say russia if you ask someone what his five
biggest problems are he is gonna say crime education i
need a job my health crime drugs aids he isnt gonna say
russia its just a plan to keep our eyes from what is really
important its just they make a problem so we dont
concentrate on the real problems cuz theyre just so
offended so arrogant that they think they have earned
everything and resentful and they can look themselves
in the mirror ask themselves those metaphysical
questions what would happen if they were born in the

projects poor black who would they be today those existential questions trading places its just a psychological defense mechanism so that they dont have to wrestle with the metaphysical questions thats all reagan is he doesnt hate black people he just cant accept he cant even let himself think about the notion that maybe he didnt really earn all of what he actually is the essence of what he actually is and who he would be if he had been born someone else thats why he cant help poor people thats why he cant help black people because its his whole entire psychological defense mechanism that preserves himself by not letting him question the fact that he is better than them not that whites are better than blacks necessarily but he personally is better because he is the president so he must have earned it he must deserve it heez not just some bumbling senile old stupid fuck that was never intelligent not even a good actor who should be taken out in the back yard and tied to a tree and nancy can come out and feed him oatmeal once a day

"Always be at the top of the heap no i already read that

High-pitched screams and cries going up-tempo are heard in the night. Going on until the wee wee hours of the morning jazz you see theres jazz when everything is OUT-OF-SIGHT. Go-ing on until dirty-oranged dawn when the bootlegged roosters crow. the indians Helicopters spin above the motel like clattering bugs as they inspect the constant stream of limousines moving to and fro afro moving on up the jeffersons to the top to that deluxe apartment in the sky of the mountain and discharging judges, generals, the Chief of Screws, and Nazarene Bishops. jesus was a nazarene not from nazareth he was a nazarite not nazarene nazarite like samson - a holy priest separate unto god - and prophesied the annunciation gabriel told mary you will have son and he will be a priest a nazarene separate unto god (The Nazarene Bishops are a bunch of drop-dead egalitarians crying into their billfolds, "We must love one another or die.") The luminaries what the hell is a luminary light can see oh can see illuminary RUTHERFORD BIRCHARD HAYES exactly i knew it was rutherford b hayes Black boy Bay. black bay Couched in the embankment the embankment of what the island of harry sam four statues of RUTHERFORD BIRCHARD HAYES. White papers, busted microphones and other wastes leak from the lips of this bearded bedrock new york and end up in the bay fouling it so that no swimmer has ever emerged from its waters alive the harlem river or san francisco bay sharks and the cold alcatraz thats it alcatraz black people are trapped on harry sam island alcatraz

i mean if we start thinking there will be an apocalypse and prophesizing it and writing about it and making movies about it and tv shows and paintings and songs about it then there will be one the indians thats right the indians were trapped on alcatraz they werent trapped on alcatraz they took it over in a protest during the sixties what were they protesting - we stole their land - we didnt steal their land - someone a long time ago that i didnt even know stole their land thats not my fault - plus its not their land someone else was here before them and they killed them and they were running around killing each other and they would have killed us if they had guns but we had guns and we had ships so we came over and killed them but if they had the boats and the guns then they would have come over to europe and killed us - so youre just saying that might is right - no im just saying that the idea that the world is a nation of men that can live in peace with the united nations or something like that is a very novel idea thats only been around for less than a century and before that people just went around taking territories and jacking people up and whoever had the best guns or the most money at the time won - but no one was inherently any better or stronger or morally right or more vicious than any other people - everyone was vicious - its just a matter of environment and whether there is plenty - its social evolution survival of the fittest like the monolith in two thousand and one that which doesnt kill me makes me stronger - that people who are worse off get better at fighting each other to get what little food while places in africa had so much abundance that nobody ever heard of war the pygmies never had any war they didnt need it because there was no competition - what was i thinking

but that cant be right because civilization started in mesopotamia by that logic it would have started in the desert or arctic where there is nothing but if there is nothing no one will survive so you have to have some balance - you need a river to fertilize like the nile in egypt and the tigris and euphrates so that there is some feeling of safety and security so that you can build things and grow - i dont know

but - but - but if people prophesy the apocalypse then they will bring about the apocalypse and then people will say see how smart they were they knew it was coming but if it wasnt for them in the first place it would have never come its self fulfilling prophecy

On the banks of HARRY SAM is a park. what - fuck it - im gonna shoot some baskets i cant concentrate ill read this again later ill read it on the plane i dont understand how you can fly - if my parents were killed in a plane crash i dont think i could fly - i love flying - i hate machines but i love to fly - what was i saying

we are gonna break into tom mccanns and steal the shoes right offa your feet - i mean we gotta get all these old stagnant fuckers outta the way truth is on the march and nothing can stop it i have a dream today - yes sir - how long - how long - not long - not long sir - till the children of former slaves and former slaveholders can sit down together in peace - how long - not long - yes sir - till the from the molehills from every mountain to every molehill in georgia - let freedom ring - and when we let freedom ring from every town and every hamlet - and every city - then we will be able to say in the words of that old negro spiritual free at last free at last thank god almighty im free at last - mine eyes have seen the glory of the coming of the lord - he is trampling out the vintage that the grapes of wrath have stored - his truth is marching on - our god is marching on - on god is marching on - our god is marching on

in the name of love - what more in the name of love - in the name of love - what more in the name of love - early morning - april four - shot rings out in the memphis sky - free at last - they took your life - they could not take your pride - in the name of love - what more in the name of love - in the name of love - what more in the name of love theres nobody like you - theres nobody like u2

but - but - these stagnant old fuckers are still in the senate that were saying nigger on the floor of the senate in the nineteen fifties and sixties and opposing integration and those are the same mother fuckers that are still in congress today they are the same people and reagan and bob hope and pat buchanan all these fuckers just have to get yourself a rocking chair and get outta my way - truth is on the march and nothing can stop it - no more auction block - just everything that is good everything that is sacred everything that is holy they trade it all in for money they dont have any appreciation its all progress and convenience thats the one worst thing in the world convenience thats what destroys everything machinery artistry all the artistry is gone there is no craft its all machinery and technology and progress and convenience and money we will trade everything to be convenient there is no appreciation for the struggles and the beauty and the passion and the hope and the prayer and the dignity of the common man well its the common man that does most of the working and the loving and the living and the dying in this world mister potter mister reagan so get yourself a rockin chair and get outta my way i dont have time for you to learn - black people dont have time for you to learn - people with aids dont have time for you to learn - the environment doesnt have time for you to learn - i dont care if youre not evil i dont care if youre only stupid or ignorant i dont have time for you to learn - you got your fuckin money - you got your fuckin mansion ranch - you got your fuckin power and the glory - just put yourself out to pasture and go to bed - i wish no harm nor put fault on any man that lives in a vault but its all right ma if i cant please him

china look at china - china germany russia the berlin wall the middle east theyre not gonna wait for you - truth is on the march and nothing can stop it

you cant stop an idea you cant stop the mind its like kubla khan its going to explode into this great big waterfall and then forge out a stream no one is gonna let you keep putting us to sleep with you we are just waking up its a sleeping giant china is the sleeping giant in the west and they arent gonna wait for you to figure out that youre all antiquated - you dont care about ideas everything that you pretend to defend everything that you pretend to uphold patriotism and hold sacred is the first thing you trample trade away auction away for tax breaks and tax cuts and trickle down and dividends you have no faith in people you have no faith in beauty you have no faith in the free market and the free mind free speech the marketplace of ideas its all the flag and the military and some bullshit which is just a means its just a means to an end and the end is the people thats your problem kant thats the second categorical imperative or the third the third the second is dont do unto others that which you would not have them do unto you thats the third you can never treat a human being as a means to an end but always as an end in themselves only just like hitler heez just like hitler - but heez not evil heez just stupid heez just ignorant - which probably makes him more dangerous because he can do it and everyone will participate and no one will know its so convincing because heez so stupid he doesnt even know it himself - but we have a strong economy and strong military which is was germany had but we are sacrificing everything in the process - because - we are sacrificing the blacks and the hispanics and the women and the homosexuals and the environment and access to the courts and right to trial by jury and free speech and free religion and art and all of our oceans and grasses and forests and animals and plants and trees and ozone and air we are sacrificing all of that trading it all in and aids and crime and poor people and education trade deficits national debt but all of the trains are running on time by golly and the stock market is up and we will be god damned if any pissant country like grenada tries to kick our ass hamburger hill what was that clint eastwood movie was that hamburger hill and john wayne airport and clint eastwood is a mayor - is he liberal - it would seem that he is conservative but he could be liberal orange country is a piece of shit

get yourself a rockin chair old man and get out of my way you still believe in that big bearded boss up there - aint ya scared luke - aint ya scared of dyin - he can have this little old life any time he wants it - love me hate me kill me anything just let me know youre there - just let me know it - standin in the rain - talkin to myself

god is dead god is gravity gods not dead god is gravity - god is - is a force that connects everything together its invisible and yet it brings everything together - love and hate it doesnt care - it doesnt care who you are it doesnt care what color you are or what

religion you are or what you believe whether youre bad
or good or evil or happy or sad and its not just people
but everything from one edge of time and space to the
other - a lot of the time we cant even feel it but its there
- gravity proves that there is no vacuum because even
where matter is lapse there is something - there is
gravity - a voice i mean a force - that stretches
everything - all is one and one is all - how does he
come up with this stuff - i dont know god is like
contacts - this invisible force that doesnt really do
anything but makes things clearer - brings things into
focus - how does he come up with this stuff - i dont
know i should call alison i love alison i should go out to
dinner with her that would be cool hey alison its tim
whats up - nothin much just gettin ready to go back to
school - yeah me too i thought maybe you would wanna
go out to dinner - sure she probably wouldnt go with
me - are you still in that fraternity - yes - no - what - i
dont think i want to eat with you - come on i wont bite
although i would like to no im just kidding - come on -
okay - what do you want you want some wine - no
thanks - come on im trying to get you drunk so i can
take advantage of you no youre trying to take advantage
of me - come on if you dont get me drunk you wont be
able to take advantage of me - thats not funny - you
know i always thought that if i were face to face with
this black man who was going to kill me i would say
look you have to do what you have to do - there is no
way i can know what youve been through and if you
think you have to kill me fine - i wish no harm nor put
fault on any man that lives in a vault but its alright ma
if i cant please him - no what was i thinking a black
man i dont know what you have gone through there is
no way that i can know what you have gone through
and if you think you have to kill me fine but i just think
youre stupid cuz you dont know who your friends are
and thats the same way i feel about some of you guys is

that you are taking such strong positions that you are alienating a lot of people who would naturally be on your side - youre a feminist - yes - how - i respect the women i have respect for - and i treat them with love and honor and respect dignity appreciation reverence - and reverence - and what about the women you dont respect - fuck em - exactly - no but the way i treat them is in a sense feminist too because i treat them the same way i would treat a guy i dont give them any preference or leniency because they are a girl if a guy is a dick heez a dick and if a girl is a bitch she is a bitch and i dont care how pretty she is - fuck her - and if she doesnt like it fuck her - just like a guy - then why if you respect a women wouldnt you treat her the same - because its disrespectful and thats not equality anyway its not language and being offensive its opportunity - thats the bottom line - and i would give do give well i dont give but i will give everyone the same opportunity which is all you can ask for - you have no right to complain about the way i feel - yes i do because language cuts everything down - you can say that you will give me the same opportunity but all you have to do is whisper slut or whore or rack or pie to the male supervisor and i am just a sexual commodity in the workplace who got to where she is because she slept with the boss and will never get above the glass ceiling because that is for men who play golf with the important clients and not women who give blow jobs particularly if they wont - which i wont - well what the fuck am i supposed to do about it

and maybe man sometimes sometimes i just want my little life just a little bit of space elbow room with my two point three children and my wife and car and house and job and little circle of friends and just myself add a little bit of beauty to this world just make it a little better or at the least not hurt it and sometimes i just wanna run everything and control everything and fix everything great desire apocalypse and everything else shake people up and make them everything jerusalem i mean how i mean how can you sort out what is you and what is you as a man and what is you as a human and then those things that arent even you but are an extension of you now a reflection of you now play soccer hunt women pong charity i mean i got my little brother and my sisters and my check to unicef and does it really matter billie could do without me and i think in the long run my unicef because there is just so many i mean how the fuck is it supposed to be its like throwing a bucket on a forest fire less than that its like a little eyedropper of water on a forest fire and if you give all of your money away then you have nothing and why does anyone have to give or not give am i just gonna set up a little shelter and live out of a mobile home like the titanic hell no because i want my beach house and two point three kids and alexandra or annie and maybe not annie i dont know who else is gonna marry me judy is a bit too old and married someone beautiful alexandra like alexandra she would be perfect but she is old and married too i wanna marry jane pauley i wanna be your hero merideth baxter bearney no she is probably a bitch sheez kind of self righteous i like joanna kerns better she would be perfect or elisabeth shue her brother goes to dartmouth - really - yeah heez in a d - does she ever come here - yeah somebody fucked her - bullshit - thats so offensive people like that shouldnt be doing that sheez so pretty why thats so offensive all of you girls you shouldnt be doing that - why not - its disgusting - its wrong - one day youre gonna be married and youre just gonna regret it - i have no problem with the church i have no problem with the church saying that you should wait until you get married and then do it only with your husband - what about men - men too - men just as much as women - i have no problem with that - its a religion -

its the way it should be - its psychological - that sex
will always be disgusting because the act of sex is
conquering its violative its intrusive its penetrating its
transgressive and ugly and hot and smelly and wet its
beautiful and wonderful and fun too of course - but its
always going to have that other aspect - that physical
aspect - and people are always going to feel regardless
of society regardless of womens lib and freedom in the
workplace and all that people are always in their
subconscious going to feel that a woman who has had
sex has somehow been violated because she has she has
been penetrated she has been intruded thats the nature
of the act and its always going to bother people - i
thinks its so wrong - i have sexual feelings for people
sure but i think its wrong it pains me its degrading and
women that i love women that i respect women who i
think are beautiful shouldnt be doing something thats
degrading - thats the woman coming off of the pedestal
because even if its you that is having sex with her there
is still something about it that is disgusting and
violative and degrading - thats the double standard - i
mean there are sociological reasons why you would
want to have women be monogamous - because you
have to know who the child belongs to and with the
woman you obviously know who the child is but with a
man you cant know unless the woman has only had sex
with one man - now that can be solved now with blood
tests but historically thats why - and also just the basic
fact that its the woman that has to live with the
consequences its for the womans protection too the first
protection is for the man so that you can know whose
child it is but there is also a protection for the woman
because you want to encourage them to be virgins
because they will have to bear the burden the men can
always run away but the woman cant - and now thats
not really a problem anymore because we have birth
control - but historically - but there will still always be

a double standard because people will always get
jealous which applies to men and women but its more
for the woman because of the fact that she is the one
that is violated she is the one that is penetrated and
there will always be a psychological fact a
psychological aspect because the man is invading the
man is conquesting but the woman is violated - and that
will never change - i once loved a girl her skin it was
bronze with the innocence of a lamb she was gentle like
fawn i courted her proudly but now she is gone gone is
the dream lover of my life time - the room knocks my
window the room it is wet the wind knocks my window
- the wind knocks my window the room it is wet the
courage to say im sorry i havent found yet i think of her
often and hope whoever sheez met will be fully aware
of how precious she is - my friends from the prison they
ask unto me how good how good does it feel to be free
and i answer them most mysteriously are birds free
from the chains of the skyway - are birds free from the
chains of the skyway - no but i want to marry its not
like julie is gonna read a letter and then come knockin
on my door and c just aint the marryin type i mean fuck
i guess i would marry c there is something special about
her very special beyond all the - i mean she is beautiful
but a lot of girls are beautiful in their own way but very
few girls are special c magical julie kendall annie maia
alexandra aunt grace i may even know only six special
girls and only one of them is a woman who is married
with two kids and one is married with three kids and
my aunt and one hates me well she doesnt hate me i
dont even know really two of them i just that would be
so great if i had a really serious girlfriend by graduation
and she came down here and we lived together and she
was real close to beth and lynn and did stuff with them
your sister wont be a mother to you when your mother
is dead and but she could be close and she could go to
school or get a job and we could cook and read and talk

and go dancing and have picnics and play basketball and swim go to destin and the jazz fest and mardi gras shit that would be so great if she just got to know what i was about anyone would fall in love with me if she could just live with me for two or three months and get to know me thats why gayle was the only girl to ever fall in love with me because she was the only girl who really got to know me i should have called her over vacation i cant believe i hid from her at the movie place god that was stupid if she wasnt with her mom - hi gayle god i should have just said it just to see what would have happened if she had just come to the north instead of running off to tennessee i mean what the fuck is in tennessee rinnggg hello - tim - yeah - its gayle - hi - hi - what have you been up to - nothing - you - not much - you know - when are you going back - tomorrow - what about you - i just got home yesterday im not leaving until next week - i would like to talk to you sometime - well im leaving tomorrow - i know but i meant this summer - im only gonna be home for the first couple weeks in june - where are you going - isreal - with your sisters are you taking your sisters - no just a few friends from school - that will be fun - yeah - well im gonna be home at that time maybe we could go to destin for a couple days - that would be nice - ill cook you some chicken you get some chicken and you put it in a pot water and some celery a bunch of celery and an onions good sized onion one of those white onions have you ever had a maui onion they are sweeter than vadalia onions they are really sweet and carrots and garlic and pepper and a bit of rosemary and you got soup or you can make moscas chicken with salt and pepper and garlic and rosemary and olive oil and broil it or there is this other chicken that i like to make where you put it in one of those huge pan fryers with some tomato paste and some cream of mushroom soup with onions and garlic and rosemary and pepper and celery salt and

thyme - what else do you cook - i love steak but theres
really nothing to it i make the best tuna fish and i make
spaghetti sauce for like my whole fraternity and chili
from swamp but i dont make it as spicy but i make
really good spaghetti sauce - its good to hear your voice
again - yeah i missed you - i missed you too - are you
seeing someone - no - you - no - how is robert - good -
you should write to him - yeah i will - do you have his
address - i have it at school - well write me a letter and
put his address on it - okay - i love your letters - will
you write me - yes do you promise - yes jesus christ -
okay - bye - bye - wait - what - will you marry me - yes
- god damn why why why why didnt i just god damn im
sittin here thinkin about c and julie and all because i
just dont want to think about her or them i dont even
know who to think about i need a girlfriend who will
have me someone with nice eyes a nice smile and a
penetrating soul an ancient soul like cleopatra helen
elizabeth or guenivere a nice blue or green aura in
motion she smiles like silence there are a lot of
beautiful people out there but they all like such teds
why do they like such teds and such assholes but i like
girls who are beautiful so why should they like
someone ugly like me

can anybody find me somebody to love i love the
way the basketball feels on my hand when it leaves
your fingers swish shit its not just male and female thats
circles and squares but nature and man because nature
is the circle the tree the pond the flower the fruit the sun
and man is the city the city block the building the
skyscraper the brick the field is rectangles and squares
and colors nature is blue and green and yellow and red
and man is silver and gray and offwhite pink i hate pink
fuckin art deco fake looking pink plaster stucco and that
orange i guess there is some pink in nature like a rose
but a rose isnt all that natural a pink rose is just a hybrid
of a white rose and a red rose which are much prettier

than pink i love white roses and red roses pink roses are kind of i hate pink i like azaleas but i like white azaleas much better than pink azaleas thats true its inbreeding thats man and mediocrity again truth is in the extremes the two extremes at the same time red and white at the same time contrast not pink yellow roses i love yellow roses maybe i should send gayle yellow roses but then she will think no god fuck it damn why cant i make this shot man is circles and nature is squares no man is squares nature is circles but man cant beat nature he tries to make a square car but he cant nature keeps beating it back to make it more like circles and planes were rectangles those old orville and wilbur wright jobs and now its circles and nature curves women hourglass we dont make hourglasses any more maybe its because women look more and more like them maybe it is too commonplace what is commonplace is boring so we need those fuckin plastic swatch watches look like they came out of a fuckin gumball machine i hate plastic benjamin - yes sir - one word - yes sir - plastics - sir - plastics - yes sir - enough said - he was right the future is plastic where have you gone joe dimaggio a nation turns its lonely eyes to you whats that you say missus robinson joltin joe has left and gone away that would be so great judy hamilton ann margaret no not ann margaret the other one ann - ann - what the hell is her name - ann margaret is the one with red hair and big tits the fat one that was in carnal knowledge i hated carnal knowledge that was the worst fuckin movie i hate ann margaret the other one is beautiful though what was her name swish nope god damn i am shooting so bad katherine ross is beautiful - you know she was only in those two movies the graduate and butch cassidy and the sundance kid and then she just disappeared - what was i thinking

i hate those fuckin swatch watches i keep expecting to pick one up without any hands on it that would be something a watch without hands a clockwork orange that is something right out of a clockwork orange tochter socher gunterfuken tochter aus elysium badumbadada da da da duh da dada da duh da dada da duh do da duh na na na na na na nuh na na na na nah nuh num

the clock takes all the life of out time all the time out of life what is it as long as life time no time as long as time is clicked off by little clocks and hands it is dead it is only when the clock stops that time comes to life and robert threw his fathers pocketwatch into the grave because for him the time had stopped oh benjy if he never had a mother i am benjy if i ever had a mother something about you cant beat time because that is your enemy i dont know i should read that book again and the physics textbook because the physics textbook describes god but the sound and the fury experiences god and god is in the experience not in the description i dont see how its nature versus man when nature is man swish there finally god the sky is awesome i could just watch the sky all day if i had to look at one thing and not be bored it would be the sky i love the way the sky looks from a plane i cant believe you like to fly if i lost my parents in a plane crash i would never fly again tim son theres been an accident beth lynn come here please kids this is the worst thing you will ever hear i know its the worst thing ive ever had to say theres been an accident your parents are dead

ann bancroft that was her name i love ann bancroft god bless you please missus robinson heaven loves you more than you will know oooh oooh oooh whats the line before where have you gone joe dimaggio a nation turns its lonely eyes to you thats one of those great lines where the song is pretty good but there is this one line which seems to say - everything - if i knew the way i would take you home - are birds free from the chains of the skyway - where have you gone what is before that

ann margaret no ann bancroft the man in the gaberdine
suit was a spy no thats from america where have you
gone candidates debate thats it going to the candidates
debate - laugh about it shout about it when youve got to
choose - every way you look at this you lose - where
have you gone joe dimaggio a nation turns its lonely
eyes to you oooh oooh oooh - whats that you say
missus robinson joltin joe has left and gone away hey
hey hey - hey hey hey

but man is nature essentially and that is where you
find out whether you believe in god or not if you think
that man his emotions his everything if you think it is
just the sum of chemical and electrical processes then
you dont believe in god but if you think there is
something more than that you do - no but thats not the
end because it can be all chemical and electrical
processes but how did it get there i mean think about
how complicated the human body is the intricacies of
almost infinite cells and nerves and circulatory arteries
and veins and capillaries do you realize how many
calculations need to be made to throw a football
without even thinking without judgment without
judgment i mean there are so many things that the body
does naturally that we cant even do or take thousands
and thousands of years but its not just that its whether
you think that the sum of the parts is less than the whole
because when you put all of the parts together there is
something else something more - this magic - this aura -
this motion something supersexual and superreal and
surreal about someone and something and the doggie
and the sky is more than the sum of its parts the
rainbow with every colour but its something else
entirely but do you think like in zen and the art of
motorcycle maintenance that machines have just as
much god and just as much holy and just as much god
as people - yes if you look at them in that way but i hate
machines i hate plastic i hate convenience i hate

efficiency and all of zen and the art of motorcycle
maintenance is about artistry like a cathedral where
they are put together with hands like art and are
evidence of the greatness in the creator but then youve
got all of these widgets and assembly lines where the
machines are created by other machines and what are
you gonna do with plastic you cant get rid of it god the
sky is amazing i love that colour you know there is a
colour of blue a hue of blue in these cathedrals in
europe from the middle ages in stained glass windows
that had never been reproduced we cant figure out how
to make it - really - and there goes michael - ten
seconds - bulls down by two - eight seven six five four
three two one and did he get it off yes - swish - the bulls
win the pennant no thats baseball and the bulls win
what do they win the championship i guess i wish we
still had the jazz the utah jazz what kind of a fuckin
ridiculous name is that so its green and red and blue
against gray and offwhite and pink like with the
apollonian and the dionysian you got the purple and the
white and the blue in heaven against the earth thats why
its the colour purple because purple is the colour of
royalty and so when she wears the colour purple she is
royalty but reed believed that you had to recreate the
language because the ideas we have of racist ideas and
slavery and racism are so deeply imbedded in the
language that we use that we have to exorcise ourselves
of this language and change the words that we use thats
why he writes in the pop style like scat like jazz gonna
put the hoodoo on bukka doppyduck we gonna break
into tom mccanns and steal all of the shoes thats where
the black panthers were in oakland i bet he was in the
black panthers what was that song that taj mahal did the
streetlamps in oakland that was a good song flip has my
disc that bastard i have to get that back no but its purple
and silver and white of the sky against brown and red
and black from the earth and thats why white is holy

and for us that is good the sky and what is up and thats
where god is thats where heaven is and hell is beneath
the earth and red like earth like fire and thats why black
is funeral because you are not white not dead not white
not black but not white and if you are black then when
you die you are not black you are white and they dance
downward to the earth while we dance upward to the
sky on our tiptoes in a ballet because they see
themselves in earth thats why its all upside down why
the black man is the devil he isnt the devil heez just not
white and if the angel then what is not white is the devil
and they have the same thing we are the devil malcolm
x is right and thats why god is above like judgment and
law rather than passion which wells up from underneath
from the earth like reds and browns and the black and
that is why god for them is inspirational rather than
judgmental and thats what blake and all of those guys
were trying to do is fuse the two because inside we are
all both inspiration and judgment reason and passion
order and law and rebellion music and art and work and
crime and hate and love the olympic and the cathonic
heaven and hell - and he has this ascension like a
disclaimer and then youve got this war red against
white hell against heaven earth against sky passion
against reason chaos against law sexual against sensual
red against white and somewhere floating around out
there pink is floating around out there with nowhere to
go i hope it just disappears because truth is a paradox
truth is in the extremes both extremes together at the
same time marbled not compromise i hate compromise
there is nothing worse than compromise and that is the
difference two extremes together marbled and two
extremes in some mediocre gray area compromise and
mediocre and compromised but truth is marbled truth is
paradox truth is the extremes together at one time
aristotle was wrong its not in the mean its in the
extremes not aristotle blake not in one or extreme or in

the other and not in some middleground but in both
extremes at the same time - i thought that was
hypocrisy - hypocrisy is not the same as paradox -
hypocrisy is the refusal to acknowledge one of the
extremes one half of the paradox even though its still
there and when it comes out everyone says that he is a
hypocrite - see its more the perception than something
that exists itself someone who lives in one extreme will
eventually be called a hypocrite whether he is or not i
dont know - so if you are on one side or the other then
you are a hypocrite and if you are in the middle then
you are wishywashy so you are damned if you do and
damned if you dont - no youve got to be at the same
time on both sides - but then you are nowhere - but then
you are everywhere - nowhere is everywhere
everywhere is nowhere is in the middle nowhere is pink
truth is red and white but never pink truth is black and
white but never gray everything is the best or the worst
i love him or i hate him thats why rocky is a great
character because everyone either loves him or hates
him thats why reagan is a great figure because everyone
either loves him or hates him what happened when ajax
died when reagan dies i will dance on his grave i will
dance on his mother fucking grave get out of the way
old man is that your answer i guess ill find my own way
- if i knew the way i would take you home god i want to
go home i want to go back thats all i want i just want to
go back time only flows in one direction thats what i
hate the most that time only flows in one direction
wouldnt it be neat to be merlyn merlyn was born at the
end of time and moves backwards into the past but then
you wouldnt appreciate anything you wouldnt
appreciate having your parents because you wouldnt
have gone through the process of loving them and you
would miss out on everything i wish i was born a long
time ago when everything hadnt been invented when
everything hadnt been done when there was something

still left to do what is there to do what is there left to invent was there left to be or write you cant be great anymore theres too many people theres nothing to invent cuz its all in stages its all little pieces little bricks cuz there are so many bricks you can build a wall you cant build a cathedral yeah but its cool cuz you got tv and technology and radios and film and cars and planes medical care no wooden teeth and toilets and air conditioning multimedia virtual reality did you see the movie brainstorm that was a really cool movie it sucked it was a shitty movie but you know how sometimes the movie sucks but it has such a cool idea that its cool thats just like dreamscape that was such a cool idea i wish i could do that go into missus hamiltons dreams and fuck her and we could have this secret dreamlife affair that no one would know about but she would know and she would have this mysterious attraction to me and remember the dreams and not know why she was having all of these dreams with me like god and her husband and michael would never know that would be great and you could go into all kinds of persons dreams and follow them around if you could turn invisible that would be neat i wish that i could go into peoples dreams and go invisible and fly - i used to have a lot of flying dreams - i would run and jump off of my diving board but instead of going in the pool i would go up in the air and fly just like swimming it was just like swimming in air and what was i thinking

dreamscape that would be so cool you could go into jane pauleys dreams and just follow her around for a while to see what she is like in real life i bet she is a bitch i bet she is a bitch but someone that you love i dont mind girls that are bitches - you want your wife to be a bitch because you want her to be smart - smart girls are bitches - not the whiny bitches - theyre dumb - but smart arrogant bitches - and plus you dont want your wife to be all friendly flirting with all of these

other guys and other men - my mom was nice - did she
cheat on your dad - no - of course not - she was nice
and friendly but she didnt flirt with people men - i wish
i was that person among those people in that world with
that past present and future and those things - i wish i
had that height weight head body nose teeth skin hair
sight hearing intellectual abilities athletic abilities
musical abilities artistic abilities knowledge will
religion courage aura magic vision personality powers
of motion vision and creation and my parents and
pawpaw and bernard and uncle g
    nowhere is medium pink tartar and well done is both
blackened prime rib that is the best meal i have ever
had in my life a cajun martini fried soft shell crawfish
and blackened prime rib from k pauls that was so good
- better than moscas - i cant say that - i mean come on
everything has its place thats the thing i mean youre
looking for different things if you want a k pauls meal k
pauls is the best if you want a moscas meal moscas is
the best if you want a ruths chris meal ruths chris is the
best domilises is the best except meatball mothers has
the best meatball domilise has the best hot smoked
sausage and roast beef and swiss - and then there are
meals like clancys and the upperline like nicer for a
date or something or antoines i love antoines is the
coolest building i mean when you walk into there you
feel like you are in paris in the nineteen twenties it is
the coolest building one day im gonna buy antoines you
gonna run it - thats the problem - you cant just buy a
place and not run it unless you trust someone else to run
it who you trust - ill trust someone - plus i dont want it
to make money as long as i dont lose money but - but -
but nowhere is medium everything will be at the sides
the best or the worst not just good or bad - but things
arent like that things arent black and white - but they
should be - they can be the both you know - you are at
the same time the most romantic and the most cynical

person i have ever met - that is the greatest compliment i have ever gotten thats the greatest compliment you can ever give someone and there is this energy this feeling and this thought that you are gonna let it go you can put moral tags on it later if you want but really that doesnt do any good doesnt change anything are you going to let things thrive even if you think they might be evil because what if it is wonderful what if beauty is ugliness you cannot deceive you cannot say that it is not what it is but you can say you have to say you must say that things are more than what they are if you see the sunset at sunset its distorted because you arent seeing the blue waves so in science that isnt what the sun is but if you say that is what the sun is all about then you arent lying because that is the sun more of what the sun is the power and the beauty but if you take a man like reagan and you say that he cares about the poor when he doesnt then you are lying making him what he is more than what he is make him see because the whole thing is power and we call what comes of this power good or evil we put moral tags on them by their pragmatic effects but thats not how you can judge things you have to judge them by their energy by this place at which they start with that intention and that passion is never wrong never evil all that lives is holy we twist it around and say that if some guys paints a blue dot on a white canvass then that is beautiful because the rational world makes some sense out of it but if its not beautiful then we dont get the beauty and the glory out of it - we dont experience the aesthetic - when we behold the work it is not beautiful - what is beautiful is that within us which gives it meaning that power that beauty that intellect - rationality - imagination - it is not the work which is beautiful - its just us - but then the work is beautiful because it brings out the beauty in us - but to be good its got to evidence the genius of the creator - like the boating party is

evidence itself of renoirs genius the sacrifice of isaac is
evidence of carravagios genius the nightwatchman is
evidence of rembrants genius - but the blue dot we dont
even know who painted the blue dot because any
mother fucker can paint a blue dot - thats not evidence
of genius - something thats good has a special quality
all its own - independent from the person watching - if
you take the blue dot and you take away the person
thats looking at it then it has no meaning - it has
nothing - but if you put carravagio in a box it still has
beauty it still has genius even if there is no one there to
look at it - thats bullshit thats like a tree falling in the
woods with no one there to hear it - yeah it makes a
sound - exactly - exactly - thats exactly what its like -
good things make a sound anyway - blue dots dont
make a sound - but the real question is do we have the
courage to let things live do we have hope and faith and
love that truth and right will win in the end but even
reagan even hitler even david duke and strom thurmond
and jesse helms its like the difference between graffiti
and vandalism we can tolerate graffiti but vandalism we
have to do something about - its like the difference
between litter and pollution - litter we can tolerate but
pollution we have to do something about - even einstein
thought you had to use force to stop hitler - but all of
these people will be discredited in the end - people will
see them for what they are - and right will win out i
refuse to accept the cynical notion that nation after
nation must spiral down this endless staircase into the
hell of thermonuclear destruction - i believe that
unarmed truth and unconditional love will have the
final word - that is why right temporarily defeated is
stronger than evil triumphant - yes but how much
damage can we afford to have along the way - that is
the question - how much damage can you allow to
happen along the way - but anyway - what was i
thinking beauty - beauty - yes beauty is not something

that you can rate - its something you feel - in your heart
- its not ten on a scale of one to twenty it is quantum it
is binary it is there or not there yes or no but beauty is
always there there is something beautiful in everything
there is something beautiful in everything and everyone
there is beauty in reagan i love reagan in humanity he
has a part of humanity with which i share im sure if i
sat down and talked with him for a while i love him but
i hate him but there is got to be some beauty to him -
what about hitler - i dont know about hitler - its hard to
say anything could be beautiful about hitler but he is a
person he came from a mother and must have had some
love some act of tenderness some act of kindness just
like martin luther king cheated on his wife no one is all
good or all bad no one is right about everything or
wrong about everything even reagan is right about some
things - stupid people are right about some things even
if only accidentally and smart people are wrong about
some things because theyre mistaken and good people
are wrong even if only accidentally out of ignorance
and even evil people must do some things that are good
nothing is black or white - everything is shades of gray
- no everything is black and white all marbled together -
they are right and wrong marbled within each person
but they are black and white not gray each thing is
black or white within that person each thing is either
right or wrong even though its mixed in the same
person right or wrong smart or stupid or ignorant or
good or bad most of evil is ignorance - i think evil is
about ten percent evil and about ninety percent
ignorance - yeah but the question is - the question is -
what is the question

the question is lets say that hitler is evil then how did
he get to be that way - i mean if its predetermined then
you cant blame him for it because its predetermined or
genetic - but you still have a choice - yeah but even if
you have a choice - lets assume free will - lets assume

that you have a choice - what makes this person choose to kill and me choose not to kill - what is it about me and what is it about them - is it genetic or environmental - because theyre bad and youre good - but what makes them bad and what makes me good - what makes me choose not to kill - because you have a respect for life - but what makes me have a respect for life - and what makes this person ultimately have no respect for life - because if you keep asking why and why and why then no one is really responsible for anything - thats bullshit - because i know that i have a choice - i can chose to be weak or i can chose to be strong - i can chose to take the easy way or i can chose to do it right - yeah but what makes you choose - because youre smart - and if youre smart then why are you smart - because i worked hard - well why did you work hard - because i am strong - but why are you strong - and if you keep asking why then its hard to see that there is some answer what makes you good what makes you smart what makes you strong your genetics - well what did you have to do with that - your environment - what did you have to do with that - but we make our own lives - we shape our own environment - we choose to better ourselves or not - we choose to better our environment or not - im not saying that - all im saying is why - what makes you choose - why do you make those choices - what is it about you - that makes you make those choices - and ultimately there is really no answer - we need to make people responsible for societal purposes - for societal purposes we have to just pretend that everyone has free will - because we cant tolerate people going around and killing people so we just create the fiction of free will - we cant have people going around raping people so we just have to say i dont give a shit - i dont give a shit why you are a criminal - i dont care if you are poor i dont care if you are stupid i dont care of you are uneducated i dont care if you were discriminated against - because none of that justifies you fucking with me - whatever the reason is that youre a criminal - what ever that reason is it doesnt justify you fucking with me beating me or raping me or robbing me or killing me - so i dont give a shit why - so for societal purposes - for due process and life liberty and property for the criminal justice system and america we have to just say i dont give a shit - you cant fuck with people - and to do that - we have to pretend like people have free will - whether they do or not - i agree with that for purposes of society - for purposes of society i dont give a shit if your grandfather was a slave - i dont care if youre poor - i dont care if you cant get a job - i dont care if youre illegitimate or illiterate or dont have a father figure in the home - i dont care if your father beat you - or you were molested as a child - because none of that justifies you fucking with me - none of that justifies you raping my sister - or breaking into my house - but for purposes of philosophy - for metaphysical purposes - as a matter of sociology or psychology or morality or ethics or drama or literature - those are all of the interesting questions - in why - why is one person hitler and one person martin luther king - why is one person malcolm x and one person martin luther king - why is one person reagan and one person carter - why is this person a criminal why is this person a student - they are both black - this person was black and poor and grew up in the ghetto and became a doctor and this person was poor and black and grew up in the very same ghetto and became a drug dealer - what is the difference between these two people - is it simply because one is good and one is bad - one is smart and one is dumb - and what made them smart and dumb - people dont have anything to do with how smart they are - but they can improve themselves - yeah they can improve themselves but what makes them want to or chose to or decide to ultimately i mean that is why morally morality is just a bunch of crap - there is no moral or immoral everything that lives is holy - thats why criminal law shouldnt have anything to do with morals - its not about morals - its not about whether someone is good or bad or motives or intentions - its just about protecting the rest of society - if someone is danger to society he should be in jail - if someone is not a danger to society he shouldnt be in jail - i dont care who they are or where they come from or why they are who they are - all i care about is being able to walk down the street in safety - or be in my one house and feel secure - or my own car - and not have to worry about my sisters going out at night and getting raped - or robbed or killed - no matter what he is done if there is some dangerous fucking guy and he only gets arrested for spitting on the sidewalk they should keep him in jail forever - and if some guy kills someone under some weird circumstances but where its clear that theyre not a threat to society let them go - i dont care - thats why its such a farce - because we look at specific actions in the past but all that matters is whether this person is a danger in the future - and then everyone looks at why people do what they do and who gives a shit because whatever the reason you dont have the right to fuck with me

and i would be pissed off too if i were some intelligent educated respectable law abiding black person - that has to suffer because of the others - thats why they have antisemites thats why they have black racists and all those blacks are turning republicans like in the soldier story cuz they have to carry the weight of that on their back - just like we do thats why i am an anti semite - because i have to carry the weight of all those loser little wormy slimy effeminate jews on my back - the jews may run hollywood but the jews are the most stereotyped people in movies even more than

blacks - they are always effeminate maybe not
effeminate but physically weak and not good athletes
and plump and out of shape and small - or they are
slimy lawyer shysters that advertise on tv like morris
bart or agents that steal all the money or just those old
people speaking with yiddish accents that are
overbearing and annoying - or they are hasids or they
are these victims of prejudice that have to be protected
just like cry freedom - and mississippi burning - thats
why the blacks hate those movies so much because they
show the good white people empathizing with or
helping or saving the poor persecuted helpless
powerless black man - and they are the heroes when in
real life the f b i didnt do anything and it was the local
black activists who brought the killers to justice - you
know paul newman turned down the movie for other
reasons - he was supposed to play gene hackman and he
objected to the movie because in a movement that was
marked by nonviolence he didnt think it was
appropriate to accomplish justice by violent and lawless
means - and then in cry freedom when instead of
stephen biko the hero of the story is the white reporter
who gets the story out - well who gives a shit about him
just make the movie about biko - its always the good
white person who empathizes with the blacks or helps
the blacks or saves the blacks who is the hero - and it is
the same thing with the jews - or else they are there to
give some background moral liberal angle on things or
else they are old yiddish comical figures or hasidic
oddities or shyster lawyers and im sure there are a lot of
jews like that - thats why it becomes a stereotype
because we have all of these bastards that ripped off
people and moralize about everything and whine about
everything - but there are a lot of jews that arent like
that - and we have to carry all that on our backs and
thats the same with blacks they have to carry the
poverty and the crime and the illegitimacy and the

illiteracy of all the other blacks - not because they are black - thats the different between a racist and not a racist - is that a racist thinks that you are a criminal because you are black - or that you are stupid because you are black - someone else thinks that you are a criminal for other reasons - but youre more likely to be a criminal if youre black - its just statistics - at least in this city - in the country all the crime is committed by white people and white people are all the rapists and child molesters and serial killers - but in this city ninety percent of the crime is committed by young black males - so if i am walking down the street at night and i see a young black male i am scared - because it is more likely that he is going to be a criminal - and that is just a fact - in that specific case he may be a student or a doctor or a lawyer or an architect or just some other regular poor or middle class black person who is nice and good and not a criminal and im sorry if i prejudge him - im sorry - it sucks - that he gets swept in under the blanket but you have to be realistic - and its not because heez black thats the difference between a racist and not a racist is that a racist thinks that they are criminals because they are black - while a non racist thinks that they are criminals for other reasons altogether

because they are poor and illiterate and rejected and neglected and dejected and infected and detected and inspected - they have no hope they have no education a lot of them are illegitimate a lot of them are abused and that is why they are criminals not because they are black but because of the homes of which they are born

but you dont cut off the arm - because the arm is not the disease - the poverty is the disease the illiteracy is the disease the desperation is the disease the drugs are the disease the violence is the disease - you dont cut off the arm you cure the disease - you get out your alcohol and your betadine and your aspirin and your stitches and you cure the disease swish - and he gets the rebound five four three two one aahhhh and the crowds going crazy in the arena they cant believe it its unbelievable whats our job we like go around and pick up stiffs or what thats great it starts with an earthquake - and birds and snakes and aeroplanes - and lenny bruce is not afraid - eye of the hurricane listen to yourself ban a murderer for hire and furies breathing down your neck - see marquis and teams of reporters battle trump tower back for barn burning blood letting symbiotic patriotic feeling pretty psyched - its the end of the world as we know it - its the end of the world as we know it - its the end of the world as we know it - i feel fine - its the end of the world as we know it - its the its the end of the world as we know it - its the its the end of the world as we know it - and i feel fine - its the time is had some time alone its the time i had some time alone its the time i had some time alone i feel fine

i hate r e m - yeah but thats a good song - yeah

but anyway - we all think that it is better to think than to feel - that it is better to be an observer than to experience something that it is better that we reserve our emotions that we dont let things get out of control for fear that it will be destructive and then we are also fearing that it will be good when you end evil you end good when you take away you are never taking away something that is wholly evil you cant sacrifice things thats the greatest evil in the world is sacrifice all that lives is holy - and they are all related to freedom to die and with it the freedom to live the freedom to destroy and with that the freedom to build but it takes a lot longer to build than to destroy thats the rub i mean it takes centuries to build a cathedral and then some fucker comes along with a bomb that he drops out of plane and its gone in seconds - but anyway - when we build plastic is backwards i mean you build a skyscraper but thats only part of progress because the other part is being able to enjoy it to experience it and to to it because that is something that you feel not something that you think should think should be true or think ought to be because beauty is something that you feel its not something that is ten on scale or five eight one hundred and six pounds is not a sunset if thats not what you feel maybe you couldnt give a shit about the sunset - fine - but what it is that is power and if it is then maybe that is payment for something else for albert einstein and thomas jefferson and martin luther king isaac newton truth is on the march and nothing can stop it - i mean look at china right now you got one million people in tienamin square in bejing and in hong kong you got a million marching which is like the biggest protest ever - and its spreading - to russia and germany and new york itll be in san francisco soon with all of those chinese people there and china makes sense because its always to the west gold and revolution and paradise new lands and pioneers from china westward to greece westward to rome westward to germany and charlemagne to france and to england to america new york and then to the west california the promise land and now to china and to russia and poland and czechoslovakia the whole thing is gonna come tumbling down the walls of jericho come tumbling down blow your trumpet daniel gabriel the walls come tumbling down into an apocalyptic sea a wonderful sea of golden reds and greens and blues whence climbs the new life a green a blue and red and gold with a mind a light no in darkness a mind of its own making out of this world revolution goodby dumbo apocalypse desire passion and love all joining all of it together with violence and separation but also joining and nineteen eighty nine on the verge of the nineties on the verge of two thousand and everyone knows that the first ending is the second beginning - you see the trick is to live in the extremes and not get torn apart by them - the man that can do that because its tiring it gets tiring im tired and im only twenty one years old i never thought that i would be so tired but youve got to keep going its time to keep on going and not to yield what is that tennyson yes or yeats tennyson to go to strive to something and not to yield we are gonna break into tom mccanns and steal the shoes right out from under them so that there is nothing for them to stand on make them touch the earth again with their toes and see what it feels like how it feels - that it is cold at night and warm on a summer day on the yoemans way he built this country thats how thomas jefferson envisioned the nation as a land of small farmers

warm a summers day and on the yoemans way he builds his ladder to the stars forsaking not from whence they came you can build castles but dont forget that theyre woven of earth and clay you can dream of lands and worlds and crosses yet to bear or not to borne is that a word fuck it it sounds good the emerald forests in the mind but its all a part of desire and the pages and pages of equations are all a product of the desire to find themselves their answers - thats passion - so lets not forget that - shall we - lets not all become robots shall we

"ptinng - ptinng" i love the echo in the bounce of the ball "ptinng - ptinng" shit i should have made that but that is where we should be going i mean you can easily see the progression you got the greeks and the romans with many gods and everything is external and dynamic and then you have one god and the focus is on the individual and then you have christianity and you start to look inside the individual to the different aspects its psychological freudian like and you got one god divided up into three parts superego ego id only they messed up the parts the father and the son and the holy ghost is all one and they look to each other half and made it the devil when they should have had the father

as one the apollonian and law and reason and order and
law with the son as rebellion and dionysian and chaos
and passion desire and lust and the holy ghost no wait
the father should be the dionysian because he is there
first the desire the chaos and the passion is there first
like the id and then the reason and law is the son born
out of that father and then youve got the holy ghost
which mediates between the two like the ego and the
son is like the superego and then but actually it is the
body which mediates between the two the body is that
physical manifestation which mediates and arbitrates
and actualizes the war between the two - so lucifer too
is god and all that lives is holy and lucifer is even well
lucifer is the father and then christ is the son and the
holy ghost is not a ghost but the corporate not corporate
corpulate corpulate the body corpulate kind of the
house for the other two no i hear a priest calling god is
beyond man bullshit god is man and man is god thats
the problem we are gods and everyone is walking
around afraid to assume the role of god everyone is
afraid of god when he is god and everyone is so afraid
of god and so afraid of being gods assuming the role of
god that we let reagan and hitler run things which is
crazy not chaos crazy law crazy we are gods and we are
gods individually and we are gods collectively as we
share ourselves with the animals and the waters and the
plants and the mountains and the wind and they with us
- that is the next generation that is the second coming
but then is that the end i mean what is after that because
living happily ever after is the same thing as dying
happily ever after - i guess we wont be able to see the
next plane until we get to it thats what true genius is
being able to see the next plane before we actually get
there i wish i could see it i wish i could see it or at least
go back to a time before it was seen on a former plane
and let me be the one to bring us to the next plane
before it comes please let me have that vision because

intelligence is not vision lots of people are smart but you can count beans on a fucking calculator but real genius is in vision - really smart people have vision please god there is no god but there has to be because youve got all of these things all of these separate parts and cells and stuff and they all work together and they all know whats going on and all these parallels i mean we are the world we have this fire inside of us and its burning and the surface is all cold under control and then we have all these volcanoes where the fire just bursts out and the lava is all fearful and scary but we love it is life and it is fire and it is beautiful and power and we love it and i mean how can all of these things be the same how can there be all of these analogies and mythologies and everything analogies if there is not some underlying meaning like a hieroglyph like the brow of the sperm whale or its intestines or the tattoo the cabala if there is no god or even if there is a god and then you have the existentialist creates justifies who justifies himself because there is no god - because why - except why told us everything about the wasp except why - who - uncle somebody

because it is meaningless if there is no god i dont like that cynical shit because even if there is no god i am here and even if there is no god there is a lot of beauty in the world i mean there are beautiful women people children all over and there are beautiful animals and plants and rivers and skies and we are here and we should enjoy it i mean if life is just a big joke then we should laugh - not cry - i mean all this the world is gonna blow up isnt the cause because we wouldnt if we cared - the fact that we can blow ourselves up in a matter of minutes isnt the cause of all this sadness it is the result - not it doesnt matter because of the bomb but the bomb because it doesnt matter - and the stuff in d c the violence and the drugs isnt the cause of all of this shit it is the solution not the solution not a good

solution but a solution result - but it doesnt matter - its
not that bleak because even if we do blow ourselves up
everything will lay dormant or something for a few
hundred years but everything is gonna regenerate even
the radioactive stuff will pass away except that it is this
halflife stuff and it never gets there then how is it
getting anywhere i mean half of half of half of half is
gonna be nothing it will never be nothing it will never
be zero it is a limit limits of infinity - anyway what was
i thinking

jung thought - but jung thought
what did jung thought think
the bells the children heard were inside them right
that it was not looking out and trying to explain eternal
events with god but an inner desire or yearing dream or
thought or dream towards god and the bells the children
heard were inside them call the roller of big cigars
but everything is gonna come back
yeah everything is gonna come back and even if it
doesnt something else will evolve but you cant stop life
you cant stop evolution you cant stop energy and even
if you could it would still be beautiful desolate places
are beautiful deserts volcanoes oceans i mean just the
water itself and the clouds and the wind there is great
life in things that are not living - in the sun - and then it
will keep on growing and if it doesnt we will be dead
anyway i mean i wont care and its kinda peaceful when
you think about it - if you could be the only one left
with the living dead water running over rocks crawling
the ice the sun rising over the formations of rock trees
and people and snakes and ants if there is a nuclear
explosion it will only be ants and roaches left because
they can withstand a lot of radioactivity with their
shells armadillos would be good and turtles but what
are they going to drink but theres enough beauty theres
definitely enough life in the things not living no you
cant stop running water running water you cant kill the

fire that burns inside - wow - this is bold - bold as love - this is bold bold as love - this is bold as love just ask the axis he knows everything yeah yeah yeah what the hell is the axis the rome berlin axis satire like this isnt true no it cant be that it must be like the true vantage point the center watching all of the things move around it like the sibyl my red is confident he flashes tokens of war and ribbons euphoria - orange is young full of daring but very unsteady for the first go round - my yellow in this case is not so mellow - in fact im trying to say its frightened like me - and all these emotions of mine keeps holdin me from being a rainbow like you - but im bold bold as love let me tell you now come on doggie lets go for a walk - come on - come on

hey mama - show boob - come in she said ill give ya shelter from the storm - i knew newborn babies wailin like the morning dove and old men with broken teeth stranded without love - do i understand your question maam for the hopeless and forlorn - come in she said ill give you shelter from the storm - even you yesterday you had to ask me where i was at - i couldnt believe after these years you didnt know me better than that - down the highway down the tracks down the road to ecstasy i followed you beneath the stars hounded by your memory and all your ragin glory - youll never know the hurt ive suffered nor the pain id rise above and ill never know the same about you your holiness or your kind of love - and it makes me feel so sorry

she has nice tits - is that - no thats not her she lives on soniat - hi tim - hi how are you - fine - you home from school - yeah till tomorrow - how is michael - heez doin real good - does he know what heez gonna do next year - no he doesnt know maybe law school maybe business - tell him i said hi - okay - you want something to drink - sure - lemonade no what would she offer me iced tea beer no she wouldnt offer me beer lemonade iced tea - iced tea - sure - you know i had the biggest crush on you in high school - really - you were wearing a yellow blouse and a pair of white jeans - i was in eighth grade and you were picking us up from sunday school and one of the other kids was late i think it was jason and you were starting to get mad - you guys had that yellow and brown stationwagon and you were standing outside of the car with the door open - and i was watching you through the window from the back - and i remember that you were wearing some kind of sandals or something but you werent wearing socks and your toenails were painted red - and your blouse was this really tight cotton yellow blouse - and i dont know if you were wearing a bra but it was kinda windy and i could see your nipples through the fabric no i wouldnt say that maybe it would get her excited no its too much she would get embarrassed and disgusted - yeah - and so i remember that you were wearing some kind of sandals or something but you werent wearing socks and your toenails were painted red - and when you went to close the door to the station wagon you lifted your arms to close it and your blouse lifted up - just a little bit - and i could see your bellybutton - and i have had a crush on you ever since

i wouldnt say bellybutton - would you say navel - it sounds like an orange - stomach - no i guess you would say bellybutton - cuz that would sound all young and innocent - she must want to fuck someone young and solid i mean she must at least fantasize about it - at least fleetingly with her old fat balding husband yeah but thats gonna be you one day - i know

she has the best boobs i could see her nipples perfectly - it just changes everything - before that you can tell the size but until you see them with a nipple erection you cant really it lets you imagine and visualize the boob - i agree - judy hamilton in that yellow blouse and white jeans - sheez ugly - i know but she is so sexual - and then i followed her around at that fair all day

sheez pretty actually - in a way

she can look good when sheez all dressed up at joshuas bar mitzvah party she looked great - she kind of sparkles - you could definitely make her look good in a painting i wish i could paint or a sketch i wish i could draw

i was in eighth grade and you were picking us up from sunday school and i can remember that you were wearing a cotton yellow blouse and white slacks like jeans and someone was late i think it was jason and you were starting to get mad and standing there with your hands on your hips and i remember that you were wearing some kind of sandals and your toenails were painted red and when he finally came you lifted your arms to close the back door to the stationwagon and your blouse lifted up - just a little - so that i could see your bellybutton - and ive had a crush on you ever since

i wish i had the power to move into and out of dreamscape i wish i was that person with that height weight head body nose teeth skin hair sight hearing eyes voice intellectual abilities athletic abilities musical abilities artistic abilities speaking joketelling and storytelling abilities charm charisma poise stature grace will religion courage aura magic vision personality and powers of motion vision and creation

so whats this sisters theory - the sisters theory is that guys and girls think about women in completely different ways - guys that dont have sisters like girls in varying degrees but its all mixed together - love likeness lust she had the three ls of dating she was lookable likeable and lustable - no but anyway - everything is thrown together - there is no religion to it - but guys who have sisters are very religious about women - and they view women as either this great perfect highly romanticized virginal being - whom you

love but you have no lust for - or a wild sexual base
creature who you really have no respect for and just
want to fuck

and the other corollary this is just as important from
a psychological development perspective - guys that
have sisters arent friends with girls - all those guys that
are all buddy buddy with girls are guys that dont have
sisters - because there is like this void there is like this
vacuum that they are trying to fill - but guys that have
sisters know what its like to be around girls and but
guys that dont have brothers - they feel this much more
powerful need to have really close guy friends -
because guys that have brothers you can never be as
close to them as they are with their brothers - but guys
that dont have brothers they have this need for realy
close guy friends because they have this vacuum - they
have this void - that they need to have a brother

you are so full of shit - bullshit - this is all
psychologically documented tested and approved - by
who whom by whom - by us - by me and martin and
swamp and bone and goon - oh - well - in that case it
must be true - you better believe it buddy whatcha doin
doggie - good boy - good boy - lets go over there
doggie - lets go where that nice lady is - yes - yes - i
know - i know oh she is a mom pie "hello"

hi she is a pie "how are you today"

okay - show boob - oh dont go inside - you scared
her off - i know - no dont go oh look at that ass oh dont
leave no no bye i love you

she looked like natalie wood i love natalie wood ava
gardner no not ava gardner ava gardner is sexy like c
but natalie wood is beautiful like her graceful poise like
audrey hepburn but she was married to robert wagner -
yeah heez a ted

if natalie wood

would if natalie would like camelot she floated down
the lady of shalott

oh well - bye - bye bye missus american pie - i used to love you but i had to kill her - i used to love you but i had to cry - and when the something something something die - singin this will be the day that i die - this will be the day that i die

now for ten years weve been on our own but moss grows fat on a rolling stone - but thats not how it used to be - and while the king was something looking down the jester stole his thorny crown the courtroom was adjourned - no verdict was returned - and while lenin read a book of marx the court kept practice in the park and we sang dirges in the dark the day the music died

helter skelter in a summer swelter - helter skelter in the midnight sun - baby jesus taken on the run - every body better get your gun- cuz the fun has just begun

i met a girl who sang the blues - i asked her for some happy news - but she just smiled and then she turned away - i went down to the sacred store where i heard the music years before - but the men said that the music didnt play - and the three men i admired most - the father son and holy ghost - they caught the last train for the coast the day the music died - and they were singin bye bye miss american pie drove my chevy to the levee but the levee was dry and good old boys were drinkin whiskey and rye singing this will be the day that i die - this will be the day that i die

theres been an accident son beth lynn come here please this is probably the worst thing youll ever hear its the worst thing ive ever had to say kids im very sorry theres been an accident your parents are dead

come on - lets go - lets go home - come on - ill race you - come on - come on - you wanna treat - you wanna treat no im not gonna give you a green one i bet those suck those are like the vegetable ones im gonna heres a brown one yeah thats good huh yeah brown are the best

NEWSWEEK **MURDER CAPITAL** The Rising Toll in Washington   i thought we were the murder

capital HOW Women Are Changing TV oh good this
should have jane pauley lets see the overheards
Conventional-Wisdom Watch good conventional
wisdom **George Bush** loser ▼ good why Old CW:
Wimp if he drops tower. New CW: Wimp if ordeal
drags on. who gives a shit **John Tower** ted ▼ good
why After this, what he'll need is a good, stiff... one
Wade Boggs who cares »➔ push Not that he cares, but
Bosox star will never be defense secretary. hmn
Olympics katarina witt ▼ well what does that mean
people wont watch it how can the olympics be down
Ben Johnson got caught. Now we know everybody
uses steroids. so whats that got to do with the olympics
- if people want to use steroids they can use steroids i
dont care - its cheating - its not cheating - its just
something people do to prepare - they eat foods they lift
weights they run they take vitamins - i dont see that as
being unfair - theyre only hurting themselves - if some
bozo wants to lose his dick and his balls to win a gold
medal if its worth it to him whats that got to do with me
- heez still the fastest person **Fox TV** up ▲ yeah up
Forget lost sponsors. CW starts tuning into
"Married...With Children." of course of course because
its so different and funny its bad its not good but its
funny and its different the only thing really like it is
rosanne **Nonsmokers** ▲ "Smokeless" embarrassment.
CW takes pleasure in tobacco's pain. yes indeed
Kitty's Back what the hell is that **K**itty Dukakis who
cares **Overheard** good "I was on federal probation for
shooting up mailboxes. I got into a fistfight. who the
fuck is this I was 20 years old. What the hell does that
have to do with Al Simpson at 57? nothing What is
this crap?" *Wyoming Sen.* ALAN SIMPSON, *on the
John Tower affair* okay that wasnt funny "I don't want
a person to be secretary of defense who does not have
advice that's worth a lot of money." what the fuck does
that mean *Texas Sen.* PHIL GRAMM "I don't want a

person to be secretary of defense who does not have advice that's worth a lot of money." what the hell does that mean i guess tower is the secretary of defense and he got paid all this money for something and gramm supports him "Men usually say such things to their wives. Usually while lying on the hallway floor." what the hell does that mean *Columnist MIKE ROYKO, on Tower's pledge of abstinence* on the hallway floor what because he cheated and she threw him out of the bedroom maybe tower cheated on his wife you wouldnt be on the hallway floor - you would sleep on the couch or go to a motel - be talking on the phone "If . . . everybody in this town connected with politics had to leave town because of [chasing women] ted kennedy and drinking, ted kennedy you'd have no government." no ted kennedy at least *Former Senator BARRY GOLDWATER* i wouldnt let barry goldwater marry my daughter was is that i wouldnt let somebody do something im not something no im pretty liberal but i would let somebody move in next door or let barry goldwater marry my daughter i wouldnt do something move in next door who what the hell song is that is that motorpsycho no no no its its its on that album or on freewheelin one of those john birch or bear mountain picnic something - anyway "I'm going to slip out of here now. I'll see you later this afternoon at cocktail hour." ted kennedy *Rep. JAMES SCHEUER* nope james scheuer *JAMES SCHEUER, excusing himself from a meeting of New York's congressional delegation* this is exactly what i am talking about if its ted kennedy theyre talking about then barry goldwater and all these republicans are goin chappaquiddick chappaquiddick chappaquiddick nothing else matters - then its a republican and its not so bad just like rush limbaugh if somebody does something or robs somebody or drinks or cheats on his wife then the first question is who was it - theres not clear standards - theres not this senator is

a shitheel for doing that because that is wrong and you
shouldnt do it - if its a democrat heez gonna say you see
here is the shitheel democrats again with no character
stealing and drinking and cheating on their wives - but
if its a republican then heez gonna say the democrats
have been waiting for something like this to happen -
because it always happens to them - this is the height of
hypocrisy ladies and gentlemen and its just what the
democrats have been waiting for - because they have no
character and dont you believe it for a second - the
liberal media and he will make up some exception and
all these explanations why he didnt do it or it wasnt that
bad or it doesnt matter and its all just who you are -
what party you are not even who you are but whether
youre a democrat or a republican - if this guy tower
whoever the fuck he is had been nominated by the
democrats then the republicans who are defending him
would be attacking him and the democrats who are
attacking him would be defending him just like oliver
north - if oliver north was had been working for carter
instead of reagan then the democrats would have
backed him as patriotic and the republicans would have
been saying its worse than watergate and a travesty and
all that its all politics - the democrats are just as bad -
its everyone and the democrats are just as bad for the
eighties i hate them too - they run congress and they
voted for everything reagan did and they should get
credit for all the stuff people give reagan credit for and
they should get the full blame for everything bad
because it takes two to tango and they were in it
together and they are bunch of sacks of shit with no
character just like the republicans and fuck all of em

anyway where was i

"I'm going to slip out of here now. no i already read
that "I kinda hate to write off a country. But it's going
to be a retreat on Bangladesh. concert for peace concert
for food what was there a flood yeah In the United

States we got all this money and we're not even holding Louisiana in place." what the hell is that supposed to mean STEPHEN LEATHERMAN who the fuck is stephen leatherman *director of the University of Maryland's Laboratory* laboratory *for Coastal Research* oh heez talking about the coastline oh that makes sense *on coastline erosion* yeah that makes sense "Far from being a 'congressional junket' junky what the hell is a junket 'congressional junket' trinket this trip will take us to areas which I believe we need to visit to understand the dimensions of the problems confronting the U.S. national security and to meet the responsibilities we face as members of the subcommittee on defense." *Sen.* DANIEL INOUYE's heez that guy from oliver north with one arm from hawaii he jacked him - what the hell is he talking about - there are no funny ones this week at all "I think the wildest place we ever had sex was probably on the bathroom counter, and if that disappoints you, I'm sorry." MARGO ADAMS who is margo adams octopussy maud adams no thats maud adams maybe its maud adams sister MARGO ADAMS, *answering reporters' questions about her affair with Wade Boggs* oh thats why they had wade boggs in the conventional wisdom heez having an affair who cares maybe sheez having the affair maybe sheez some important person why is this news

"I think I had duck one time. what I went 0 for 4." what BOGGS whats he talking about *testifying in Adams's palimony suit about his superstitious belief that there are "hits in chicken"* what is palimony it sounds like a horse palimo what is that horse palomino thats the horse i guess sheez suing him for a bunch of money thats why its in the news i guess but who makes the news i mean whos in charge who accepted that who approved that who allowed that to happen

QUALITY IS YOUR RIGHT

yes it is - i demand quality **Radio Shack** thats quality **Perestroika Isn't Working** what is this Mikhail Bocharov is a pioneer

"We still need more freedom from central authorities here," he complains.

Across the Soviet Union, as Gorbachev observes his fourth anniversary in power this week, the verdict on perestroika is that, so far, it doesn't work. what - i thought
perestroika was just a good will of feelings and friendliness between us and russia and the u s i didnt know it was like a whole system
Shortages of food and other consumer goods have worsened since the reforms began; the standard of living has actually gone down. see thats all people care about is the economy they dont care about freedom of speech religion due process trial by jury access to the courts all people give a shit about is taxes aids crime poverty they dont care - all they give a shit about is the economy taxes stock market standard of living you have to work out the kinks you have to give it a chance maybe the recession is for other reasons - it will come - it took us over a hundred years to get the kinks out - they cant go back now anyway once people have a taste truth is on the march and nothing can stop it no more auction block it was only a matter of time just give them mcdonalds and that will be the end of them - once they see how easy it is how easy it can be - once they see that you can go into a place and get big mac and french fries in two minutes for two dollars complete with ronald mcdonald clown people and batman kids meals theyll never turn back - plus it will kill them all from heart disease - we didnt have to waste all our money on atom bombs all we had to do was give them

mcdonalds - psychologically defeat them and kill them slowly from the inside out – anyway

Soviet communism-have become serious problems.

"The old system continues to crumble while no new one has been put in its place," says Washington economist Jan Vanous,

What has changed in the Soviet Union is much less important than what has remained the same.   As always, any reform that threatens the Communist Party's monopoly on power will be rejected get out of the old road if you cant lend a hand - for the times they are a changing - dont stand in the doorway dont block up the hall - for he who is hurt will be he who has stalled - the battle outside ragin will soon shake your windows and rattle your walls - for the times they are a changin
to whom do those tits belong **Why do most lovers get together at night?** because thats when they see each other - they are working during the day - she looks kinda like c **AT&T** The Right choice.
Cops: We're Losing the War It's time to change the premise of the corrections system from one of rehabilitation to one of simple justice not justice well its not justice its specific deterrence BY KENT W. PERRY lets see what this loser has to say
I've been a cop for nearly 18 years.   During that time ive kicked some ass eaten some doughnuts skimmed some drug money fucked some whores and I've been shot, punched, kicked spat upon and cussed. vietnam war veteran yeah bein a cop would suck if i were a cop i would be so prejudiced and violent and

Lest I sound lest where did he get lest self-pitying, let me hasten to add that I really like my job. Most of the time, anyway. By any reasonable standards, police work has been good to me. In each of the last three years my salary (with

overtime has exceeded $50,000 where the fuck do you work i think cops here get like sixteen   My family and I enjoy the benefits of comprehensive health and dental care as well as ample sick and vacation time. I'm also relatively untouched by strikes, seasonal layoffs or the vagaries of the economy.

So what's my beef?

a knowledge of meaningful accomplishment, a sense of being valued - are largely nonexistent. This has as much to do with the paradoxes inherent in American society as it does with the nature of police work.

Cops in America are caught between a rock and a hard place spot. place Faced with an ever-growing crime rate washington of staggering proportions fettered by a chronic lack of manpower and funding

And it is a war. Though undeclared like korea and fought against an enemy not easily labeled, it is nonetheless being waged daily throughout the country. Its cost in dollars, as well as forfeited lives, is incalculable. Worse, perhaps, is an accompanying spiritual erosion. exactly People no longer feel safe - and in truth, they're not. Pick up any newspaper, turn on the radio or the TV and you're bombarded with a stupefying litany of violence and lawlessness. So inured to crime have we become   that   even   the most   senseless   murders   invokeperfunctory indignation. exactly theyre all statistics theyre all just statistics how do you expect them to have any respect for human life when you treat them all as statistics

We shake our heads in sorrow and pay lip service to the notion that "something" ought to be done. Meanwhile, we barricade ourselves in homes that have become fortresses and view every stranger with suspicion and distrust.

yeah heez right about that **Jameson** is that scotch no irish whiskey ZENITH INNOVATES AGAIN if basketball A Trap Can Catch More Than A Mouse welcome to the roach motel where palestinians beat the drums of rampage and the brussels of freedom wash against the suds of my commission where GINGIVITIS im a yuck mouth cuz i dont brush **Murder in the Nation's Capital** Panasonic **Quality is Job 1.** Henessy **You're a Wanted Man** If you're concerned about hair loss... ...see your doctor. and remember im not only the president but im also a client **Networking Women** here we go

On and off camera, a fresh breed of women is seizing control of prime time. The new leaders of the pack are 'Murphy Brown' and 'Roseanne.'

WARD: What type of girl would you have Wally marry? i wonder if she fucked wally missus brady fucked greg i wonder if merideth baxter bearney fucked michael j fox

JUNE: Oh, some very sensible girl from a nice family. One with both feet on the ground, who's a good cook and can keep a nice house and see that he's happy. see that he's happy. yeah well whats wrong with that as long as sheez happy - because sheez living vicariously through him - she is happy only of he is happy - yeah thats wrong - but if she doesnt want a career why should she have to have one - it would suck to be a girl and want to just have a family and be a housewife because there is so much pressure on you to

go out and get a job and have a career - well dont you
think sitting around the house every day cooking and
cleaning and washing and watching the kids would get
boring unfulfilled would be pretty unfulfilling - yeah
but going to some piece of shit job or even a good job
and doing the same thing day after day would be pretty
boring - i would probably rather play with the kids and
watch tv

I feel like June Cleaver on acid.
- "Murphy Brown" 1989

Her age is forty something

Marlon Brando

She's also a killer
PMS
National Hockey League

Shirelles

Sonny Jergensen, for the way he bounced up after
"being hammered from behind on third and long." Her
favorite diversion: busting the chops of her 25-year-old
boss.

still wearing a retainer Murphy Brown to drive i hate
murphy brown sheez so
not not funny - the jokes come from miles away - its
like heres the set up - here it comes - here it comes -
here it comes - there is goes - its so not funny - its so
bad - i cant believe that anyone likes something that is
so objectively bad - but its good because it portrays
women in a completely different way - yeah but that
doesnt make it good - that might be good - the effect
might be good but just because something has good

effects that doesnt make it good - its just like madonna with her crap always about it being art like that gets her off the hook once you answer that question but thats not the question the question is whether its good art its shocking but that doesnt make it good art is art but that doesnt make it good - shocking is shocking but that doesnt make it good - but it opens peoples minds - but that doesnt make it good - it has nothing to do with good - it can be something can be good and shocking or bad and shocking or good and not shocking or bad and not shocking - why cant it be shocking and also be good - plus its not that shocking - what - you show your boobs - big deal - people have been doing that for years - interracial couples - people have been doing it for years - chains and whips chips and dips its all cliche - its all stereotype - theres nothing really shocking and theres nothing good about murphy brown Nielsen's Top 10) Mur i mean its good that they are having strong women characters who have careers and arent dependent on men - but that doesnt mean that the show is good - they can make a show where they have a strong woman who has a career and is smart and pretty and intelligent and independent and also good - with good dialogue - and funny jokes and integrity to the characters - and to the plots and the dialogue - everyone is a stereotype - every one of those characters even murphy brown is a stereotype - sheez not the old stereotype the marcia brady carol i mean carol carol brady stereotype or june cleaver stereotype - sheez a new independent woman stereotype - she has no depth to her - sheez completely predictable - you know what she is going to say ten minutes before she starts to say it - thats not good - its political it may be socially good or culturally good or politically good - but its not dramatically good - it has no integrity - it has no art it has no drama its just a stereotype - theres no integrity - anyway - what the hell am i reading - and where the

hell is jane pauley sheez the most respectable woman
they got - thats who is candice bergen is trying to be is
jane pauley so why dont they just talk about her

Its name is womanpower. It is stamping an imprint
on both sides of the camera, reshaping the male and the
female images on the screen as well as the sexual
makeup of the industry that manufactures the images.

feminism
    The feminization of television has surprisingly
little to do with feminism. At its roots lies an intriguing
demographic shift: female viewers have seized control
of the prime-time dial as the networks' male audience
increasingly drifts to the cable channels (where else
could they find "Full Contact Karate" and "Reform
School Girls"?). At the same time, market research
reveals that women have become the principal
purchasers of the products most advertised by prime-
time sponsors (e.g. cosmetics and household goods).
Such findings have spawned a theory: the network that
most endears itself to the lady of the house has the best
chance of survival. The theory also comes with a
corollary: shows that capture the viewers sponsors prize
most – women between the ages of 18 and 49 – can
charge "Cosby"-close ad rates even though they rest a
tier below in the ratings. thats smart
    A second explanation for TV's sexual role its not
really sexual its gender role reversal can be found
behind the cameras. on the casting couch - god i hate
that there is nothing more offensive than those old
bastards on the casting couch thats so wrong bob barker
fucking janice when sheez eighteen years old and old
hairy bald fat ugly cokehead producers fucking
madonna in the ass so she can make some pissant video
- thats so wrong i wonder if jane pauley ever fucked

anyone producer when she was young walter cronkite c b s no who was n b c

Opportunity Act

Let's begin

"Nightingales" (women in nursing school) - "A Different World" (women in college) - "Studio 5B" (women in television) - "Designing women" god is that show a piece of shit "The Golden Girls" oh my god old women (women in retirement). come on Now add such female-centered shows as "A Fine Romance," "Day by Day," "227," "Murder She Wrote," i hate murder she wrote she was a pie when she was young though what was she in samson and delilah or something cleopatra one of the classics angela lansburry what a i hate that show and ill tell you something else i would not want to be her friend - if you are a friend of hers or a family member you can be guaranteed that you are either gonna get killed or you are gonna get charged with murder - but you dont have to worry cuz angela lansburry the pretentious fucking nosy full of shit mystery writer will push her old tits in the way and solve everything - yeah but in the meantime youll get fucked in the ass a few times - yeah   Disney staff whats distaff characters - traditionally confined to serving as dutiful appendages missus cleaver

Love fest: Few shows are working better than Candice Bergen's chic-collar but its so bad - whos in charge - who conceived this who approved this who allowed this to happen - i mean there are so many people to make a movie or to make a tv show or anything - so much money goes into it and so many people - there are writers and rewriters and then

producers and directors and actors and you would think
that someone along the way would just say hey - stop -
this isnt funny - this isnt good - this isnt good - i dont
see i mean in the whole scheme of things murphy
brown is pretty good i mean its bad but compared to
most of the shit out there and i just dont see how so
many people can spend so much time and so much
money and ostensibly so much effort and talent i mean
these are supposed to be professionals these are
supposed to be the best the cream of the crop and even
just other people - its their job - and i just dont
understand how you can have so many people and its
bad - you have so many rewrites - the screenwriter
writes it and then the studio gets their hands on it and
they have people rewrite it and rewrite it and then the
director gets his hands on it and then the actors
collaborate and improvise and add all this stuff - and it
still comes out bad - can you imagine how bad the first
script was - originally - how does this stuff get made -
how - who does this - who lets this happen - i mean i
dont understand how can you make something bad -
whats the point - why doesnt someone just say no - stop
- there must have been some point along the way when
we could have said no - but we missed it

"Hey, Murph!" norm So many female newscasters
are pies copying her unstructured jackets, oversize
jewelry and thigh-high skirts that, when W magazine
conceived a fashion spread
Jane Pauley there she is when W magazine
conceived a fashion spread on women anchors, it chose
Jane Pauley, Kathleen Sullivan and . . . Murphy Brown.
thats all theyre gonna say about her - norm - whats
shakin norm - all four cheeks and a couple chins

TV trends define their cultural eras. That's a valid
assumption: only a fool would deny that an

entertainment form with a nightly following of 50 million

postfeminist '90s

What are the women who inhabit today's network series telling us about the post-Reagan, postfeminist '90s? Don't expect unanimity; every video movement invariably harbors a few course-defying exceptions. Nonetheless, this one seems to be sending some unmistakable messages:

It's OK to work: Sue Ellen Ewing of "Dallas" why do they put quotes around everything you know its a tv show Sue Ellen Ewing of "Dallas" supposedly heads a Texas movie studio, and Elyse Keaton of "Family elyse thats how you spell elyse i thought you spelled it with an a like alice but pronounced aleece she is such a mom pieof "Family Ties" is billed as an architect, she is but for all we see of their workaday lives, they might as well be full-time homemakers. Not so with the female doctors on "Heart Beat"

It's OK to be alone: A record proportion of TV's female population lives without husband or children. Are they lonely and miserable? Not really.

ago: "When Mary Richards threw up her hat in the air for the first last time, it stayed up. The contemporary TV woman is

making it on her own." must be mary tyler moore at the beginning - her name was mary richards i thought it was just mary tyler moore m t m sheez like the richest woman in the united states - i thought oprah was - no she makes the most now but mary tyler moore has it all saved up - she has the rights to all of those m t m shows - thats exactly what it is its - mary tyler moore - you have the strong independent female reporter at the center of the show youve got the bald nice flaky friend who might be a fag youve got the stiff weird other ted knight guy youve got the jew editor producer not really similar but - and then you got the extra chick just thrown in its just a remake of the mary tyler moore show the only thing they did was replace the fatherly knowing jew editor in one and the young neurotic tedly jew producer in the other - other than that its the same exact show - they couldnt even think of a new setting - its tv - wait was ed asner an editor - it was tv - he must have been the producer - i always thought he was an editor that was another show

It's okay to mess up: By now even casual prime-time visitors

Superwoman linda carter no that was wonderwoman cathy lee crosby she was the original wonderwoman the outfit was more like a superwoman outfit her face was so bony she was beautiful in coach what a piece of shit movie but she looked just like alexandra i guess her face filled out but she was so beautiful alexandra i wish

Women's Place in TV History

The women's movement in TV has been evolutionary, not revolutionary. June Cleaver stayed home and nurtured her nuclear family. Mary (Tyler Moore) Richards got a job, but only as a go-fer for the guys. she was i thought she was a reporter Chrissy in "Three's Company" was most liberated in a bath towel. Alexis in "Dynasty" has power - but that makes her evil. Meanwhile, Claire Huxtable, as televisions's current paragon mom, can do everything but convince us that she's real.

50 NEWSWEEK: MARCH 13, 1989
look at those tits *Suzanne (jiggly Chrissy) Sommers (left), Joan* terry was so much hotter she never wore a bra like farrah fawcett i loved terry

It's OK to mouth off: roseanne "Do you *eat* with that mouth?" yes you fucking bitch i do - since you asked

"Murphy Brown" came away equally dismayed: "Murphy has no compassion or mercy. She seems so hardhearted." Oh, well, no one ever extolled television for its abhorrence of excess. And yet only the most pig-skinned reactionary would mourn the days when Lucy had to beg Ricky for a measly $5, or when Harriet Nelson would implore Ozzie: "How can I get a permanent if you wont tell me if you want me or not?" The liberation of the TV woman has lagged abysmally behind that of her real-life counterpart. Even Mary Tyler Moore's single working girl – acclaimed as a breakthrough in her day – seems, in retrospect, inordinately timorous. (How many times did she cry on Lou Grant's shoulder?) Besides, Mary was soon swept away by the "jiggle" wave. Feminists may have been igniting their bras, but the the only heat generated by the video bimbos of the late '70s was strictly hormonal this is the worst writing (How many ways did Suzanne Sommers find to loosen her towel?)

The early '80s brought a few reforms. "Hill Street Blues" that was the best show ever - all in the family - hill street blues - all in the family - the early cheers - before diane left once diane left they went to shit - the only funny one after that was the jeopardy one - be that as it may alex

Grumbles Steenland: "In the real world, women work to keep out of poverty and to send their kids to college. They are fatigued and short-tempered. These women
never lost their tempers. It's an impossible ideal." its like playboy thats whats causing all of the divorce because all of these women are trying to live up to these ideals that dont even exist - women in playboy dont

even look like women in playboy so how are regular
housewives supposed to compete - i dont agree with
that i think that things should be as beautiful as they can
be like poetry or art if things are ugly what is beautiful
and godlike about humans is that we can make it
beautiful we can make it have harmony even if its
shattered and i thing things should be as beautiful as
they can be - but then people are only going to be
disillusioned they are not going to be happy with their
wife because they want christie brinkley when even
christie brinkley doesnt look like christie brinkley and
the women are not going to be happy with themselves
which is why we have all of these eating disorders like
anorexia how much anorexia do you think there was
before television and movies and playboy magazines - i
dont know

Cheetos-popping

Enter, with a megaton blast, Roseanne.   This
Cheetos-popping, blue-collar curmudgeon is being
haled as the medium's first authentic working mother.

Nixing Nixon: The message of "Murphy Brown" is,
in its opposite fashion, no less revolutionary its not
revolutionary its completely camp
Here's a woman so unsuited for motherhood that,
confronted with caring for three abandoned children,
she tells them bedtime stories about Haldeman and
Ehrlichman.   When they cry, she tries to bribe them
with a stack of 10s and 20s.   When they act up in a
restaurant, she snarls.   "Stop throwing food,   you
rotten little Huns!"   Within   her   profession,
however, Murphy commands awesome respect. oh
yeah sheez the best dines with Cronkite - jousts thats
the whole problem she is so successful that you cant
take it seriously - if they just made her like a normal

newscaster then people would believe it - the local writer tom cruise maybe if sheez lucky the police commissioner a woman that pulled her baby out of a burning car - but they think its so funny or so cute or whatever that no one takes her seriously because obviously not even barbara walters or jane pauley or diane sawyer eat with this president one night and go out with the secretary of state for lunch and are all chummy with gorbachev and all that shit so everyone knows that its just a joke and they never try to infuse anything with real stories - theres no creative anything on that show dramatic tension - they never try to develop a story - where this person kidnapped this little girl and the father gets her killed and she has to interview the mother or - its just as effortless as any other sitcom - theres a plastic structure and a one line theme plot and then you have a series of back and forth leading up to one joke - and then a series of back and forth leading up to her joke - and then a back and forth leading up to miles joke - and then at the end they sing aretha franklin - its crap - thats all cheers was - yes but the genius of cheers is that it wasnt pretending to be anything else - it didnt have to invent a structure because it was just about people that sat around in a bar - and thats what they showed you - people sitting around in a bar - it wasnt about news reporters who theoretically go interview all of these presidents and whatnot and then come back to the bar - it was just lets have people sitting around in a bar - so there is more integrity to it - and it was just done so well - it was a sitcom but it was just done so well the dialogue was so good and it was so funny and there was so much tiny genius to it - the little things all four cheeks and a couple chins - that most shows dont pay any attention to - and there was a drama to it just by the chemistry of the people - they were such good characters that you knew them you felt like you know them - they are your

friends - just like anybody else like actually people that
you do know - and so you didnt have to artificially
insert drama - like all in the family - but all in the
family was much better - it was much more like a play
each show was a play and you had the drama of all of
that family tension all of those dynamics and the way
they dealt with issues that show where archie explains
prejudice is the greatest television show thats ever been
made - which one - when he gets drunk with meathead
in the basement and somehow they are talking about
prejudice and meathead says they were wrong arch -
my father told me the same thing and they were wrong -
no he wasnt - he wasnt wrong about nothin - your father
that loves you - your father that takes care of you - heez
the breadwinner - he protects you - he plays ball with
you - he loves you - how could he be wrong

and then that show when he is talking about religion
and he wants to baptize little joey and but they dont
want to baptize him and he says religion - no no no it
wasnt the baptize one it was another one when they
were saying something i dont remember and he says
use force which one was that was that the one when
they baptize no but something religious strike no
permission what would they need permission for other
than baptizing joey without permission

i dont know

permission - thats the last thing we need is
permission - no use force - its the christian way - and
edith says that aint the christian way - and he says yes it
is - when we went into the jungle and we got all the
black people - you think we tried to reason with them -
hell no - we drug them right down to the river - and
then held them under until they found god - and then
when we brought them over on the ships they were
singing - because they were happy - because we
showed them god - use force - its the christian way - its
god judgin archie - not you - god

Only a woman could invent that line
what line
"This must be particularly hard for you . . . knowing there's no one special in your life and you're probably not ovulating anymore." Only a woman could invent that line oh yeah thats genius - but its the little things thats what they dont understand its always some plot to destroy the world or save the world its just not that interesting such a large scale its like when david letterman started out and he would have the woman who collected potato chips that look like nixon and the guy that went back to take his s a ts that was funny but you have some actress like susan sarandon on and what the fuck does she know what is she gonna say thats interesting - i was coming here on the airplane and the funniest thing happened this guy asked me if i wanted to be in the mile high club and i fucked him right there on the plane so what are you doing now - well i just made this movie i was over in paris - how is paris this time of year - its beautiful - and who was in this movie robin williams isnt he a real pain in the ass to work with - no heez wonderful - heez a genuis and then we did our benefit for the rain forest who gives a fuck i wanna see your next door neighbor with the wifebeater shirt that complains about the jets and can do the entire you talking to me scene from taxi driver and how his wife was cheating on him with the pizza delivery girl who turned out to be a lesbian - homeless guy - thats a good interview

"Friendly Fire"

"Women's Room"

ABC balked

sexism

Down in the video trenches, however, females still grapple with stubbornly resistant forms of sexism. At last count, male TV writers earned an average of $43,000 a year, nearly a third more than their female colleagues.

Director's Guild awards. "Heart Beat"

"You still get men's fantasies of the way women talk and relate," she complains. "The only place I see women playing poker or talking in sports analogies is on television. It just isn't

realistic." well thats cuz television isnt realistic - the only place i see men playing poker or talking in sports analogies is on television - you think that its bad because its sexist but its bad just because its bad - if women wrote the shows they would still be bad - they would be different but they would still be bad - they would be murphy brown

its just as unrealistic and bad as any other show and they got that - and if you want more then write them - get some women together raise some money hire female writers and produce a bunch of chick shows - they have women with money oprahs got money between oprah and mary tyler moore they could buy their own network and you can have just as many bad chick shows as we have bad male shows the a team - instead of a bar you could have a beauty parlor steel magnolias bridge game or country club and you can have bad unfunny meaningless dialogue about fashion and changing diapers and sports analogies what analogies clothes analogies no cars no bridge no what do women make analogies about - they tell you what they feel they dont beat around the bush with analogies thats what makes them women - but they can have their own shows nothings stopping them - i mean

"Charlie's Angels" now that was a good male show farrah fawcett never wore a bra you could always see her nipples it was great all you have to do is make a show with guys walking around like at a club you can have a male health club and guys sittin around in saunas and playing racquetball and lifting weights and stuff and guys will like it cuz they will be sitting around with guy talk saying derogatory things about women you should have a bridge club if you dont like a poker game - and dont try to make a plot just have a weekly bridge game and thats what you show - women talk about women and how they talk when they are together and you have one women who has a career she can be a lawyer or a news reporter or something that would be good cuz she could comment on current events and how the media is too powerful or too sexist or theres too much concentration on appearance and fluff rather than substance and how do they make the news not just about violence and all that stuff - and then you have one women who is like a house wife and a volunteer or something and one weird chick who is like a widow or a divorcee or something the professional is single and she is like a widow or a divorcee who believes in reincarnation and astrology and sheez always late maybe sheez an artist and does pottery and all that stuff - and then one woman who is like has a part time job maybe like a real estate broker or is in advertising or one of those things that a lot of women do and its not completely full time and has a family too and maybe she has affairs and is controversial or something - and you get women to write it and they play bridge and its very realistic and men wont watch it unless you get huge pies to play them but you dont do that you just get normal women attractive but not models just normal beautiful not beautiful but attractive women like judy hamilton or someone and maybe the newscaster is pretty but not like joanna kerns not miss america just like a pretty girl like faith daniels or cokie roberts or someone and attractive but youre not resting the laurels of the show on something superficial its substantive its the the dialogue and there is no drama its just internal drama the problems and the dilemmas and the drama that the women bring to the table every week - and its satire and they talk about current events and whatnot and then you have the drama of the game who wins and if people are into bridge you have real hands and people can kind of follow even if only subconsciously but its got to be authentic thats the most important thing integrity

"Most of the women on this show are preoccupied with men rather than with their jobs," fumes Cherle Rankin, a Massachusetts psychotherapist who served in Vietnam as a red cross worker.   vietnam - vietnam - vietnam

"They are bimbos or hookers, always dressed in seductive clothes. They're a GI's fantasy. By God, they sat around a bombshelter talking about makeup and boyfriends."   vietnam - vietnam - vietnam - yesterday i got a letter - from my friend - who was fighting in vietnam - vietnam - and this is what he had to say - tell all my friends - that ill be coming home soon - my time will be up sometime in june - dont forget to tell - he said - my sweet mary - her golden lips as sweet as cherries - and he was fighting in vietnam - vietnam - vietnam - it was just the next day - that his mother - got a telegram - it was addressed from vietnam - now missus brown - she lives in the u s a - and this is what she wrote and said - dont be alarmed - she told me - the telegram said - but missus brown your son is dead - and it came from vietnam - vietnam - vietnam - ooohh ooh vietnam - vietnam - vietnam - somebody please stop that war bob dylan said in nineteen sixty nine that vietnam was his favorite song - really - yeah was it nineteen sixty nine maybe it came out in the early seventies whenever it came out - its so weird because its such a good song its so happy almost you wanna dance around in spite of what youre singing about

Whew. C'mon - lighten up! well thats enough of this its obvious that theyre not gonna say anything about jane pauley - and it came from vietnam - vietnam - vietnam - vietnam - yeah hea vietnam

time to watch some tube - come on doggie - come on - what is this

Terms of Endearment

X X X is that jack nicholson yeah its when he plays that old astronaut i hate this movie A FILM BY JAMES L. BROOKS i wonder if thats albert brooks brother is that washington STARRING SHIRLEY MACLAINE oh god i cant watch this "and robert strauss in billy wilders stalag seventeen" hogans heroes

AMC
classic movie
A PARAMOUNT PICTURE
is this in black and white i cant watch black and white "here we go wwwoooooo" look at her "oh yeah" oh sheez a grimbo a tattoo what a scumbag i hate mtv "come over here - and all you eligible bachelors you go over there - we are gonna catch the garter" what is this "come on show us some leg" CNN "i dont want to comment on the situation" hockey - hockey this looks like an afterschool special this is h b o why do they have an afterschool special on h b o "our ladies team in charlottestown has had great success" joe "the same pain relief that trainers use - flexall forty four" "keeps my hands from hurting" "nothing works faster than flexall" "flexall really penetrates" "opportunity for a fast break here" oh this is terms of endearment SAM COMER stalag seventeen look at this stupid

mutherfucker i hate mtv why dont they put on remote control or a madonna special or something everything else they have is shit "frank zappa once said that talk journalism is people who cant write doing interviews with people that cant think for people that cant read - what do you think about that mister lydon" sounds about right who is mister lydon "i think that" JOHN LYDON Superstar i dont know who he is - obviously heez not a superstar or you would know who he is "zappa sounded like a rock critic himself when he said that" he must write for a magazine called superstar some rolling stone imitation "people need information" they need to combine if you could combine playboy newsweek life the new yorker and vanity fair into one magazine it would be so cool "we need information and journalists provide that - i think they go over the line sometimes when it gets too personal but" if you had the playboy interview and you had a set of facts quotes and stuff which was like a combination of the newsweek overheard perspectives section and the playboy funny facts section or poignant not necessarily funny but poignant and then a lot of different photojournalistic essays that are sensual but not like playboy but like vanity fair kinda in between but all artistic you would have one section on a beautiful women with sexy but tasteful but not explicit provocative but not explicit and then you would have a life like photographic series or two on a couple topics and then you would have the portraits that go with the stories and interviews and fiction like in playboy and the new yorker and vanity fair a movie review a music review a book review an art section and good ads quality ads with quality photographs - you have like selective ads so they dont take anything cheezy - and then some cartoons political like in newsweek mike luckovich and funny ones like in playboy but not as lewd with the same underlying themes but not drawn so crudely and then the kind that they have in the new yorker that would be cool - you could make it like a new orleans magazine - national but based in new orleans - and it would tell you everything going on in new orleans for tourists and you would have one local story like wynton marsalis or interview and then one national interview like playboy and one local story and then several national stories - that would be cool

"side of fries make" there she wrote serve it to "that a baked potato" "we are gonna sue her for malicious prosecution - not only am i gonna sue her but attorneys think that we will be able to sue the two attorneys who filed the suit" "why dont you just win the case and let sleeping dogs lie" cuz heez a shithead "no - because i think that if i could sue those two attorneys" i can save america it will be a public service to everyone because "let me say first that i loath sexual harassment - i abhor it" oh thats what heez gettin sued for - fuck you - you know you did it "there are some women who are using it for financial gains" isnt that ironic - its kinda like selfhelp affirmative action "but i wanted to work at home" what the heck is this looks like australia i bet its that dingo movie with meryl streep but thats not meryl streep the deer hunter is such a good movie agnes of god it looks like australia - how do you know youve never seen australia - isnt that neat - i mean everyone says that tv sucks and people should go outside and play or read and all of that stuff but we know so much more so much of our knowledge about the world comes from tv - thats scary - thats why its so bad that tv is bad because people get all of their information from tv and if its wrong then it can do a lot of damage - no i think that people can decipher between what is real and what is not - and what is good and what is bad - you dont give people enough credit - they know the difference between the ten oclock news and hill street blues - they know but we have so much extra knowledge i know what australia looks like i know what people there talk like i know about their economy and i have never even been there - you couldnt do that without tv - even bad tv is good - its entertaining - it can be educational even bad tv is educational if you can take some kernel of knowledge or wit from it even if unintended - a lot of times you can see something poignant in a tv show or a movie that the people making it didnt even know about - it just slips in fortuitously but if youre a good watcher you can make something out of anything - its like modern art - objectively its bad but you can make something out of it because of the genius in you

but all of our knowledge is second hand thats the thing - we hardly know anything of our own accord from our own personal experience - everything that we know comes from secondary sources television movies radios schools computers songs books magazines newspapers magazines we dont experience hardly anything probably only like - ten percent of your mind is original personal experiences - everything else is garbage that comes in from the outside which is bad but its good too - it makes us lazy but it makes us smarter - and we know each other better what the fuck is africa to me but when i watch it lions on the natural kingdom and the discovery channel then its real and i care about it and thats good there just has to be a balance and you cant accept everything - you have to take it for what it is - just entertainment value if its wrong but then look for all of the little insights that are in there little pieces of meaning or little pieces of genius that they probably didnt even intend thats why you always have to judge the argument and not the person because no one is right all of the time or wrong all of the time - even good people say bad things even though they have good intentions theyre just wrong - even smart people make mistakes and even stupid people say things that are right even if only accidentally even reagan says he must have said something that was right even if only accidentally and if you automatically disagree with him then you will be wrong and martin luther king cheated on his wife even though he was right about everything else thats why you have to look at the issue regardless of what other people think about it - who is backing it and who is against it - just like abortion because that doesnt make any sense

and it also gives us kind of this national conscious - where we all have this set of characters and plots and symbols and phrases and quotes that we are all familiar with - even though we have never met each other if someone in seattle starts talking to me about the brady bunch or the godfather i know exactly what she is talking about and it conjures up these sets of images and symbols and memories and characters and ideas that are different varied for each of us but there is a commonality to it - and this is the first time in the history of the world that that was possible the bible - except the bible - the bible is really the only thing thats even comparable

"when youre rea" what is this - you know you watch things - or listen to things - and you are aware of them - but youre not really thinking them - its like when youre driving and all of the sudden you think what - was i just driving - i could have been in an accident i wasnt paying any attention or was i i must have been aware - but you can like be listening to music or watching tv or and studying or talking and you are aware of things you are listening you hear the words but youre not really listening you are thinking - youre aware of all of these things these sights and sounds and memories and smells and what you are reading and what you are hearing and what you are thinking but it all comes down to this one line - this one voice that is actually - thought

im tired oh jesus dean martin - auto racing - what the hell is this the ratings game "seventeen lawyers - on retainer - and you manage to work it so that in a free market - a so called free country - i cant buy some shitass stock that any other asshole can buy - youre destroying the capitalistic system - while everyone else in the world is embracing it - my boys and girls are fucking it up" i didnt think they used bad language during the day - rockford files "mom" look at this fag "sorry - we didnt mean to be trespassers" "our new" "election in november that was about money and economics and greed - it was about" look at that fuckin monkey - heez checkin out its asshole "in new jersey says the healing process begins" the garden state what are you growing there smokestacks "no one gets the stars to talk" look at this grimbo Chaquita ratings game - doritos "you can respect - and ultimately it should be does it have a good beat that you can dance to it" jerry lewis "theres another kind of beat when you do interviews" oh jesus bowling "one dollar for me - one dollar for him - but you should always be getting back from the relationship - so pay attention to that - are you" 3. Is you're giving not equal to what you're getting? look at that turtle "after he kissed my brother" what after he kissed my brother "whats this all about" good question "whats the story with you"

"he was cute" oh my god this guy is such a flamer "now you have known about your brothers sexual persuasion" brother - i thought he kissed her brother "yes" "right - i mean - its no" "its no secret at all" "no heez open" who is this "i get the feeling that you like it - i mean - is the the first boyfriend is this the first" oh he must be her sister and her boyfriend kissed him whos not there "no" what a flamer

but - i just dont understand why anyone cares - i mean why do you care - its disgusting - but a lot of things are disgusting the thought of you having sex with your wife is just as disgusting - i just dont see why you care so much that you would take action - i mean its one thing to sit around and say shit but its something else entirely to take action - to actually want to change peoples conduct - i mean thats exactly what you cant do - you have no standing to do that - you have no standing just because something bothers you to change someone elses life conduct to make them do anything thats exactly what you cant do - i mean im offended by a lot of things - and i can be offended - but i cant say you cant do that just because it offends me you have no standing - i just dont see why you care - so much does it keep you up late at night - fine - its disgusting - who cares - you gonna make people miserable just because youre offended - fuck off jesse helms - fuck right off and die - youre offensive - but i cant do anything about it - and i really dont care - i mean the thought of jesse helms fucking his wife is just as offensive as two fags going at it

"flowing into the" basketball "the only way to preserve the integrity of the elections process in these the closest of elections is indeed to hold a new one" she must have lost   PREVUE   maybe she was being gracious maybe she won 40 Bravo | Jewel of the Nile "even though the accident was described as terrible one in which the automobile was totally damaged" "abortion and euthanasia are threats to democracy and peace - thursday the pope will be" i thought the pope got shot "what he calls a growing culture of death - and wants everyone to understand a full respect for life" thats good "but is he moving" "from hitler - and here are the british threatening death to anyone in palestine found helping the jews to escape hitler - now you mentioned that anyone caught there they would send you to cyprus - but what was life like for the jews in cyprus"

"cyprus was almost as horrible as the death camps" this guy must be israeli palestine is a huge ratfuck if they had just taken their people in in the first place -

yeah but they were just the poor nomads who lived
there and we pushed them off of their land and gave it
to the jews - yeah and the jews said live here with us in
peace and they said fuck you and left and fought and
youve got all of those arab countries youve got egypt
and saudi arabia and iran and iraq and syria and jordan
and lebanon who could have easily absorbed an extra
few hundred thousand people but instead they put them
in camps - they put their own people - their own arab
brothers - in camps - so that they could just breed more
and more hatred and use them as pawns to fight against
the jews - if they had just said okay come and live with
us then there wouldnt be any problem and slowly
maybe some of those families would peacefully
emigrate back into isreal but instead they to their own
people and put them in camps just so they could breed
hatred against the jews - and they made their own
people pawns in their war only a pawn in their game
and thats what caused the problem

big bird "hard times - im gonna get them" what is
that it looks like a cricket its a mammal what happened
to big bird - basketball - "everyone - the company"

"i didnt know it would be this bad when i bought it"
what the hell is that guy stripes no thats not stripes did
he buy that thing - oh god is she grim - professional
wrestling - stalag seventeen - mtv - gary busey what is
this - thats not gary busey it looks like gary busey with
a moustache "twenty inches" "talking about celebrities"
"maybe a tornado watch later" jeff daniels terms of
endearment i wonder if heez married to faith daniels
sheez hot i would love to fuck her no thats disrespectful
i wouldnt - sheez very - sheez not - you wouldnt do that
to her - sheez more straight laced i wonder if sheez a
mom - sheez really pretty smart she seems smart but
more laid back than jane but still not sexual i love her

"well - we have over half a million more prison cells
than we did twenty five years ago and we have about

eight times as much incidence of violent crime - so obviously - putting criminals behind bars is not really solving the crime problem" that is such bullshit if we didnt have all those prison cells you would have ten times more crime - its just because you cant see what would have happened if not - we can see what did happen - but we cant see what didnt happen - there is no control group - you have this fact and you have this fact but there is no causation its like well it worked the cold war worked communism is falling russia is turning to democracy and china and everyone else and reagan is taking all of the credit but it would have fallen anyway - because truth is on the march and nothing can stop it - you can only stop truth so long and we dont know what would have happened - maybe communism would have fallen sooner and maybe we wouldnt have bankrupted ourselves in the process - i mean jesus christ we have a four trillion dollar debt we have got silos full of missiles that have absolutely no use and countless other arms - we have tons of poverty tons of illiteracy tons of illegitimacy tons of homeless people tons of people dying of aids the environment is going to hell in a handbasket nobody likes blacks anymore no one likes mexicans no one likes the japs and no one likes gays women are bitchin about abortion and sexual harassment and e r a and theres just no respect - thats not reagans fault thats not the republicans fault thats everyones fault - thats the biggest problem - theres no respect - theres no reverence - for anything - people dont love anything - its not even that they have to love i dont care if you love me i just want you to respect me - theres nothing to look at where have you gone joe dimaggio a nation turns its lonely eyes to you but what was i talking about - the crime - yeah everyone is always trying to make us choose prevention or deterrence prevention or deterrence prevention or deterrence when obviously you need both - democrat or republican liberal or conservative both - you need both - you need prevention and deterrence you need defense but you need to take care of people at home you need to build things its always either or - its always this choice or that choice - why do we have to choose - the answer is always neither - cuz both plans are stupid - or both

"omelettes" oh i hate debra winger "putting on as you alluded to those last minute touches for the big show" "you clean" "young um" auto racing - danny devito - wrestling - nixon - circus - basketball - was that nixon it looked like nixon - terms of endearment - stalag seventeen - mtv - "come on out" this guy must be a stripper "ooohhh" "oh" "wait - wait - all right" oh he is pissed - he is so pissed - look at her she loves it and he is so pissed - she is a slut - look at this guys fuckin package its not that big he must be on steroids - got that weenie bikini on national tv these people have no self respect these people - she would fuck him she would definitely fuck him damn he is pissed i would be pissed what is she doin suckin his dick - oh its a belt - this is grim "jason is one of the strippers" look at that weenie bikini that is so grim "what is your name" "jason simmonds" "jason is one of the strippers from shaniquas favorite strip club" shaniqua - what the hell kinda name is shaniqua look at this guy what a fuckin flamer "okay - you can go right on out - now look heres your hat" "beauty and the beaches and just to honor spring break" fuck off "im not really sure why things that come out of a machine for a circus ticket as opposed to an eagles ticket it should cost the same" the eagles who would go buy a ticket to see they eagles they would have to pay me - to sit through that - don henley i hate that pretentious mother fucker is almost as bad as bono or sting bonos the worst now i used to like u2 but bono is the worst "transactional costs - but you get charged by the ticket - not by the transaction" look at this wench - who is this whore "in my mtv show and a cold sore from my lover" what the fuck is goin on "but when i received an offer from a top medical school" i wouldnt let this bitch touch me with a ten foot pole probably got aids crabs she already said she had herpes probably a cold sore she is filthy - god - no the thing about abortion is that the people who are so gung ho to fight for the rights of the fetus while they are inside the mother are the same people who dont give a shit about them when they get out - yeah but that just means that those people are hypocrites that really says nothing about whether abortion is right or wrong - you are judging the person rather than the issue again and no one is right about everything or wrong about everything - thats the problem with politics - if youre allied with someone then you support everything and everything they do is right and if youre allied against someone then everything they do is wrong and thats just not true - everyone is right about some things and wrong about some things because theyre mistaken or because theyre just right or out of ignorance or because theyre hypocrites or because youre a hypocrite or just because - they could just as easily say well you bleeding heart liberals who care so much about these poor little welfare babies and their irresponsible and illegitimate and illiterate moms all of these drags on society you care so much about and want to throw all of our money away on how come you dont care about these fetuses these poor innocent babies inside the mothers womb - because that is what you would think naturally you would think that liberals would want to protect life and value life over economics and convenience while conservatives would want to sacrifice life for the health of the greater good for the good of economy and saying hell we have too many people these are just gonna be poor unwanted unproductive uneducated criminals that are gonna be on welfare or in jail and living on the public dole while the liberals would be saying you cant kill life you cant stamp out life because you dont know what these people will be and you just have to have faith - you just have to have hope - that we will find a way to care for these people and that everything will turn out okay - the liberal is gonna hope the liberal is hope the conservative is fear - the liberal is gonna have hope and faith that he is gonna grow up to be a martin luther king or an einstein or a freud while the republican is gonna fear that the person is gonna be a criminal or a homeless person or a welfare mom cuz a liberal should be hope faith courage the innocent and noble savage roussuea - that left to his own devices man is good - free marketplace of ideas and kubla kahn and if you let things grow if you let things develop if you let things live if you just have hope then we will get to the next level we will get to the next plane to the future to the apocalypse the marriage of heaven and hell to god

if youre a republican then you fear - then man left to his own devices is evil and stupid and flawed it goes back to original sin - so he must be protected and controlled - capped - dammed because they dont have faith they dont have faith in capitalism and democracy that communism will die they have no faith that truth is on the march and nothing can stop it because no lie can live forever - yes sir

yes sir - i dont know - sometimes its a case of rape or incest or the womens life is threatened - yeah but thats in like one percent of the cases most of the time its just for the sake of convenience - economics and convenience - its just letting people be weak - take the easy way out - people are beautiful and strong but they will be uncourageous and weak if they have the opportunity they will eat mcdonalds its bad for them and it doesnt taste good but its convenient and cheap so people will buy it by the billions - and i mean i mean we have this institution these institutions and they are here second they are secondary its a social contract the power begins with the people and is vested into institutions for the common good - now if these institutions cannot support the life that we have then we should change the institutions - the institutions - everyone has the idea that these institutions are irrevocable permanent unchangeable being - the institution cant be wrong - the institution cant be changed - and people are judged by their value with respect to the institution - what is your value in terms of the economy in terms of the church democracy the government if we cant fit people into the institution you change the institution - if its not working then change it - its ours - we created it - its there to serve us - if its not working if it cant accommodate us then change it - so it can accommodate us - dont change our lives so that we cant accommodate the institutions change the institutions so that they can accommodate us

because rousseau said that government is a chain of the strong that is used to chain the weak while neitzsche said that government is a tool of the weak that is used to chain the strong but if you let people grow no but people have to be secure in life liberty and property you cant have complete anarchy people have to be secure in life liberty and property or they wont build anything but the true geniuses the true great men obermen will create anyway they will create for its own sake - and that is the best form of art anyway - i mean do you think julius caesar or alexander great could have accomplished so much in a democracy - yes because we have produced in two hundred years a lot more great people than that - jefferson frank lloyd wright einstein no he was in germany and austria but he developed all that stuff when he came here - you know a lot of people say that his wife invented everything not everything but the theory of special relativity and that he just took credit for it because everyone was so sexist that they knew no one would accept anything if it came from a woman - what about madam curie she won the noble prize didnt she plus its not important who it actually was what was important was the idea - einstein is just a concept its just an image its just a symbol the reality behind it makes no difference - anyway what was i thinking

we had jefferson edison ford bell frank lloyd wright the wright brothers benjamin franklin melville faulker ayn rand wallace stevens twain we had martin luther king and winston churchill was in a democracy was it a democracy yeah parliament they had parliament and he was the prime minister we put a man on the moon we created cars and trains and boats and planes and atomic energy the wright brothers television telephones computers film - yeah but maybe that was just the time and it would have been invented anyway and maybe greek and rome were just the times and the world was ready and anyone would have done it i dont know but america has this the great thing about america is that we are free - in a greater sense than actual freedom - there is this theoretical freedom and pride the land of the free and the home of the brave oh say does that star spangled banner yet wave - oer the land hand of the free eeeeehh - and the home - of the - brrraaaaaavve boom boom boom baboom badum dubba dubba no but - clarence darrow inherit the wind even if there is no true freedom even if there is a bunch of racism and discrimination and waste and pollution and poverty and crap just the promise - just the image - just the symbol is something - everything else can be worked out everything else we can fight over and work and hammer out the kinks but the idea - the promise the hope the constitution the starting point fountainhead social contract - you can say what you want about thomas jefferson he had slaves and all that shit but he was a fucking genius he was a giant his faith ultimately in people even black people was so great he even introduced a bunch of legislation on he was the first one in virginia to introduce legislation for the freedom of slaves he was in love with one of his slaves and the only reason it wasnt in the constitution was that they knew it wouldnt pass - jefferson wasnt involved in writing the constitution he was in france but he wrote letters to jay about trial by jury the purest form of democracy and more sacred and fundamental even than the right to vote and it was jefferson who really pushed for the bill of rights and he the only reason he kept his slaves probably is because he knew that if they were free they would just get harassed and lynched by others - or maybe he was just an elitist racist bastard who talked a good game and raped sally hemings - but you cant judge people with such a historical perspective i mean slavery today is just different - i mean the idea that people should not have slaves is a relatively novel idea in the realm of history the romans had slaves the greeks had saves the egyptians had slaves even the blacks had slaves in egypt and in carthage and in all over the place the muslims had slaves before they were traded to the europeans im sure the japs and the chinese had slaves and basically all of those feudal medieval systems the people the peasants and serfs were basically slaves of the overlords or the shoguns or barons or whatever there is technically very little difference between a peasant or a serf in the middle ages and an actual slave - so the idea that slavery is abhorrent i mean it is abhorrent but that realization is pretty novel in terms of world history you cant say that jefferson wasnt a genius just because he had slaves you cant say that he was evil just because he had slaves maybe he wasnt perfect maybe he could have been stronger he should have been stronger he should have been better the people who are smart have a higher duty they have a higher obligation because if they dont no one can - the people who are smart enough and rich enough and intelligent enough that they know right from wrong that they know good from bad or are rich enough that they can afford to be good - they have all the more obligation to do it - because if they dont no one else can no one else will because no one else can - and its not even the person thats important anyway you cant judge the idea by the man because the words themselves all men are created equal it was like a prophesy to be fulfilled even though they still had the three fifths and the slave laws and women couldnt vote and the indians once those words were etched into the fabric of our society it was only a matter of time because no lie can live foreever truth was on the march and nothing could stop it - plus if he were living today could you imagine he would be like f d r and j f k and lyndon johnson and robert kennedy and brandies and brennan and holmes and learned hand all rolled into one if we just had someone or something to believe in where have you gone joe dimaggio who will be my role model now that my role model is gone gone he slipped back in the alleyway there were hints and accusations spinning in infinity there were angels in the architecture they were spinning in infinity in the museums infinity goes up on trial - voices echo this is what salvation must be like after a while - but mona lisa always had the highway blues you can tell by the way she smiles - she sure has a lot of gall - to look so useless and all - muttering small talk at the wall - while im in the hall - how can i explain - its so hard to get on - and these visions of johanna - they keep me up past dawn

but theoretically life is more important than economics and convenience but its someone elses economics and convenience its the same thing as fags i have no standing to tell someone else what they have to do just because i am offended - it doesnt affect me - it offends me i think its wrong on some theoretical sense but why should some woman in michigan not have an abortion because i think that we should have more reverence and respect for life - you cant make people have reverence - you cant make people have respect just like you cant make people straight you can make people have reverence and respect a lot easier than you can make them straight it doesnt matter whether its biological or environmental because no one would choose to be gay - why would you choose to do that just so people can think youre a fag and give you a lot of shit whats the point obviously its not their choice and even if it is there choice no one else has any standing to object to it it doesnt affect them in any physical or tangible or concrete way - i mean how can i tell someone in kansas that they cant do something they want to do for whatever reason just because i think its disgusting - i mean

its just like the very same thing as why we shouldnt have drugs be illegal no thats not really because of standing thats more economical it doesnt make sense economically to pay police officers to arrest people for drugs when we can take the drugs and sell them from state stores like they have in new hampshire for alcohol and take the tax money and use it for rehabilitation centers and drug treatment centers and education and research and advertising campaigns because its not the drugs themselves that cause as much damage as the fact that its illegal - thats why it costs so much - thats why its so hard to get - thats why everyone is killing everyone over it - if you took the monopoly away from colombians and drug czars and gangs and gave the monopoly to the government you wouldnt have drive by shootings - you wouldnt have gang wars - you wouldnt have people stealing things cuz they cant afford to buy drugs - you wouldnt have people shootin up with aids from dirty needles passed around parks and crack houses a thousand times i mean why do we want criminals and drug dealers and crime lords to get the money when we can take the same money and use it to fight drugs - healthwise and educationwise and advertisingwise but no one is ever gonna let that happen because of fear yellow freakin fear because everyone is scared that there are going to be so many addicts well there are so many addicts - and its not the addicts that cause the problems its the salesmen - and the problems that the addicts cause they wouldnt cause so much if the drugs were cheaper and we could use the money that is now going to criminals and crooked cops and crooked presidents and c i a guys and the contras to fight addictions with hospitals and rehab centers and education and advertising and you could let the cops fight other crime and you could clean up all of the dirty drugs and make them clean so people dont get bad l s d and marijuana laced with angel dust and bad acid and all that other shit and you have an age you have to be over that age and you have very strict laws about being high while driving like d w i and enforce those laws strictly and enforce the use of minors very strictly but no just possession and illegal sale but there wont be illegal sale because it wont be profitable - but there will be because you will have some drugs that we wont legalize and they will be on the black market cuz people will want more and more and more and try new things and with stuff like coke you can die on the very first time like len bias and so if you legalize it even if they dont have a lot of people who will get addicted they will try it for the first time and they will die and it will be too late or a bad acid trip - yeah thats true - its a ratfuck - its a complex problem but i just think that overall in the long run if we legalize them

anyway - on to bigger and brighter things - but its all the difference between what people can do and what people should do - i am the most liberal person in the world about what people can do but the most conservative about what they should do - just because someone should be able to do something that doesnt mean they should do it - but that doesnt mean that we should not let them if you want to have an abortion you should be able to do it even though you shouldnt do it - you should be able to take drugs even though you shouldnt do it - you should be able to cut your hair like some fag and wear an earring and get a tattoo but you shouldnt do it - people should be able to have sex with whoever they want but they shouldnt do it they should wait until they are married and only do it with that person but they should be able to do it with whoever they want - as long as they want and there is consent - even incest or statutory rape - well incest is disgusting but i dont really understand statutory rape because the theory is that the girl cant consent but if you are the same age as the girl then its okay - it doesnt make sense - it seems that if a fifteen year old chick is mature enough to consent to having sex with a fifteen year old then she is mature enough to consent to have sex with a thirty year old i mean when i was fifteen i wanted to have sex with forty year old women that shouldnt be a crime it doesnt make sense its like that rape where its rape just because the woman is drunk that doesnt really make sense - just because you are drunk a lot of people have sex when they are drunk when they would have done it anyway i mean maybe its with their boyfriend or their wife i mean their husband or something - but if the guy is drunk too then is he raped - that seems kind of sexist like a drunk woman cant consent but a drunk man can - i would have had sex with a lot of women drunk that i wouldnt touch sober - so in that sense the alcohol vitiates consent but that isnt rape i mean if the girl is unconscious or something thats one thing but just because the girl is a little tipsy and drops down her inhibitions especially if you are drunk too that shouldnt be a crime "hey tim"

hi guys - how was school

"good"

what did you do

"we had a math test and played softball"

i didnt know you had a softball game - you should have told me - i would have come to watch

"it was just a practice game"

how did you play

"we won"

i don't give a shit about the team - how did you play

"i got one single and one out - i almost got a double but the freakin umpire called me out"

"she was safe"

you guys wanna go to dinner

"okay" "yeah" "i gotta go change" well go change then i am so hungry i want some wanton soup some fried wantons roasted pork with mustard and moo shoo i hate that plum sauce - how was your day lynn

"okay"

did you get that stuff you needed

"yeah - i need you to call mister horseshoe and get some money because we had to pay for the air conditioner"

okay - you have to call vena and make sure she is coming tomorrow

"when are you leaving"

i dont know - sometime in the morning i need a ride to the airport can you take me to the airport

"sure" good i need to call grandma before i leave ill call her tomorrow morning she might not be up i better call her tonight "did you ever see rain man"

yeah i saw it

"did you like it"

yeah it was good - dustin hoffman was good - the movie was good but - it wasnt really that good there was nothing - there was just nothing new or memorable or important or substantive about it - i mean it was a cute story it was interesting and fun to watch but its not like - the godfather - i mean you cant compare it to the godfather or the deer hunter or cool hand luke - whats that movie with al pacino one flew over the cuckoos nest nineteen seventy five jack nicholson beat out al pacino for the oscar but al pacino should have won the bank robbery dog day afternoon thats it - you cant compare it to dog day afternoon or cool hand luke or network or a clockwork orange or two thousand and one - i mean even other barry levinson movies are better tin men was great tin men was much better than rain man

"i never saw that"

oh its excellent - danny devito and richard dryfuss - it is really good

"okay im ready"

and do you really think even dustin hoffman i mean once you get into the character i mean its almost kind of a parrot - i mean i wonder if its really that hard

"dustin hoffman in rain man"

yeah

"oh i thought he was great"

yeah but is it really that hard i mean i think it would be harder to try to play a real person

"he was a real person - who was an idiot savant"

but is that harder or easier to play a person that is not an idiot savant

"i don't know - but can we go eat - im starving"

you ready

"i think the hardest thing would be to do comedy"

thats what they say

"lets go"

is chinese okay

"yeah" wanton soup fried wanton barbque "did you ever read bonfire of the vanities" yeah it was pretty good - i thought it was gonna be terrible but its was actually okay - i dont know if it will ever be this great book - but it will be one of those books that really captures the times you know like the great gatsby isnt really a great book but it really captures the times of that age

"i like the great gastby" the twenties were a lot like the eighties - it was okay

"i heard theyre gonna make a movie out of it"

they have a movie with robert redford - oh you mean bonfire "bonfire of the vanities"

who else was in that movie - jane seymour

"i dont know"

she was brett ashley in the sun also rises thats what im thinking

"theyre gonna get tom hanks to play the main guy" master of the universe what was his name - what was his name - they shouldnt get tom hanks "i dont know" tom hanks is terrible "rusty sabich"

no thats presumed innocent

"i always get that book confused with presumed innocent" heez not terrible - yeah me too - heez not terrible heez just terrible for that they need someone "and melanie griffith is gonna play the woman" oh my god thats terrible - she was italian melanie griffith isnt italian looking - i wonder if she is gonna show tit she usually shows tit thats all sheez good for sheez the worst actress - she is the worst actress

"i know"

she cant even like deliver a line

"i know"

sheez like on the bottom tier - you know theres like three tiers of actresses - theres like actresses who can actually act - and play characters - become characters - meryl streep or jodie foster - and then you have women who cant really play characters they always play themselves but theyre likable - and they can at least deliver a line - like meg ryan or someone like that - and then you have the third tier of people who cant even play themselves - they cant even deliver a line - like melanie griffith - she is the worst - sheez like sean young - they cant even play themselves - plus you need an italian - you need a dark voluptuous sexual dark mysterious italian stupid well melanie griffith can be stupid but not stupid - dizty - and conniving - but conniving - thats gonna be terrible

"i know"

oh i gotta tell her about that book jane austen batwinger abbey - you know what book you would like - its this book by jane austen called northwinger abbey no northanger - northanger abbey - its like this gothic novel but sheez making fun of the gothic novel - its like a satire - not satire a parody - its like a parody - its not really a parody i dont know what it is i dont even really remember it - i hated it but i thought you would like it

"thanks"

no well you like all of that romance garbage and this is like that but better quality - beth should read the color purple she would like that not the nellie letters just the celie letters you can skip the nettie letters

"good evening"

hello we have three

"would you like to sit in smoking or non smoking"

non smoking please - beth you know what book you should read

"what"

thank you

"youre welcome"

um - the color purple - you would like that - its written like a group of letters between these sisters

"didnt they make a movie out of that"

yeah steven spielberg made it and all the black people were pissed off because - i dont know why

"i loved that movie" i always cry at the end

and when she sings miss celies blues

why didnt black people like it - it wasnt like cry freedom and mississippi burning or to kill a mockingbird because they did focus on the celie and her family and not some white savior that rides in on his white horse and saves the poor blacks or who isnt sympathetic at the beginning and then learns to love - they didnt like the color purple because they werent poor enough and had laura ashley curtains - thats so stupid nobody could watch that movie and think that she had some kind of idyllic life - but i agree with the other criticism - but i kind of understand that because most of the audience is going to be white that is who you are trying to reach and you want them to experience the same journey as the protagonist from indifference or actual hostility to understanding - but you are just creating a barrier the audience can do that for themselves its once removed plus you are undermining the message if its a message its not even a message or it shouldnt be its a drama in and of itself "can i get you anything to drink" coke i wanna coke - what do you guys want

"iced tea"

"iced tea please"

"a coke and two iced teas"

thank you - but you have to skip all the nettie letters - you just have to read all of the celie letters

"okay"

"nettie is the one that lived in africa"

yeah

"and the book is the letters between the two of them"

uh huh

"thats cool"

you should read it - who should play tom hanks - you need someone who is like a yuppy investment banker guy waspy michael douglas no younger and goofier who was the guy beneath michael douglas in

wall street charlie sheen no heez kind of a shithead heez
not naive enough maybe tom hanks would be good heez
not serious enough though actually tom hanks is better
in serious roles he was great in nothing in common no
that was really jackie gleason who was serious that was
just a good movie but that movie with sally field i hate
sally field he was good and serious in that movie the
punch line i hate sally field she always has to give some
big long moralistic speech that movie with paul
newman was good i love paul newman heez too old you
need a wasp - robert redford no too old warren beatty
too old michael douglas too old and too serious - whats
that guys name - whats that fags name "shhhh"
"timothy" with blonde hair in sex lies and videotape
"james spader" yeah james spader he would be perfect
"tim"
   what
   "dont say that"
   why not
   "its not nice"
   yeah he would be perfect - james spader would be
perfect for bonfire of the vanities
   "yeah"
   "are you ready to order"
   yeah - we want three wanton soups an order of fried
wantons an order of roasted pork - you want eggrolls
lynn
   "yeah"
   an order of eggrolls - an order of mooshoo pork -
you guys want mooshoo pork or kung po shrimp
   "i dont care"
   "me either"
   uh - an order of moo shoo pork with a couple extra
pancakes and an order of combination fried rice -
thanks - you need an italian chick lorraine bracco she
would be perfect they need to ditch melanie griffith and
get her but melanie griffith is such a draw thats the

problem so many people want to go see her even though sheez bad its like kevin costner sherman mccoy thats his name sherman mccoy - sherman mccoy lynn - thats the name of the guy in bonfire of the vanities

"oh yeah"

isnt that right

"i think so" oh this looks good - thank you - i love wanton soup - this is so good - this is so good - the place where we go at dartmouth the wanton soup is like brown

"thats the way it is at five happiness" oh i love the crab ragoons - really

"yeah"

i love the crab ragoons there - they have great crab ragoons - and they have this really good dish called double feature - with chicken and shrimp

"what was that place that aunt grace took us to in the quarter"

ginns - it closed down "yeah that was great"

it closed down

"really"

so beth whats new

"nothing"

no boyfriends yet

"no"

good - keep it that way

"she likes this guy named tad" "shut up" "but he doesnt like her"

tad - what kind of a name is tad - thats just one letter away

"from what"

ted - or tard - both

"can you come home to see my play"

when is it

"may sixth and seventh"

ill try - i wonder if thats green key weekend that would be perfect ill come home go to the play maybe judy will be there for jason go swimming wait is that jazz fest - is that jazz fest

"no its the week after"

oh - then i cant come - then i cant come

"tim"

im just kidding - unless i have a paper due that monday or unless i have mid terms ill come

"promise"

i promise - ah pork - gimme the mustard - you guys can have the two egg rolls - i just want wantons and pork

"you sure"

yeah i just want wantons and pork - i need some sweet stuff for the wantons - there we go - oh this is good im not gonna have food like this for a while should have gone to eat seafood we gotta go to skunk hollow oh i gotta take annie there she would like that i wonder if robert is gonna come up "you should come home for the last weekend of jazz fest and just stay the whole week until beths play"

if i can i will - but i can never get anyone to come with me and i dont want to go to the jazz fest by myself

"well robert will come home - he always comes home"

yeah but he usually comes home for the first weekend cuz the second weekend is too close to exams

"oh"

"tim do you like pete seeger"

i love pete seeger - where have all the flowers gone "me too" whats that song about san francisco not san francisco silicon valley little boxes thats it little boxes on the hillside and we go and raise a family "you guys like the worst music"

okay little miss heavy metal

"its good music"

bullshit

"you like something to believe in" so give me something to believe in - lord arise "we like good music - you like shit"

"beth"

what

"she shouldnt say that"

why not

"cuz sheez a little girl"

thats a bunch of crap - you can say whatever you want - my best friend died a simple man - he was the king of the vietnam vets - he fought a losing war on a boring shore and his country didnt want him back "you have no religion"

me - im the most religious person you know

"you"

sure

"if you are the most religious person id hate to see what"

what

"nothing"

what

"well - you are kind of cynical" no im not - im not cynical at all

"you are the most cynical person i know"

no im not - im the most romantic - i am - the reason im always down on things is because i care about them so much - i love them so much - you can only hate something that you love - if you dont care about - if you dont have a reverence or a respect or a religion - about things - then you are indifferent - but im not indifferent - i love things so much that it bothers me so much to see such beautiful things made so ugly and complacent and lifeless - it makes me mad that people dont have any respect for themselves or for god or for each other - they dont have any respect for beauty for what is good - for what is spiritual and aesthetic and holy everything is so conventional and easy - everything is so complacent and lifeless - thats what makes me mad - not that i dont have respect for things but that i do - not that i dont believe in things but because i do - i love everything - i love reagan even - because he doesnt even know who he is or what he is doing - its like that thing about the beginning of things if a worshipper were to make a mistake would not god know his intentions - if you look at the intentions - if you look at the intentions - if you look at the beginning - or end - and everything is so beautiful everything has - so much potential so much genius - so much genius so much power and so much potential - that - that you just cant stand it - all the disrespect appreciation theres no appreciation reverence theres no reverence - the only thing i hate is disrespect - not disrespect because of the words you use or the phrases you say - but real disrespect - at the beginning - at the intentions - not that i would want to split the spiritual wholly from the physical because there is a physicality to the spirit and a spirituality to the physical - but when your car is more important than your friend or when your stereo is more important than the music that you listen to on it - the projector more important than the film no thats not good no one has that much love for a projector a television - or the tv more important than the program or the projector more important than the film - when people look at paintings and all they see is the oil and the dyes - when they dont see the hand behind it they dont see the painter or the god in it it pisses me off - and i dont hate the people i love them - because i know that they are much more than what they are much more than what they seem to be - everything is much more

"so is this spiritual force a jewish force"

its jewish but its also christian and muslim and hindu and buddhist and greek - thank you

"combination fried rice"

thank you

"moo shoo pork"

thanks - can i get another coke please - and two more
iced teas - thanks - but god is the same - the jewish god
is the same god as the father in christianity - the father
the son and the holy ghost the father is our god - and
heez really the same god as allah - i mean the koran is
obviously different from the old testament and certainly
the two religions are different but they are different
because of the differences between mohammed and
moses not because of the difference between allah and
god - and christianity is all paul - its not even jesus -
because jesus wanted to remain tied to the jewish faith -
he was a reformer - but he was essentially a jew - not
one word of the torah shall pass away - i mean on the
night before he died even he was having a passover
seder - so he must have intended that people continue to
recognize the jewish holidays and the jewish faith and
he even says in matthew that think not that i have come
here to abolish the law or the prophets - i come here to
fulfill them - till the end of heaven and earth not one
word of the torah shall pass away - but then paul came
along two hundred years later and was trying to convert
all of these people and started saying you dont have to
do all of this stuff - you dont have to keep kosher - you
dont have to obey the ten commandments - you dont
have to observe passover or channukah or yom kippur -
you just have to accept jesus christ - and thats where
christianity began - but the father is yahweh its the
same god as adonai - and the differences between
judaism and christianity are not differences between
god and christ - they are differences between god and
paul

and then hindu and buddha and everything is a
stream - its a river - that is my religion - rintrah roars its
head while hungry clouds swag on the deep - roses
grow where thorns once grew and on the barren heath
sing honey bees - the cut worm forgives the plow -

everything that lives is holy - and all of these things move forward - plunging speeding ahead - speeding and slowing - backpeddling at times - but things move on - and you can pollute you can damage you can infect you can blow the whole thing up with nuclear arms - but you cant stop it - we move on - life moves on - even in the things not living - in the rocks and the oceans and the rains and the clouds and the stars and the sands - life moves on - beauty moves on and within - there are two visions - first that everything is glorious closed unto itself - if you take a drop from the stream - and its discolored ugly spastic dumb and then you take it and you remove it out of the stream and you watch the light pass through it and you watch it crawl down your finger and then all of the sudden its beautiful - and what is discolored and ugly and spastic and dumb becomes colorful holy complete because if you stripped the mind of all your senses five everything would appear as it truly is - infinite - holy and infinite - and if you could see the past the present and the future all in one instant then you would see that the water at mile one is the water at mile five is the water at mile seven is the water at mile twenty - and the same is true of people - you got two guys and theyre playing ball and they cant hold on to anything couldnt catch a cold in winter and you look at them and you say that these people are spastic ridiculous stupid foofy dumb and yet thats only when you have the context of lynn swan and joe montana and jerry rice - but you take them away from all of that - you strip away and you look at them - the two - pass the rice please - thanks - those two closed unto itself themselves - and what you have is awesome and wonderful and right - a guy playing catch with his dad - or his friend and the sketch - its like and then in the extension you are sitting in class and you see this guy across from you and he is moving his pen on the page a bit and he looks up - and he looks down - and he moves

the pen across the page a bit and again he looks up -
and you have this revelation that he his sketching the
guy next to you - but then you remember that the guy
sketching him is gay - and then you think oh this is so
gross a faggot sitting across from you sketching another
guy - but then you think that if a beautiful girl were
sitting in the class then you would be sketching her if
you could sketch and that would be beautiful - and you
are him and he is you - and it isnt gross anymore - its
beautiful - and thats my religion - thats my religion -
that we arent ever born and we dont ever die - we are
all a part of this beautiful stream of life - even in the
things not living - they have life - and any element in
this stream which doesnt respect this beauty - or
diminishes the beauty of the energy of this life pisses
me off

   so if we are all just a part of the stream - then we not
as well not might as well not i mean then do we matter
as long as the stream keeps going - oh well we have to
be individuals because we need to make it shine like
each of the colours in the rainbow that comes together
to make light and music like each of the instruments in
one great symphony and we are individuals but the way
in which we are beautiful is not just in the way we are
individuals some of it is but some of it is the way we
are part of the stream and that doesnt make us any less -
as those cynics would have you believe - thats what we
are - is just another drop in the stream - but that makes
us more because we are part of the stream and that is
why you cant sacrifice and compromise - thats when
you just become just another drop because its not you
anymore but what you have conceived beyond yourself
thats why i hate the premises of this version of
christianity because it takes all the life out of the stream
- as if the stream had a life of its own which it does but
only in that we share our beauty with it and of course
she shares her beauty with us

gold and rose the color of a dream i had not too long long ago misty blue and the lilac too never to grow old - but i never laid eyes on you not until that faithful day i wanna be your hero - mighty youngblood wishes he was famous - mister moses just wants someone to believe - you believe in miracles - i believe in you if you believe in me i really want some more wanton - i wanna be your moo shoo pork - mighty youngblood wants a pancake - mister moses wants a wanton sitting inside of me - you believe in wantons - i believe in wantons fortunes i believe in fortunes if you believe in me "can we get a movie for tomorrow night"

sure

"can we get caddyshack"

"oh jesus we have seen that a million times"

get the deer hunter

"is that the movie about vietnam"

no

"yes it is"

not really

"its in vietnam"

yeah part of it is - but its not about vietnam - thats just part of the metaphor - its just an instrument but thats not what its about really "lets get soul man" oh my god "lets get gone with the wind" oh my god "okay" i hope they have a good movie on tonight maybe ill watch cool hand luke or the jericho mile "have you seen the movie little big man"

i think so what is that

"with dustin hoffman - heez like half indian or something"

yeah ive seen that - its a vietnam protest movie

"its not a vietnam protest movie - its a western like a comedy"

yeah but its really a vietnam protest movie - i mean think about it - it was made in sixty eight or sixty nine - and if you listen to the dialogue its all about how the white men has given himself this mandate that he has this god given right - whats it called - social darwinism no not social darwinism some kind of imperialism - i dont remember - its some kind of manifest destiny - thats what it is - manifest destiny - that he can take over all of the land from all of the inferior races because he is spreading the word of god or whatever and the movie is reminding you that the indians are human beings like the people in vietnam that you are killing - remember they call all the indians they dont call them indians they call then human beings "oh" yeah - and they have that line in there that there are many white men in the world - but very few human beings

"thats cool"

its all about ethnic cleansing harry s truman but harry s truman wasnt an ethnic cleanser - thats kinda crap - he would have dropped the bomb on the germans if they were still fighting and they are white and european - yeah but it was based on the myth that the japs would fight until death and never give in or surrender - yeah but you dont know that thats a myth - maybe its true my yellow in this case is not so mellow but that im trying to say its frightened like me and all these emotions of mine keeps me holding from giving myself to a rainbow like you - but im bold - bold as love let me tell ya now im bold - bold as love come on baby now im bold - as love - just ask the axis - he knows everything

could we have the check now please - thank you - that was good - that was good

"yeah"

"yeah i love the pancakes"

have a little chinese tomorrow morning maybe theyll have good food on the plane i hope they have a croissant like a croissant with ham and cheese or something those fucking eggs are so disgusting i hope they dont try to give us eggs why do you try to do

something you know you cant do - it will probably just
be a roll - you guys wanna get ice cream
  "yeah"
  "i think we have a bunch at home"
  do you have work tonight
  "i have a little bit"
  what do we have at home
  "we have coffee" i love coffee "i think we have
some mint chocolate chip" okay - okay well we can just
go home if you guys want
  remember when we used to go to grandmas with
mom and we would always get coffee ice cream no beth
wasnt born yet and lynn was too young
  "what does your fortune cookie say"
  "i havent opened it"
  "we have to bring one home for doggie"
  "thats his favorite food"
  "and popcorn"
  i thought he liked ice cream
  "he likes ice cream too but not as much as fortune
cookies - thats his favorite" IF YOUR DESIRES ARE
SIMPLE THEY WILL COME TRUE i wish i was that
person with that height weight head body nose teeth
skin hair sight hearing eyes and voice musical
intellectual athletic artistic abilities speaking joketelling
storytelling abilities charm charisma poise stature grace
will religion courage aura magic vision personality
powers of motion vision and creation into out of and
through literary adventures photographic adventures
artistic adventures dreamscapes and fantasies see hear
visualize imagine understand remember and know
make myself felt heard seen understood and known
  $36.80 thirty six is three sixty plus one half one
eighty six dollars **TIP $6.00 TOTAL** forty two eighty
$42.80 - lets go
  "you got the food"
  yeah i got it

"i have the fortune cookie for doggie"
"have you seen mister redburton"
yeah how much weight has he lost - about sixty
"i think about sixty five"
i bet i weigh more than he does
"how much do you weigh"
one seventy - one seventy five
"thats about what he weighs i think"
i dont think thats healthy
"he has been going to the doctor like once a week getting his blood pressure checked and all that"
yeah - but i think once you go on a diet like that it screws up your metabolism forever - and then if you start to gain weight again you will gain it more - and it will be impossible to lose - thats why you have to have a high calorie diet
"high calorie"
yeah - you eat a lot of calories - maybe not as much as you would but a normal amount but you just make sure that a lot of the calories are from fibers and that none of the calories are from fat - especially saturated fats or cholesterol - and then exercise
"or cholesterol"
yeah - but saturated fats and cholesterol is the same thing - because as soon as you eat saturated fats your body immediately turns them into cholesterol so its the same thing as eating cholesterol - or vice versa
i just dont believe in dieting - i just dont believe in dieting though - i mean its so sacrificial - i mean you are denying yourself things that you love - i dont know - i guess as long as heez happy then its good
"well maybe he is just happy looking good instead of being happy enjoying certain foods"
yeah - i guess its the same thing
i wish i was like a nazarite separate unto god like a knight or a puritan or a monk like beckett or like galahad or robert de niro in the mission or joan of arc

and i was a vegetarian and didnt do anything that wasnt pure or unclean consecrated in thy service my will be lost in thine but i could never be a vegetarian i love steak hamburger its against my principles not to enjoy eating but what if i loved tomatoes and mushrooms and potatoes as much as steak and ribs and hamburgers it would be so boring - but you know that you can only eat meat because you dont actually have to go through the process of preparing the food you couldnt kill a cow or a pig so how is it right to let some nameless faceless person be the executioner - i dont know - you dont have to be confronted with the choice - but it seems so natural to be one with the earth and hunt and cook and prepare your own food and take only what you need like the indians - thats crap - if you were truly strong like a puritan you would be a vegetarian - a puritan nazarite cabalist ascetic hebrew knight

"if i could lose five or ten pounds"

why

"cuz i need to lose five or ten pounds"

no you dont - one thing is that butter

"what"

that imitation butter stuff - is so buttery - have you tasted it or smelled it - i mean i dont see how it could be good for you - throwing all those chemicals into your body instead of real butter - from milk

"yeah but butter is like everything thats bad for you in milk taken out and pressed together into like one bad concentrate - its like the stuff they take out of skim milk before it becomes skim"

yeah but its so buttery that if you ever go off the diet you are gonna need to drown your food in so much butter to get that taste that youre used to - youre gonna need like a stick of butter for every little pinch of molly mcbutter or i cant believe its not butter or whatever its called molly mcbutter - dum - dum - dum - molly mcbutter - hello doggie hello doggie "we have fortune cookies for you"

"wait"

what

"the alarms on"

oh - god i hate it when you lock this fucking thing lynn you know if they can get through the deadbolt then they can get through this little dinky thing

"well im used to locking it"

hello doggie - hello

"we have fortune cookies for you"

time to sit down and watch a little television - o five - mark harmon twenty kung fu sixteen oh good broadcast news "i can read while i sing - i am singing while im reading both" come here doggie yeah i always do that i always talk to myself - i dont talk to myself i talk to people that arent there - yeah me too - and i always sing - yeah but what was i thinking

yeah but you can read and think something be thinking something else and listening to the tv all at the same time and you are comprehending what is going on you are aware sometimes it moves in and then fades out but then you have that one actual line of thought that you are hearing or thinking but its in words and ideas i mean you have what you are seeing but you dont think that unless you are actually reading you dont think sights you have visions but you dont think them

hello doggie - did you like your fortune cookie - yes yes - i know - i know

"what" oh this is the good part "give a minute please - this is tough" tom is the devil - tom is the devil "okay lets take the part that has nothing to do with me - let me just be your most trusted friend now - the one that gets to say all the awful stuff - okay" tom is the devil "yes" tom is the devil "you cant end up with tom because" heez the devil "totally goes against everything you believe in" "yeah - being a basket case"

"i know you care about him - ive never seen you like this about anyone" certainly not me "so dont get me wrong when i tell you that tom - while being a very nice guy - tom" is the devil "is the devil" yes "this isnt friendship - youre crazy - you know that"

"what do you think the devils gonna look like if heez around" "god" thats awesome i wonder if that was on purpose i never noticed that thats amazing "taken in by a guy with a long red pony tail - come on - whats he gonna sound like - achachchchchch - no im semiserious here"

"youre serious" yes "he will be attractive - he will be nice - and helpful - and get a job where he influences a great godfearing nation - he will never do an evil thing - he will never deliberately hurt a living thing - he will just bit by little bit lower our standards where theyre really important - just a tiny little bit - just coax along - flash over substance - just a tiny little bit - and he will talk about us all really being salesmen"

and he will get all the great women

"and he will get all the great women"

"hey aaron"

"what"

"i think youre the devil"

"you know im not"

"how"

"because i think we have the kind of relationship where if i were the devil youd be the only one i would tell" i wish you were two people so i could call the one who was my friend and tell her about the one i like so much there you go thats the sister and the girlfriend and thats why in the end she cant be the wife - so anyway what was i thinking

oh yeah the devil is yeah well it could be that but you gotta think about all that blakian sensuality and sexuality and beauty in hell and the devil is earth and

opposed to not earth not me not you not us - what - i
dont know - you cant escape where you come from but
why would you want to - so bob dylan is proteus
reinhart and wordsworth and faulkner and then you
have jimi hendrix and blake who have the bigger
thomas violent rebellion and then the heaven the lotus
eaters the tennyson heaven and kubla kahn a stately
pleasure dome decree where alph the sacred river ran
into a sunless sea - i saw a damsel with a dulcimer in a
vision once i saw - she was an abyssinian maid and on
her dulcimer she played singing of mount albora - if i
could revive within me her symphony and song - then
something something twould win me and something
something long - and i would build that dome in air that
sunny dome those caves of ice - and all who came
should see them there and all should cry beware beware
- weave a circle round him thrice - for he on honey dew
hath fed - and drank the milk of paradise

thats not it im missing i need to get a coleridge
collection lets see if i have something maybe its in a
collection or something MADONNA   *ROLLING
STONE* i wish they had better pictures of her she was
much hotter when she had blonde hair material girl she
was fat then yeah she looked better she had some meat
on her - she was voluptuous - now sheez too slim too
muscular she was much more sexual before like
material girl that is when she looked the best - but even
borderline and lucky star burning up - she was fat - she
wasnt fat - she was just normal i mean - now theres a
good blakian figure potential what a waste i mean sheez
got this sexual this religious breaking of symbols the
six six six and the virgin and the boytoy shakes people
up i mean its too much sex for her to handle its like eula
coming into frenchmens bend and its just too much
energy like the spotted horses and she is desired and
repulsed at the same time - its great - all that sexuality
and then also that violent sexuality thats brash and

kinda disgusting kinda perverse repulsive you gotta
hatefuck her you gotta hatefuck that bitch but then she
could have that softness and sensuality because she
really has a great voice like in love dont live here
anymore she sounded just like barbara striesand - yeah
but i think thats done up in the studio because her voice
sucks i mean if you hear her in concert she is all out of
breath and her voice is all cracking she has a terrible
voice im sure the running around on stage and dancing
makes it worse she gets out of breath but im sure her
voice is really done up in the studio plus she really cant
dance - i mean everyone talks about her dancing but i
mean - its her job - she really doesnt dance that well
considering the fact that thats supposedly her job - if
you go out to any club on friday or saturday night you
can see ten or twenty people that can dance as well or
better than her i mean sheez supposed to be a
professional but i mean compared to a ballet dancer
thats the thing i mean - you take the worst violin player
in a two bit symphony like new orleans and that person
has twenty times the musical talent of any rock star -
yeah i mean thats true plus the bottom line with
madonna is that sheez stupid - i mean there is just no
getting around the fact that she is just plain stupid -
there is now no way that she could be any kind of a
great figure because she doesnt understand the essence
of anything she thinks that just because it is shocking or
because it makes people think then it is good and so if
she opens peoples minds and all of that bullshit that
relieves her of having the responsibility of making
something that actually has quality that has integrity its
like the cosby show they rely on rudy to be cute and
that relieves them of the responsibility of doing
something that is actually funny - she relies on her tits
and on the other crap and thinks that that because it
shocks people or opens peoples mind even though its
really not that shocking or novel - its all pretty cliche - i

mean what does she have a chain and a whip and a burning cross - big deal when you have pornos with triple penetration and bestiality and people fucking each other in the ass while they give blow jobs to some teenage hermaphroditic midget i dont think madonna is really doing anything too shocking that hasnt been done before - its all the setting - even though the things she is doing arent shocking its just that thats not what people expect to see on their television when its not a pay channel - its not that people are really shocked because its something new that they havent been exposed to - they are just shocked to see it in that forum - no one is shocked to see tits they are just shocked to see tits in life or vanity fair or rolling stone because they have never seen them there before - theyve only seen them in playboy and penthouse - just like if you say fuck on tv no one is shocked by the word fuck they are just shocked to hear it on the cosby show because they never do - its never in that forum - sheez not doing anything new - sheez just putting them in a different place

its the same thing with movies - if they throw melanie griffith or tom cruise in a movie it doesnt have to be good because millions of people are gonna see it anyway it doesnt matter how good it is - they should just pitch the movies to the stars and then they can go to the studio because tom cruise can make any movie he wants - any studio will make any movie with him so it doesnt make any sense to go pitch a script to a studio or a producer - and then have the producer go to tom cruise you might as well just go to tom cruise cuz whatever he decides is gonna get made he can find any studio or he probably has the money to produce it himself - and then find a producer - thats what i would do - so basically youre gonna have actors deciding what movies get made - they do decide - some loser goes to paramount with some piece of shit idea for a bad movie

and says im thinking tom cruise in the lead role and
melanie griffith as his seductive aunt and they say that
sounds good - and if tom cruise and melanie griffith say
yes they make the movie and if they say no they say no
it wont work - what was i talking about

but whos in charge - thats the real question - who
conceives this who approves this who allows this to
happen - how do bad things get made - how do so many
people put so much time and effort and investment into
something and its bad - but madonna could be the muse
and the minstrel and the female bard but its all just a
waste because she doesnt know what to do with herself
because they got her playing the roles of idiots in bad
movies at least marilyn monroe was in a couple good
movies the misfits niagara some like it hot even though
she played an idiot they were good movies she wasnt an
idiot in niagara and in the misfits she seemed to be an
idiot but everything she said was perceptive she was
always innocent and full of love she was so unsexual i
cant believe that she was a sex goddess i find her so soft
and innocent and angelic and nonsexual ava gardner
was sexual jane wyman was sexual patricia neal was
sexual but marilyn monroe is the furthest thing from
sexual sheez like a child sheez like an angel you cant
have sex with her you cant make love to her you cant
fuck her none of those really beautiful women are sexy
lauren bacall is not sexual grace kelly is not sexual -
theyre pretty - theyre beautiful - theyre wives but you
cant violate that you cant penetrate that - thats so
disrespectful - thats so disgusting - and wrong

i mean you fuck raquel welch you fuck ava gardner
you fuck barbara bach judy hamilton terry on threes
company farrah fawcett susan sarandon merideth baxter
bearney madonna but you dont fuck marilyn monroe
you dont not even fuck make love to you dont even
make love to marilyn monroe or grace kelly or lauren
bacall or jane pauley or joanna kerns - i mean you dont

even make love to michelle pfieffer maybe you could
make love to them but you would never fuck them -
that is just so - wrong

disrespectful and wrong - but madonna - sheez got
that bigger thomas with the crucifix between her breasts
god she has beautiful breasts she would be the best sex
in the world i bet she is the best sheez had a lot of
practice and sheez got her boy toy and her fire and
leather and rape but she cant get the innocence back the
gold and rose when the wind cries mary and little wing
and bold as love she can be bold as hate but she cant be
bold as love anymore - and she may not be able to be
the other side any more at all because she doesnt really
command that respect because to be shaken up to feel
youve got to have that respect youve got to have that
fear - no one is scared of her anymore - maybe there
was a time you could have but no one takes you
seriously anymore - youve just become a caricature of
yourself - you may not like me but you damn well
better respect me she cant say that because you may not
like the devil but you damn well better respect him and
then now she tries to do all this meaningful stuff like oh
father promise to tell and like a prayer whats that other
song spanish eyes and its a shame - but she doesnt write
those songs - yeah who does write those songs
PROFESSOR   LONGHAIR   PROFESSOR
LONGHAIR PRESERVATION HALL l m n o p
THELONIUS MONK   THELONIUS MONK
THELONIUS MONK TAJ MAHAL   WYNTON
MARSALIS WYNTON MARSALIS where is it LED
ZEPLIN II LED ZEPLIN III MADONNA here she is
MADONNA "BURNING UP" MADONNA LIKE A
PRAYER look at that i bet thats not her its probably a
hand model why the hell did she put perfume on these
things that is so fucking annoying all my records smell
like shit she looks good there looks like kendall lets see
god this smells - jesus CHERISH   uh   LIKE A

PRAYER   (BY   MADONNA   AND   PATRICK
LEONARD)   whos that guy leonard leonard theres
some composer maybe its like his son leonard bernstien
something leonard i dont know well i wonder how
much of the song she wrote and how much was written
by patrick leonard she probably wrote one line   TILL
DEATH DO US PART   i dont know what that is
EXPRESS YOURSELF   PROMISE TO TRY   who
wrote that   (BY   MADONNA   AND   PATRICK
LEONARD)   again   OH FATHER (BY MADONNA
AND PATRICK LEONARD)   SPANISH EYES (BY
MADONNA AND PATRICK LEONARD)   i guess
theres no way of knowing i guess she probably writes
about half of the songs hal leonard who is hal leonard
that guy on barney miller - i dont know hal something

but the stuff is good even if she didnt write it or
would at least be good if it werent done in such an
insincere way with synthesizers and drum machines and
disco beats the most generic pop george michael
unaesthetic and ungenuine unauthentic way its a shame

oh well - i want a farm house grow some corn and
garlic i wonder if you can grow garlic or rosemary and
peppers bell peppers and hot peppers put them in a
bottle with olive oil and vinegar grow grapes and make
vinegar and wine and olives and apples and oranges
gotta have an orchard and some horses milk cows and
pigs not to kill but just to have the play around and dogs
and stuff i would love to have a farm and house and a
pool and with a little river and a boat house where you
can go fishing and water skiing and then a house on the
beach with a sailboat thats what i wish i had a place in
the french quarter with one apartment and then a few
apartments to be rented out and a few parking lots with
a balcony and something to rent out on the first floor
and a house in destin on the beach with a sailboat two
sailboats a hoby and a real sailboat and then a farm
house in florida on that river near destin with all of that

produce and all of those vegetables and animals and a
swimming pool and a boat house and fields and a farm
with a fishing ski boat and rocket stuff and bb guns and
bows and arrows and radio planes and fishing and
boating and farming and skiing and sailing and scuba
diving and music art literature photography av film
computer clothes and sports stuff toys and games
collectors items miscellaneous paraphernalia furniture
appliances utilities tools money stocks bonds trust
funds mutual funds memberships subscriptions and
accounts and i was that person with that height weight
head body nose teeth skin hair sight hearing eyes voice
intellectual abilities athletic abilities musical abilities
and artistic abilities knowledge will religion courage
aura magic vision and personality

my yellow in this case is not so mellow - in fact im
trying to say its frightened like me - and all these
emotions of mine keeps holdin me from giving my life -
to a rainbow like you but im - im bold - bold as love -
let me tell ya now - im bold - bold as love - come on
baby now - im bold - as love - jut ask the axis - he
knows everything - yeah yeah yeah one law for the lion
and the ox is oppression the dead lion is a living dog no
the what a dead lion right is a living dog right a dead
dog is a living lion thats tomorrow maybe tomorrow
gold and rose the color of a dream i had so jimi hendrix
is the blakian figure i mean heez got the bigger thomas
rebellion and revolution and violence with the way he
dresses and smashing guitars and burning and the star
spangled banner i love the star spangled banner upside
down and all that sexual energy and assertion and then
also that sensual muse the bard minstrel innocent
inspiration like the piper and the lamb the piper at the
gates of dawn inside the gates of eden there are no
truths outside the gates of eden - at dawn my lover
comes to me and tells me of her dreams - without any
attempts to shovel a glimpse into the ditch of what each

one means - at times i think there are no words but
these to tell whats true - and there are no truths outside
the gates of eden that dreamlife is waking life is truth is
reality reality is truth that is all i know in life and all i
need to know beauty is truth - but this dreamworld gold
and rose color of a dream i had and castles made of
sand when the wind cries mary waterfall and little wing
fly on little wing imagination like the dragon
imagination is like the dragon because its a snake man
is a snake man is the dragon - man is the dragon - he is
a reptile - a serpent - that crawls along its belly - but it
has wings because it can lift itself through imagination

and so anyway its like fly on imagination live on o
muse o poesy lift me to the sun and color it rainbow is
that a color white fly on so its him and blake and the
two extremes and then its bob dylan the proteus reinhart
from all narrations all vantage points the axis kinda
with wordsworth and faulkner just ask the axis he
knows everything fly on little wing let it go and so to
fade away ay ay - to let it go o - uh huh - and so to fade
- fade - fade away - im wide awake - im wide awake -
im wide awa ake ake - im not sleeping - oh no - no no -
im not sleeping - oo oo oo ooohh - if you should ask
well maybe they tell you what i would say - true colors
fly - in blue and black - through silken skies and
burning flags - colors crash collide in bloodshot eyes -
if i could - you know i would if i could if i could -
through myself - set your spirit free - id lead your heart
away - see you break - break away - into the night - to
the day - that was the greatest album that was so much
better than the joshua tree they peaked with that album
and then they got popular and that was the end of them
thats what always happens with tv shows - all tv shows
are the best in their second year - their first year they
are just starting and feeling their way around and trying
to find the characters and work out all of the kinks - and
then but then the second year then all of the kinks get

worked out and the characters get well defined and then
it gets good and at the end of that year - during that
summer between the second and the third year then its
gets all the hype and then it gets popular and goes down
and everyone talks about how great it is when really its
not even that good anymore and all of those people
really never even watched the show when it really was
great like destin - and but - no but and then they run out
of ideas and they have to resort to gimmicks - plus you
get to know the characters as well as the writers - thats
what happened with cheers - you knew the characters as
well as the writers did and norm can only say what
norm can say and you know in a given situation exactly
what norm is gonna say thats why diane was so good
because she was so fresh everything was so fresh and
unexpected kirsty alley never says anything funny you
always know exactly what she is gonna say you always
know exactly what carla is gonna say carla is the worst
she is the worst - but even cliff and norm the writers are
trapped into cliff and norm and they cant say anything
that cliff and norm would never say and you know them
as well as the writers so you always know - so thats
why the show just has a half life of about five years and
some show did that i think it was the dick van dyke
show or some old show that went off at the height of
popularity because the creators realized that they
werent gonna be able to think of anything fresh any
more and believed - the producer believed that you
should just end every show at five years

but the second year is always the best - and im gonna
tell you the same thing i love you but i think youre
stupid cuz you dont know who your friends are - so you
say black what if the guy was white would you say the
same thing - i dont know it seems you know cuz you
know a black man it aint been quite right for him and
because we expect him no we ask him to play that role
so everything works - if he doesnt play that role it

doesnt and we love i have more for them i think - but of course its all just white liberal jewish guilt and its all self creation and delusion thats probably just as offensive to blacks as bigots the invisible man thats probably what ellison was saying or part of it - wright actually wasnt max a jew and bigger hated him even more than the people who wanted to kill him - but i just feel this attraction almost i have so much love for them they are so romanticized in my mind - its like grace - i just see poise and stature and grace - but its superiority in a way and prejudice when you have sympathy you are setting up a superiority where you are above its just as offensive - its still the invisible man - but how can you tell the difference between sympathy and empathy - and respect

but because i expect him to play that role does that make me evil no cuz i cant do anything about it - except know that - love him except love him you are not responsible for what you feel you are only responsible for what you do with what you feel - who wrote that i dont know its a good quote anonymous i thinks its anonymous - anyway the black man sees life - its him first and its last last but what comes in the middle it aint all up to him i say it aint all up to him - amen - i say you wake up and you lie down to rest but what comes in the middle it aint all up to you - i say it aint all up to you - and if you rise up - they cant put you down - i say they cannot put you down - amen - and if they put you throw i say if they throw you down they better be ready to lift you back up again i said they better be ready to lift your ass up - hallelujah - because all that lives is holy - i say all that lives is holy - amen - yes sir - i say the dead lion is a living dog - i say - i say to all of you mistahs and mastahs and uncle toms of your own making dog is just god from the other side thats right i say dog is just god from the other side - yes sir - and what you consider to be right what you consider to be

white i say love thy neighbor - i say hallelujah - truth is
on the march and nothing can stop it - yes sir - cuz no
lie can live forever - no sir - from every town and every
hamlet - from every mole and mole hill let freedom ring
- yes sir - mine eyes have seen the glory of the coming
of the lord - he is trampling out the vintage that the
grapes of wrath have stored - he is something and is
something from his terrible swift sword and his word
shall be their sword - his truth is marching on - his truth
is marching on - his truth is marching on does that star
spangled banner yet wave - oer the land of the free -
and the home - of the - brave

one law for the lion and the ox is oppression

thy life immortal tochter aus elysium i say rise up
now hallelujah amen i say nothing shall i say nothing
shall separate me from the love of god - i feel the eagle
stirreth in its nest - and every sparrow falling like every
grain of sand - i say each and every grain of sand the
sparrow rises now to the eye of god amen amen - can i
have a hallelujah - hallelujah - hallelujah - hallelujah -
and if they say if roy rogers brings himself to say if
john wayne and harry sam bring themselves that it is
chaos to rise up then i know i feel it in my blood
hallelujah that i know that god rises up from within -
god himself reaches out his hand and picks me up into
the sky and let him not forget his ancestors from the
distinguished lands of virginia and pennsylvania that
the origin of their own kingdom was brought forth from
the inspiration of god against reflection soft in thine
own mirrors in the face of god - a shadow but the
shadow knows hallelujah rob serling no thats twilight
zone who did the shadow orson wells i dont know but i
got to get some money so i can buy all of this stuff cuz
pretty soon theyre not even gonna be making albums
anymore thats why ive got to start getting all this stuff i
got to get the holiday collection and the ellington
collection and the armstrong collection and both miles

davis collections colombia and riverside prestige no its prestige the thelonius monk is riverside ive got to get that too because you just cant listen to jazz and blues on disc especially blues it just doesnt sound right without all of the crackles and pops especially if its acoustic - and then you got that hiss and it doesnt sound better unless its recorded digitally and theyre all a a d its just convenient cassettes are convenient too but albums have this aesthetic quality that the others just dont have - i mean there is just this beauty about the album - the way it feels in your hand - and watching it spin on the table but everything just has to fall to what is easy and convenient and conventional everything falls to mediocrity everything falls to compromise o brave new world upon us pumping plastic pulcitating pulsing plastic world oh paupers plastic in plastic coffins shit im gonna listen to bam puh dam padumpah dum doom lets see i should have got this on album i have my dads album thats right its one of these plastic cover ones MILES DAVIS COLLECTORS ITEMS god that was stupid MILES DAVIS KIND OF BLUE i love that album that is one of the best albums ever MILES AND MONK AT NEWPORT kind of blue blood on the tracks the unforgettable fire piano wizard live and beethovens ninth **ALL STARS WALKIN** BAGS' GROOVE if i just had those five albums i could just listen to them over and over again forever **SKETCHES OF SPAIN** heres the plastic ones sketches of spain live at blackhawk birth of the cool here we go +19 no this is miles ahead here it is PORGY AND BESS this is the best album cover i wonder whose hand that is cleo lane no sheez not on this one sheez on the one with ray charles cicily tyson werent you married to cicily tyson - oh yeah but that was later - i thought she was an intelligent black woman but she was an ignorant bitch like the rest - is that what he said - something like that - she was corretta scott king in that miniseries - she was in everything her and sidney portier were like the only black people anybody ever put in movies louis armstrong was in singing in the rain not singin in the rain one of those shitty bing crosby movies great society high society not great society great society was johnson bing crosby sucks

did you ever see dances with wolves - no it sucks - how do you know if you havent seen it - one because costner is in it - two because it focuses on the white kevin costner character and he is riding in like a white night to save all the indians instead of focusing on the indians themselves - and three because at the end they just tell you that all of the indians died so that you can say to yourself aw thats a shame without having to actually experience the pain of seeing it happen like in the mission that is what was great about the mission - youre full of shit its a great movie - how could it be great with costner heez the worst actor heez like in the fountainhead when they have the critic and they get in a room and everything thats great they say is bad and everything thats bad they say is great so that pretty soon people wont know the difference - and they have the power and they can convince themselves its like a defense mechanism that they can compete when they know they cant compete with howard roark or robert de niro or martin scorsesse or bob dylan or faulkner or joyce - and costner is just emblematic of mediocrity just a completely mediocre actor who is elevated to some status arbitrarily so that we wont know the difference anymore between good and bad

but what is good good is just relative no good is not relative - good is absolute - good has its own indivisible quality which is not dependent upon the time or the politics or the circumstances which evidences its own greatness - its got nothing to do with enjoyable its got nothing to do with funny its got nothing to do with shocking its got nothing to do with entertaining its got nothing to do with boring its got nothing to do with moral - its a separate quality all its own - yeah but what is it - it has to do with integrity it has to do with the synthesis of content and form its something that can only be done in the way that it can be done - complete it should not require explanation or excuse to tell you why its good it should be evidence of its own goodness in and of itself

and i think it has to do with being true to its form in that it can only be what it can be a poem or a movie or a painting or a story or a building or a legal brief or a song everything has its own form like you cant make a movie of the sound and the fury or ulysses or moby dick and the godfather has so much more than the book there are so many things you can capture on film that you cant get across in a book a lot of people always say that the book is always better because thats what you are supposed to say to be intellectual and all that but a lot of times the movie is better the godfather is better lords of discipline is better the one flew over the cuckoos nest is much better you cant make star wars anything other than a movie you can but its not the same its like music needs the music to support the lyrics if you read them like a poem they just come out hollow and silly and trite even good lyrics in a good song - its kind of like howard roark and frank lloyd wright where each piece of land has its own essence which is only suited to one unique structure - marriage of content and form and substance marriage of heaven and hell

frank lloyd wright may have been a genius but he is responsible for some of the ugliest buildings that have ever been built not just his but particularly all of these hacks that came after him all half cocked that used him as an excuse to build these monstrosity creations

bam puh dam padumpah dum doom summertime and the livin is easy the fish are jumping and the corn cotton is it corn or cotton is high your mamas rich and your pa heez good looking so hush little baby i dont want you i dont want you to cry summertime one of these days youre gonna rise up singing spread your wings and go to the sky and ba duhduhduh hush little baby i dont want you to cry what is porgy and bess hey baby you seen porgy and bess we can make it the two of us you and me i can eat fifty eggs - fifty eggs - nobody ebber eat fifty eggs - my boy can eat rusty nails broken bottles rusty nails any damn thing - he was smilin - what he look like drag yeah what he look like - he was smilin - that ol luke smile - right till the end - and if they didnt know it fore they knew it then that they werent ere gonna beat him - yeah luke was a good ol boy - a natural born worldshaker - badoobadeh dumpahdoom ohyahayah zabim zadam kaka boom kaka tah tah ta tooom buddupadadadada yaya rinnggg hello tim - hey how are you - fine - you home from school - yeah till tomorrow - how is michael - heez doin real good - does he know what heez gonna do next year - no he doesnt know yet i dont know - tell him i said hi - okay - you want something to drink that would be great if she got drunk i could cook her dinner and we could drink and eat and talk all night - is bob here - no heez out of town - im just trying to figure out what to have for dinner - i could make you dinner no we would have to talk for a while she would see me and stop me and then we would talk for a while and then she would complain about being alone and she would have been laughing and talking and really enjoyed seeing me and then i would offer to make dinner - you ever watch that show - yeah that is really funny i love that - did you read bonfire of the vanities and

you wanna stay for a while - come sit over here - god when i think about being in college again those were great times i would love to back and meet her in college i bet she went out with all of these guys but the times were different back then girls werent that promiscuous a lot of women were virgins when they got married - i bet she wasnt a virgin - i bet she was - no she must have had at least one serious boyfriend she probably fucked a few people - did you and bob meet in college - yeah - i was a sophomore and he was a senior and he asked me out for some ice cream and then we went to a dance - i hated him at first - but he took me to really cool places and then i started to like him and then he had a serious girlfriend from before who kinda got back into the picture and we broke up for a while and then i moved back here for the summer i was on vacation and i was getting dressed to go out and the doorbell rang and i thought it was my friends coming to pick me up and but when i opened the door he was standing there with a dozen red roses and he picked me up and swept me away and we got married two weeks later and we have been happily married ever since - totally happy - you never even had like a seven year itch or anything - there was a time when i missed flirting with boys and dating and stuff but it passed pretty quickly - did you ever um - did you ever um have any fantasies about younger men - i was just curious - and i thought well i mean i guess all boys have their fantasies about an older women - and i guess a lot of mine have been about you - and i thought well i kinda thought that maybe when a woman gets older maybe she starts to get depressed starts to feel that maybe she isnt desired anymore - and i guess maybe i thought it might help you in some way to know that you are - desired

you know i had the biggest crush on you in high school - really - you were wearing a yellow blouse and a pair of white jeans - i was in eighth grade and you were picking us up from sunday school and one of the other kids was late and you were starting to get mad - you guys had that yellow and brown stationwagon and you were standing outside of the car with the door open

- and i was watching you through the window from the back - and when you went to close the door to the station wagon you lifted your arms to close it and your blouse lifted up - just a little bit - and i could see your bellybutton - and i have had a crush on you ever since

i dont know if you were wearing a bra or not but it was windy and i could see your nipples perfectly i wouldnt say that and when you went to lift the door to the stationwagon your blouse lifted up and i could see your bellybutton and i have had a crush on you ever since i have just one rule for the vacation - yes - while we are in the room we dont wear any clothes god that would be awesome just walking around naked with her all of the time o god i should say something but if you actualize them they should just be fantasies cuz when you actualize them thats what nine and a half weeks was about - things are great as fantasies but when you actualize them its hell and heaven its got fear and hope and love and all the sexual and violence and transgression it is everything marriage of heaven and hell the apocalypse of everything that is the whole of this world in having an affair im gonna do it im gonna tell her no she would probably tell her husband and laugh about it - that would be cool if you could tell her and she would just keep it as this special secret between you and her that no one would ever know not act on it not do anything but you would just share that energy that connection and no one but she would tell her husband she would definitely tell her husband and they would laugh about it together at you and then michael would find out that would be so embarrassing - so - im sure michael had a crush on some older woman - he would probably have a crush on your mom if she were alive - my mom was pretty

whats on the other side of this thing   Prayer (Oh Doctor Jesus)   jes crew grew jes crew   Fishermen - Strawberry and Devil Crab   black man is the devil   My

Man's Gone Now It Ain't Necessarily So Here Come de Honey Man thats it thats a great song That's Soon for New York i gotta get this thing fixed i would love to just watch her walk around the house naked or half naked i love women half naked not in underwear but like fully dressed on top and naked on the bottom or dressed on the bottom and naked on top like a woman in jeans with nothing on top or slacks - white or black slacks well even a skirt just standing there that is great with not in underwear that is so much more erotic its like a painting or - i love that - if you could just watch people and then make love from a distance doing the dishes or cooking or just watching someone and you could make love to them with your clothes on at a distance so that you could see them in motion in a painting or something and make love with some force the physical part with some forcefield or some energy or something - some gravity - i am gonna learn how to do that after i learn how to dreamscape - where do you sleep - i sleep in teamachus - where is teamachus - its where the sky is all purple there are people running everywhere and then a little orphan girl comes up and curls up next to me like a pup under the stars all diamond stars all green and red and the forests are crystal with this blue white clear crystal forest and these lakes like lakes these green no that would be ugly these red crimson lakes and ducks and geese of white all white against the purple eagles piping into hollows at the gates of dawn and fawns with black red stripes like zebras where on plain they dance in rainy seasons where the monsoons wash and whip and wile across the bitter lakes where pancake husbands laugh with dying children who were once reborn and torn out of the sky the purple sky where milton tomcats rusty nails and bottle chains are laughing with the crows and owls and calling cawks and eagle hawks with earthworms dancing the cut worm forgives the plow

albatross youre an albatross around my neck and
theres an albatross all fluttering in light and sun like a
sun like no other sun a big blue sunset harvest sun and
washed in silver like the moon red moon do you protect
the orphan i do but she doesnt need me where the bees
are swimming on our heads as we are sleeping and the
fish and the cacti - where jumping lakes and turtles fly
up through the air against the purple sky and scrub
themselves beneath their gills where baby blue azure
foam rocks at gates of midnight where the edges meet
the land the universe beyond

goodnight johnboy

here we go - there is a world named teamachus
whereupon the sky is purple and the earth is green - and
from this earth grows acorns of gold and crimson lakes
crawls serpentine rabbits and snakes and upon the earth
grew men whose constitutions bled of the same blood
and pounded the same heart and contemplated as of the
same mind and pulsed of the same veins and were alike
except in the way that one man is violet like the sky and
the other was olive like the branch - and so these men
parted on their separate ways and the one - abraham -
the one violet looked to the sky and it was good - and
what was not was not good and so he created the rituals
of the sky - of the bird - and the plane - and he leapt
about this man who became tribe who became nation
the nation of abraham who had made by his way which
they lived beneath the sky above the land - purple
above the green - and all that is born of the sky - holy -
while - all that is born of the land base - and so the
clouds down to abraham - down to the serpentine
rabbits - down to the snakes - down to the earth and
below - and so it went to the gold and the acorns and
the green and the gold - and so he moved beyond - and
beyond and beyond because it was all on the horizon -
and all the here the crimson and the green was bad but
everything at the horizon was good - and so he travelled

always to the horizon - to the west - across the crimson fields and waves of grain and foam and mist where he came upon the nation of isaac and it was his brother but they had been separated for many centuries - and the nation of isaac was green in constitution - and they had dwelt for centuries upon the thriving green and the sacred serpentine and all the acorn and the tree - and the sky was all purple and not holy not he because god was vegetable and earth and thriving - springing from beneath - the land and it was full of animal and music and song and wine and dance - and so this man was foreign to this nation of his brother abraham - to his conceptions lofty ideals and notions of all the higher things higher up there sacred and holy and above - and so abraham looked to the sky ominous oer that subordinate green in the land and then to his brother nation and threw him down beneath subordinate to his ominous self - so you are saying - i am saying if the ground were white and the sky were brown we would be over in africa digging their graves - its as simple as that - its as arbitrary as that - because its all psychological we dont even know it - its in the psychology from the moment you are born - these faces that shape what must be or what you think should should is kind of a dangerous word you know i mean should you should take a bath you should brush your teeth you should see because youve got these mythologies you have got these mythologies in the eras these dowries of myths when one dowry dies there is this war until the order can be restored with a new dowry - and thats what we are doing right now - trying to form this new dowry to replace the christian myth - because we are no longer in the christian world - because that world died neitzsche said it after the fact with all of these revolutions the french revolution the american revolution and thats the war - thats the end of the monarchy because the myth is dead - why do you think we look back to the magna carta with such importance it was meaningless when it was signed - we just hold it in great stead now because we know that what was to come - we think that they somehow had a notion of that would be a thousand years well not a thousand seven hundred years early and the myth is dead so now we have to secularize government and whatever because we have just swum we swam out of it because it didnt really die because nothing ever dies - its just reincarnated and you had the ancient dowry reincarnated into the classical dowry reincarnated into the christian dowry and now its time for a new one the american dowry we dont believe in god we believe in ourselves

we believe in the law - our heroes arent priests or politicians - theyre police officers gunfighters soldiers the common hero the innocent and noble savage the guy who jumps into the fire - the atticus finches and the george washington carvers and the george baileys that do most of the living and the sweating and the living and the dying in this world mister potter - cary grant in north by northwest - horatio alger the great gatsby from rags to riches the person that can make himself from nothing - our heroes are inventors edison and franklin and bell and the wright brothers and ford - we believe in money - we believe in capitalism - we believe in invention - our heroes are tv people and movie stars theyre common people and real people elvis and john wayne god is dead and now we have all of this new found power but at the same time we miss him - because there is no one to show things to - and there is no religion - and no reverence - and respect - and because we love him

priests are like these old antiquated odd strange figures that dont even belong anymore - thats why all of those ministers developed taking their place - cuz theyre not priests theyre just showmen - theyre just salesmen

youre replacing capitalism for god - thats why you have jimmy swaggart and jim bakker and billy graham - youre taking this old monastic noble ascetic marriage between man and god and you are placing it into the stream of commerce - so that its a good - its a service - religion is a service now you pay the money and you get the service - relieve your guilt - have a place to go on retreat - hear speeches get entertained

and kings are like fools the royal family and all the presidents there is no divine will there is no genius there is no intelligence - they are just like everybody else - which is good but where are all role models now that my role model is gone where have you gone joe dimaggio a nation turns its lonely eyes to you but its not just psychological there are a lot of physical factors - its not all metaphysical a lot of it is physical - like whether you can grow things the climate the landscape the soil because in africa it was so plenty that they didnt need to invent the plow or the hoe or the other tools for agriculture thats why you have so much more advanced culture in europe - because the soil was rocky and it was hard to make things grow necessity is the mother of invention and tools become arms its like the monolith in two thousand and one - and the only reason the americans beat the indians is because they had guns the only reason that the americans europeans got all of the africans is because they have guns - its ironic because now africa is of such necessitous circumstances and everything is starving and dying but historically they didnt need anything the pygmies had so much food that they could take whatever they wanted they never even heard of war but the vikings invented ships and the greeks because they had to get from island to island the egyptians had to invent all of those tools they were first probably invented the wheel there is this balance in mesopotamia and what about egypt because that was in africa on the nile the first great civilization after mesopotamia on the tigris and euphrates - so it cant be that simple - who knows - there has to be this balance - so that you can have enough to be strong enough to survive but it has to be difficult so that there is competition so that people get to the next level and have to invent things - its like two thousand and one

there is evolution but its not physical evolution its cultural evolution evolution has stopped because we can correct any deficiency - people say we will get big eyes but we wont because there is no disadvantage in having small eyes - you can just get glasses you can just get contacts - there is no handicap - everyone reproduces - there is no biological natural selection everything is cultural not internal differences but external because of the tools we use its not that anyone has evolved any race has evolved more than any other race because its got nothing to do with biology or genetics - its just social - its technological - its something that one person teaches to the next and then they can learn it not something that is passed down and weeded out genetically from one generation to the next generation - thats the problem with hitlers idea of a master race because its got nothing to do with the gene pool its got to do with knowledge - and skills - its about knowledge not about intelligence - and there is a religious and mythological evolution - that goes along with this sociocultural revolution - from outside forces to one god who resembles man and now to ourselves we are the gods of our world i am the god of my world - i can make the world whatever i want of it - i miss my parents because i love them but i can do whatever i want now im not in their shadow

isnt that terrible i feel so guilty whenever i think that - but you know - what you know what i miss the most - what - when you do something and you go to show it to them but theyre not there

its liberating but its frustrating - and its sad - its the losing of gyres theyre coming apart like william butler yeats and we have these wonderfully powerful myths and some are returning to the old and rewriting the fall of hyperion and prometheus unbound and faust and then you got these new gyres dowries of irish folk songs but then these melancholic assholes came along and they werent really bards or prophets they were just scientists really and so they got all of their bleak facts mixed up with god and spouting all of this i am therefore i think - i exist therefore i essence and all that crap - because if there is no god then it is not i that i can justify my own actions then there are no justified if there is not god then no actions are justified justification or meaning - so they just cry or destroy or cry or say i dont give a damn - but if life is a joke then the least we can do is laugh - not cry - because the romantic hero and the existentialist hero is the same person except that the romantic hero is romantic and the tragic hero is tragic - but so you have these cycles these gyres as they are called and systems come and go from samaria and isreal and babylon to egypt to greece and rome and the old testament and the odyssey and such i guess there are only three and then they swim into rivers like bulges tides of chaos the huns and goths and visigoths upon their horses black and carry torches to burn the dowries downward you got caligula who said bring me the head and he ate his tongue and fed his eyes to the jester who was vomiting in the baths and he called this woman in to run her lips across his penis while he strummed his guitar while the city burned he watched it burn no that was nero - and so out of all this fire rises - the dowry of nazareth like lazarus because this man was born in this small town to the north where

the wind hit heavy on the borderline and they carried
him in quilts and he rose up on the water to slay his
father with a dagger that he stole from the blacksmith
shop and he cut up his arm until he bled and fell and so
he rose up on the dowry and you have paradise lost and
the inferno and then god is dead and the dowry falls so
they try to bring in the next but some people just have
to hold on like reagan and renquist and bork and jesse
helms and falwell because they are scared - because
here they can be the lion - in a christian world - they are
the lions in the coliseum they eat up the christians and
tell them that its for their own good but its crumbling
and they keep putting up the scaffolding to try to save it
but not even the founding fathers could have conceived
what would be anymore maybe jefferson can but theres
no slavery anymore and now you have also got stanley
kowolski - he is king of his own castle its a world of
thunder and lightning and blanche with all her delicate
pastel lights cannot survive - and then youve got this
system of laws and order and this hierarchy and right
and then its broken in revolution a series of revolutions
and war and suddenly the master is gone god is dead he
isnt up there anymore and there is this great freedom
because he isnt over you now and now i am the master -
and thats the romanticism - but then youve got the other
side - the existentialist - the fatalist - who realizes that
the fact that there is no longer not only god the judge
god the master god the lawmaker king but the other god
is gone too - the provider - the protector - the savior -
and some of them have to hold onto their plantations
and others some try to get back way back to kenya and
zimbabwe and zaire and voodoo like the iliad or the
odyssey or something no cuz voodoo is actually a
fusion of christianity and whatever they had before i
dont even know what that is - and then you got others
that move on for something something beyond a
reincarnation and maybe its gonna start with chaos and

war but youve gotta keep on because because because
you do

because you do

so the black man is the devil - of course the black
man is the devil and the white man is the devil too
malcolm x - he is the devil in our society he is the one
who rises against the white clouds above his head the
rebel and the violence and all the things that are
chathonic and dionysian - the dope and the wine the
chaos and the violence and the war and the rebellion
and he is the criminal and the musician and the athlete
that is the stereotype - is he - i dont know but thats the
role he plays or is forced to play or is expected to play
or pretends to play like a role like an actor because its
expected - its written - and unwritten - but dont forget
that it goes the other way too - god is dog from the
other side - and the white man is ominous and
judgmental and oppressive one law for the lion and the
ox is oppression and we are cloudlike and vacuous we
have no rhythm we have no passion we have no heart
we have no imagination we have no desire we are
stagnant and oppressive and the enforcer of arbitrary
rules and laws we have no culture we have no art but
fake ballet and lifeless petty little nice little things that
do not threaten that do not challenge that do not
encourage one to feel or to appreciate no thats not true
because we have rembrandt - we have beethoven - we
have the great cathedrals and milton and shakespeare
but what about now - what is white culture now -
television - elvis who stole everything from black
people thats where the music comes from - john wayne
and bob hope - bad comedians - sterile books -
senseless television programs - stupid films - boring
food - punk and pop and stolen popular music
ridiculous stupid art - white culture there is no white
culture - culture is almost by definition not white - jews
have culture - yeah we got people with yiddish accents

jewish mothers and bagels - yeah but we got einstein
and marx and freud - e equals m c squared its a jewish
thing you wouldnt understand - i heard einsteins wife
did everything and he just took the credit the three most
important men in modern age were jewish - marx -
einstein and freud or is it einstein freud and christ the
three most important people in world history is with
jesus with modern history its marx actually paul is more
important than jesus - i mean jesus was god if he was
god but paul really made him what he was in terms of
religion - he may have been god but without paul no
one would have ever known - but anyway in terms of
modern life really darwin is probably the most
important - the three most important people are
probably darwin einstein or einsteins wife and freud
and not even freud maybe freud probably thomas
jefferson - those are the three probably the three most
important people who have had the most effect on
america and our life and our philosophy and the way
that we think about things are thomas jefferson einstein
and darwin - well einstein is not that important from a
practical matter on an everyday basis its probably the
person who invented the computer or edison or henry
ford no but einstein or his wife completely changed the
way we think about the world - the theory of relativity
and taking things out of this analog theory and quantum
physics and relativity its like taking an analog world
and making it digital - and then relativity and now with
hawking and the earth worms and the black holes the
worm holes at right angles that time is at right angles -
and going to the moon - atomic energy - that just
fundamentally changes everything - not only physically
but the way we think about the world - thats darwin and
flight the wright brothers no but freud changed
everything about the way that we think about ourselves
- he made us look to ourselves and even though a lot of
his theories have been disproved or rewritten it changed

everything about the way that we think about ourselves - the way we think about the mind - that we even do think about ourselves and our mind - its like moving from judaism to christianity - from one external god to one internal god with three parts the father the son and the holy ghost is like the ego the superego and the id - anyway one or two out of three aint bad when you only have like two percent of the population if that - one or two out of three aint bad

what if you could go back - before einstein before darwin before faulkner and joyce before the motorcar before the wheel before the duchess faced horse - when we rode daft and bareback

but what if you could go back to like seventeen fifty and you could be like thomas jefferson and faulkner and melville and ayn rand and darwin and einstein and freud and edison and whoever invented the train and ford and you could be blake and coleridge and dylan thomas and joyce and beethoven and frank lloyd right and bob dylan and you could write the constitution without slavery without the three fifths and with a prohibition on slavery and with due process and equal protection from the beginning and the declaration of independence and the star spangled banner and all of those folk songs and the marriage of heaven and hell and america and jerusalem and a man for all seasons and the crucible and inherit the wind - and invent the train and the railroad and steel and darwin and einstein and freud and architecture and moby dick and billy budd and the sound and the fury and the fountainhead and the rime of the ancient mariner and the nightingale and kubla kahn - and david arthur alexander elizabeth and joan - and you would have america and canada and mexico as one place from the beginning with the indians and the blacks and the europeans from the very beginning with no slavery and all of those natural resources and all of that land and you would have like

central cities set up connected by railroad lines from
boston to new york to philadelphia to d c to miami to
new orleans to mexico city and chicago and from
mexico city to san francisco to seattle and back over to
chicago and to boston and montreal and each city has a
railroad line and an army base and a naval base and a u
s bank and a courthouse and a federal building and an
arms munitions plant and a mint and a militia and then
you also have one in havana cuba and one in honolulu
with national parks and a great protection of resources
and better liberties secured america its such a promised
land its such an eden and gold and to the west and
paradise - and we shall build jerusalem both heart and
heart and hand in hand

i once loved a girl - her skin it was bronze - with the
innocence of a lamb she was gentle like a fawn - i
courted her proudly and now she is gone - gone with
the season sheez taken - anyway what was i thinking

the black man likes watermelon well of course he
likes watermelon do you like fried chicken of course i
like fried chicken everybody likes fried chicken white
people like watermelon and white people like chicken
its probably because of the cost - watermelons were
probably really cheap and the only thing they could
afford in the summer cuz they couldnt afford to buy ice
cream thats probably where the stereotype got started
its just like the stereotype about the jews being cheap
got started because in the middle ages - because the tax
collectors would come around to collect taxes for the
church and naturally the jews didnt want to pay taxes
for the church so they got the reputation of being selfish
and cheap and also because christians under whatever
edicts couldnt lend money - thats why jews were the
bankers - because there was something in the bible like
its something like neither a borrower nor a lender be its
not that but its something like that - and that was
interpreted as meaning that you couldnt lend money -

even though you can borrow it it doesnt really make sense - so when people needed to borrow money they would go to the jews because they were the only ones that could lend it thats how the jews got to be bankers - and then if they got into trouble they would just come back into the ghettos and slaughter all of the jews - and then they wouldnt have to pay the money back - but anyway - they have these stereotypes do they like basketball of course i do and would rather fuck and steal than learn to read well maybe thats true and maybe thats not but it is a role and pretty soon the roles are gonna change the year two thousand theres gonna be an apocalypse and the roles and the roleplayers will become one or maybe they will just reverse upside down doomsday rapture helter skelter but then then youve got to have something after that - thats what we forgot - that you have to have something after that - maybe a beautiful paradise of gorgeous mulatto men and women who can synthesize both at the same time the black and the white the dionysian and the apollonian the olympic and the chathonic the passion and the reason the heaven and hell orc and urizen leviathan and the albatross the serpent and the bird and we will build jerusalem both heart in heart and hand in hand

which is really the dialectic as thesis and then antithesis and then synthesis is the marriage of heaven and hell but it cant be a marriage which is just a grey blah compromise but something new that gets you to another plane like a child

i have this great desire that everything be all the time at once - i wish everything could be all the time at once i wish it was then and i was that person among those people in that world with that past present and future and those things - i wish i had those powers of motion vision and creation call the roller of big cigars and bid him whip concupiscent curds - let the wenches dawdle in the dresses they are used to wear - and if her horny feet protrude they come to cold how cold to show how cold she is and dumb - let the lamp affix its beam - the only emperor is the emperor of ice cream - and if the dying elephants and milton tomcats call from the beyond - where mountains rush with waves and teams of horses the only emperor is the emperor of ice cream - the new york nightingales and bales of cotton that were gathered long ago do not leave any cloth to sew the withered seam - the only emperor of the emperor of ice cream - and if i were to dream to dare to dream the least of dreams they couldnt miss be counted - the only emperor is the emperor of ice cream

the end of knowledge or worse than that the end of feeling because you stop feeling the fear numbing it just gets to be this numbing pulsing in the back of your brain stopping you from pressing forward to jerusalem or theyve forgotten or maybe we will just blow the whole thing up i dont know i dont care its like a truck an eighteen wheeler out on the freeway and you stand in front of it and you try to push it back but you cant so then you call your sister and you push it again and you cant so you call your brother and your father and your mother and your friend and pretty soon it seems like you have an army of people and it seems like you can move it and you push it back for about a few feet and a few more feet and you keep pushing and you get about a mile or so and then you stop and you push and you cant push anymore and you look and another truck has pulled up behind because he has built another and so maybe you can and maybe you cant because you cant stop the energy the force and thats why it doesnt matter because they keep on - the beauty keeps on - the rainbows keep on - and the forests the emerald forests of the sky are free the way they seem tonight the moon

over china sings again to me - cliffs of honey fall into
the sea but i dont care the war wont last till right do i
know the whole thing i think so - the emerald forests of
the sky are free the way they meet my eyes this night -
the moon oer china sings again to me - cliffs of honey
fall into the sea but i dont care the war wont last till
right - the emerald forests of the sky are free - knights
thats right the knights in armour rode on wicked glee
and yet their torches burned so very bright - the moon
oer china sings again to me - cartoons do you now
name me harmlessly or shattered dreams of i forever
dressed in white - the emerald forests of the sky are free
- athena lend your arms to me i say and manfred mind
me with your might - the emerald forests no the moon
over china the moon oer china sings again to me - the
sunsets lain beyond the shores decree the mountains yet
surpassed its height - the emerald forests of the sky are
free - the moon oer china sings again to me - and so
anyway that was the whole thing so anyway what was i
thinking

life goes on - the rainbow and the forests and the
rocks and the sunsets and the suns and the sunsets and
the waters and rains and the oceans and the streams the
dust and sands and waterfalls the rocks the clouds
volcanoes and the mountains and the cliffs they just
keep on beauty keeps on life keeps on even in the
things not living because youve got this stream and you
can damn it but it just keeps on going until it explodes
because there isnt any beginning and there isnt any
ending i seen the beginning and now i seein the endin
from ocean to ocean to bay to gulf to river to ocean to
bay because where did i begin - the sperm and the egg -
right the sperm and the egg and before that - the testicle
and the ovary - and before that - the blood and before
that the food and before that earth and excrement and
plant light the sun i was always something and i will
always be something and so you arent ever really born

and you dont ever really die its the law of conservation of mass and energy of existence that nothing ever ceases to exist its just changing forms like proteus reinhart who is reincarnated into new life and not just people but all forms of waves and energy and life stories and myths and it might take a billion years but you are gonna be part of a living creature again somewhere somehow and not even in the living living but in the living dead the rocks and the earth and the soil and the energy and the light and the sun and you will be everything and everything will eventually be you of the whole universe is you and you are the whole universe beyond time beyond this time if you could open it up so that it is now everything everything all is one and one is all and you are god and jesus and lucifer and hitler and kennedy and einstein and newton and king you are the sparrow and the albatross and the serpent and the snake serpentine rabbits the tree and the flower and the rock and all of these which are you but not you never not you but you

"you saw it first on n b c" well who gives a shit that is a stupid fucking ad they make such a big deal about being there first what difference does it make youre gonna hear about it eventually if its important and youre not gonna remember where you heard it because if you remembered where you heard crap like that they wouldnt have to make commercials telling you where you heard it from - and they break into the important shows then it really pisses you off - youre trying to watch cheers or hill street blues or something and they interrupt to tell you that we dropped a bomb on lybia or something - well who cares - like i am supposed to do something about that between now and ten oclock - i cant find out about it on the ten oclock news or at least between programs - i mean if there is a storm or something that you have to know about that is one thing but they interrupt tv for any damn reason and then they

run commercials bragging about the fact reminding you
that they pissed you off thats not good business hey
lynn

"what"

did i tell you about the sales gimmick of the
twentieth century

"what"

you know how on cheers sam can only drink spring
water cuz heez an alcoholic

"heez an alcoholic"

yes

"i didnt know that" good christ - of course heez an
alcoholic thats one of the main premises of the show

"thats kind of weird that a recovering alcoholic
would open up a bar" good christ - exactly - its called
irony - anyway - if you notice he always drinks out of
this clear bottle with no writing on it or anything else -
so you make seven up or something and you just put it
into a clear bottle with nothing else on it - itll sell like
hot cakes - the advertising is wide open - what is it - i
dont know - give it to mikey - he will try it - he will try
anything - it tastes great - what is it - its nothing - well
nothing is really something

"i bet people would buy that just like they bought the
pet rock" but i think you have to put stuff like bar
graphs and nutritional information the government
makes you that would be cool if it were just an empty
bottle with a bar graph - but you have to put the
nutritional information - there is no nutritional
information it just has no nutritional value you can
assume the worse - my other idea for a commercial is
you know those bugle boy jeans commercials where the
guy is by the highway

"yeah"

but then the girl always leaves without him it doesnt
make any sense - so you have the chick drive up and
she says excuse me are those bugle boy jeans - no -

theyre levis - cool - hop in - and the guy jumps in and
they drive away together

"thats good"

im gonna call coke and levis - but really except for
that there is nothing to do thats what they dont realize
thats really the ultimate reason why they cant run the
country not just because its our future at stake and not
theirs but also because they think that there is
something for people to do if they were industrious but
there isnt - they dont realize that people are graduating
from college good colleges ivy league colleges and law
schools and business schools and medical schools and
there just isnt anything for them to do - they are looking
for jobs - they want to work but there just isnt anything
for them to do - we dont need anything - everything that
we need to get done is pretty much getting done tell me
what you want me to do and i will be happy to do it - its
not like the fifties - there isnt all this potential for
growth - we have more people who need to be
employed and more things to be invented we have more
things so we have less things to be invented - we need
less things - everyone has a car - everyone has a tv -
everyone has a v c r - and the people that dont dont
have them because they cant afford them not because
theyre not available - not because they need to be made
- we have computers and faxes and telephones we have
enough mcdonalds and wendys and burger kings - we
have exceeded our demand - and there just isnt
anything for people to do - those old ideas are
antiquated they dont work anymore - its not just a
matter of being industrious its a matter of being too
efficient - its a matter of supply far exceeding demand -
you dont need two hundred and fifty million people to
support two hundred and fifty million people - thats
why we have to enter new markets international
markets - but then they are going to grow - i mean that
will only temporarily solve the problem - and all at the

same time its getting faster and more efficient
exponentially faster and more efficient so that two
hundred and fifty million people arent really even
necessary to support five billion - plus you have all the
other people that need to produce something so they
can have money to buy what we are producing - and
why do we want to produce all of this crap anyway -
what does it amount to - its just pollution its just plastic
its just crap anyway - whats so great about producing
something - everyone has put all of this credence in
wall street that we should produce something build
something instead of living off the buying and selling
of others - but thats exactly what we dont need - we
need to produce less - we need more services - we need
more lawyers and brokers and consultants - we need
more people who live off of the buying and selling of
others - agents and consultants and investors and
brokers and advisors - because we cant just keep
making plastic and plastic and shit - theres no where to
put it - theres no one to buy it - theres no one who really
wants it - theres no one who needs it - and no one who
can afford to buy it even if they wanted to - we can
make cars that last so long that people dont need to buy
another car - its just

you know what robert wants to make
"what"
you know how they have those laugh tracks on tv
"yeah"
well he wants to make portable ones so that people
can wear them around their neck
"thats funny" a bing bing bing bing boom bah boom
"getting to know you - getting to know all about you"
oh baby come on and get to know me too you grew
your love grew and mine too oh baby if you get the flu
you know what you can do ill make you chicken sou p
ow all right "michael dukakis is in the news again - not
as a national figure but in his home state of

massachusetts where huge deficits" did you really vote
for michael dukakis - yep - how could you vote for
bush - because he was running against dukakis - see
progressives know why they just dont know how -
while conservatives know how they just never ask why
- thats how i can vote for a pathetic ridiculous
snivelling little fuck like dukakis over a rational strong
decent man like bush - first of all i dont know if bush is
decent bush could be evil he seems decent but he also
seems cold - heez smarter than reagan and yet believes
the same things and with reagan you could just chalk it
up to stupidity - maybe he got that way accidentally but
bush knows what he is doing so maybe he really isnt
that decent - second of all decent isnt necessarily good -
i would rather have someone with good intentions fuck
up than have someone with bad intentions do the job
right - first of all is that the job thats what you have to
ask yourself cuz they know how to have a strong
military strategically and whatnot but is that what we
want and the economy is good but who knows whether
its gonna fuck something else up in the future the wage
price controls of nixon completely screwed up the
economy with all the inflation and stagflation in the late
seventies when they were lifted and the economy just
flows in a natural flow - you can have all these inflated
things but we are selling out to the japanese and then
that is gonna crash and then we are gonna be right
where england is and japan will take over and then they
will crash and it will be something else and you always
have fluctuations that go up and down maybe just some
people get elected at the top and some get elected at the
bottom and there is nothing they can do about it - and
the things they try to do to try to fix it just end up
fucking other things up later - thats why we just
shouldnt do anything with the economy - the federal
reserve shouldnt set the interest rate they should just set
a prime a median number and let the market sort out the

interest rates at whatever the market would bear the federal reserve shouldnt be engineering because whatever they do good now is just gonna fuck up something else later and they shouldnt do anything with the money in circulation they shouldnt constrict it or make it more available they should just basically have it on the gold standard not tied to gold or the price of gold but just a constant amount of money in circulation that always remains the same - and they should stop social engineering - but if you are going to do social engineering then you dont focus on the rich - you focus on the poor - because of the multiplier effect economically the trickle down theory doesnt make sense its voodoo economics because of the multiplier effect - not the multiplier effect but that other thing - the consumption function which is then multiplied by the multiplier effect - because if you give a poor person a hundred dollars he is going to spend all of it but if you give it to a rich person only part of it is going to get spent - a lot of it is going to get saved - it makes more sense to create more demand so that more products can be purchased which will in turn give more money to the companies so that the companies hire more people to manufacture the products and make more money and pay more taxes because you are getting one to one on your dollar because every penny is spent - but if you give a million dollar tax break to a corporation they will hire some people but most of it is going to get saved or paid out in dividends or reinvested - but then those people who get the dividends will buy products - or it is saved or reinvested a lot of it is just paper money - its paper profits - that doesnt get translated through the economy and so if you give a hundred dollars to poor people to stimulate the economy you get a one hundred percent dollar multiplier effect on your investment but if you give a hundred dollars to a rich person you only get a seventy or eighty percent multiplier effect on your investment - it makes more sense to stimulate the economy by creating more demand - plus look at the psychological factor - we shouldnt be saying the government shouldnt be saying we are gonna help the rich first and then the poor people can have whatever happens to trickle down - we should give it to poor people and let it bubble up we should have the bubble up theory - we shouldnt have any theory - the government should not be involved in social engineering it shouldnt be involved in stimulating the economy - but dont you think its okay for people to say as a country that we want to take care of each other i mean obligations aside just ethics not morals but ethics or just charity that we are going to provide people with basic food and clothes and shelter and medical care - i have no problem with that - but thats not social engineering - yes it is - and then what happens during the lean years and what happens as a result of the programs because its going to have some prospective recurring effect its better if the government just stays out of it altogether - well i dont have a problem with it but anyway - if youre gonna do something then you should try to help the people who need it its just a matter of priorities - and what about spirit - what about culture - the culture we have now is the absence of culture - bring it out to the extremes if you look at communism - it doesnt work - well we dont really know if it works cuz no ones ever tried it - russia - no russia is not really communist its more of an oligarchy thats a political term yeah economically its more socialist its a capitalist system - a totalitarian system which is kind of capitalist where the government is the owner of everything - i dont even know how you can have communism on a national level there are too many people aristotle said you have to have more than a thousand but less than a hundred thousand for communism you need to have like more than ten but less than a hundred - you cant really have a communist market - it doesnt make sense - you can have it in a village or a community or a town but you cant have a national market thats communist - but anyway if you think about communism as a theory in the abstract in the extreme assuming it could work it is based on love and sharing and trust but if you put if you look at fascism everything works fine on a political level on an economic level and the state is strong and all that good stuff but thats only with respect to the outside because on the inside everyone is so full of fear and hatred and mistrust that they cant even enjoy it and its based on exclusion and separation and hate because if your eye causes you to sin then pluck it out or your hand cut it off the jews and the gypsies and the blacks and the catholics and the those guys because youve got that health here in reaganism except youve got to cut off the blacks and the homeless and the poor and you got to sacrifice the homosexuals you got to sacrifice the oil states of texas and louisiana and denver and you have to give up the farmer and the small farmer and the trade deficit and the deficit deficit and worse because i dont even care about the socioeconomics because thats only what people do but culture is what people are - the culture and the music and the art and youve got this wasteland now - this yuppy wasteland of plastic music and plastic art and plastic television plastic books and plastic food - and we have to go back or forward the olympic and the conflict between the olympic and the chathonic the apollonian and the dionysian and it doesnt even have to be actualized in socioeconomics - we dont need another vietnam or civil war - but people do have to fight battles and not bullshit battles of today on the cosby show where the winner is predetermined by some self proclaimed upholder of moral decency or some conventional formula or arbitrary code of political correctness and ultimate shit because that age is over -

its all over - its about the apocalypse rapture now the
marriage of heaven and hell and we have to perform
this marriage over and over again through some art or
explication of that war in our actions towards our wives
towards our life and men and women between the eagle
and the ox and the lion and the tyger and the serpent
and the mule and the lamb we have to explicate and
assert ourselves reagan can no longer - in xanadu did
kubla kahn a sacred pleasuredome decree "what" where
alph the sacred river ran through caverns endless known
to man into a sunless sea "what are you talking about"
if i could build that dome in air - that sunny dome -
those caves of ice - and all who came would see me
there and all would cry beware - beware - weave a
circle round him thrice - for he on honey dew hath fed -
and drank the milk of paradise

"what the hell are you talking about"

coleridge

"whats that"

heez a poet

"oh"

a romantic like blake and byron

"oh"

the rime of the ancient mariner - the nightingale -
kubla kahn - christabel

"never heard of him"

well what kind of show are they running at that
goddamn school

"i dont know"

"they probably taught it and she doesnt remember"

"shut up beth"

"you shut up"

"you shut up"

you both shut up "fuck you" i deny defy spurn back
and scorn ye

"what the hell is he talking about"

you have no power upon me that i feel - you have no power upon me that i know - the mind which is immortal makes itself its own requital for its good or evil thoughts

"heez crazy" what is that thing from hyperion "i know - he is" the gods thrown down there must be a golden victory - there must be a golden victory - there must be gods thrown down and trumpets blown of triumphs calm and hymns of festival - upon the gold clouds metropolitan - voices of soft proclaim and silver stir the strings of hollow shells and there shall be beuatiful things made new - for the sky children - thea thea where is saturn

"im trying to do homework - go away"

i could teach you more in one hour than all those fuckin idiots can teach you in a year - they dont know anything - let be be the finale of seem the only emperor is the emperor of ice cream

"youre crazy" "i would love some ice cream" you know that nietzsche said "i thought you already ate some"

"no"

you know that nietzsche said that manfred was the greatest oberman in all of western history - even greater than faust "who cares" "go get us some ice cream"

"yeah go get us some ice cream"

we have some downstairs

"i know"

"go get it for us"

"yeah go get it for us"

Dr. Jekyll and Mr. Hyde haight ashbury greetings from ashbury park A WRINKLE IN TIME   thats a great book have you read it "what" a wrinkle in time "no" The Yearling what the hell is the yearling

"i dont know"

"i think its a horse" is it a horse a male is a colt whats a female "i think its really bad" a mare - really -

no thats grown a calf no thats a cow veal is it a calf i
dont know cliff notes FRANKENSTEIN 3.75 three
seventy five thats more than the book we live in an age
where the cliff notes cost more than the book

though much is taken much abides - and though we
are not now that strength which in old days moved earth
and heaven we are what we are - one equal temper of
heroic hearts - beat down by fate and time but strong in
will to strive to seek to find - and not to yield

did you ever read frankenstein

"no"

you how it got written

"how"

shelly - who was friends with byron - was with
byron at a lake house and his wife mary shelly was
there - and they had this contest to see who could write
the scariest story - so they stayed up all night - writing
their stories - and when they woke up the next day they
each read them all - and mary shelly won

"thats cool"

so there is this war of the bird against the snake and
youve got these birds the windhover and the albatross
and it descends out of the sky and its godly and the holy
eagle and the eagle is the symbol of our country but in
mexico where man is red and not white but red youve
got both on their flag the eagle and the snake and india
the snake is holy and - it is holy there - it must be cuz
you got all those charmers the spirit god is in the snake
and then rudyard kipling an englishman comes over and
he writes the story of the mongoose that kills the snake
because the serpent is the one that rises out of the
ground that dark man the devil the dragon orc who rises
up on his wings against the white english establishment
and monarchy and there you have mans biggest fear in
the world a dragon a serpent a ghandi a martin luther
king a spartacus a cool hand luke a jericho mile - every
time i plant a seed - they say kill it before it grows -

they say kill it before it grows - and i say bah dah dah dah dum dum dah da daahhh i i i i i shot the sheriff - but i didnt shot the deputy - and that is the god of the american myth a secular hero all of our heros are secular not priests but sheriffs and policemen dirty harry wyatt earp astronauts those are the real heroes pioneers - and but anyway if you have a snake a dragon that can rise up that is mans biggest fear fear thyself because man is the dragon it is a creature a dirty creature that crawls along its belly and yet can lift itself up through imagination it is like a great tower in the desert who can look forward into the future and backward into the past but is powerless to move no but i wish it was then and my parents and me and my family and friends and the world and that past present and future and those things

but that is the dowry is the constitution - that is what is protected - that is the bible - we dont believe in god we believe in ourselves but the whole point is to make us holy - its not to secularize the world its to make it more religious - its to hold us to a higher standard to make us and everything around us god - its to say that god is everywhere not that god is nowhere - we should have more respect for each other - not less if there is no god - because there is god in all of us - we have to rise up to gods level not bring him down to our level - that is the point

reverence - reverence - it is all about reverence people have no reverence people need to have more reverence not less - people should feel empowered people should feel liberated its an overwhelming responsibility it is the responsibility of gods and men so lets use it - lets not crawl deep into the caverns of our innermost protective hiding places in our closets and under our beds my yellow in this case is not so mellow everything that lives is holy im bold as love but so anyway we have the constitution which is like the architect of the next dowry the next myth the next gyre which is very revolutionary but at the same time very conservative because they were scared of all that new energy and they couldnt get to the next plane but they sensed it - they knew it was coming - and now it is ready to be born slouching towards bethlehem to be born - its still chirstian though its written differently but theres still no room for hell because youve got all these codes all those codes of the west ten steps and draw mister never draw first never allow yourself to be called a cowboy or a cheat coward a coward or a cheat dont shoot until you see the whites in their eyes and soldiers what heroes soldiers are these days you can go to fuckin grenada and they will still make a bad clint eastwood movie about you

and oliver north who doesnt even play it by the book but its always the overall spirit its how its interpreted thats why we have problems with dirty harry and oliver north who go outside the law but its always ultimately to protect the law or at least the system - but in norths case it was imagined - yeah you cant really compare oliver north to dirty harry - but he is still revered - yeah thats the thing its our values not theirs that are important ultimately and its like the crusades and we have our own crusades its manifest destiny just like arthur is just the king david story rewritten into the christian myth and so we keep going back because we miss the old things because we love them we love the cathedrals we love chivalry we miss chivalry and knights we miss the beautiful plantation homes and the castles and the palaces but they were all the governments and the church but now we all have palaces we have the world trade center and the empire state building and everything else - but we miss the plantation houses because there is a lot of beauty in the old plantation houses the porches and the columns and wells cathedral ceilings chandeliers the oak trees with the spanish moss and then youve got the sacrifices though - lets not forget the ransom that was paid for those houses - for that beauty - lets not forget about the blood and sweat and tears - lets not forget about the whips and chains the burning crosses and the lynchings because a lynching was not just going out and hanging some poor innocent black fuck a lynching they burned him alive while they hung him and castrated him alive - one of the most vicious things you could do to a human and they called the blacks animals - but you wouldnt do that to a dog - if you had a common sense of humanity - they didnt burn them and castrate them - yes they did - where do you think strange fruit comes from - what do you think theyre talking about - thats what smells thats whats burning the strange and bitter crop - go read going to meet the man - really - yeah im serious so lets not forget about the price that was paid for all of that beauty and all of those peasants and serfs in the middle ages when some evil knight would come into a village and rape all the women and burn the fields and raze and slaughter everything lets not forget about the slaves in greece and rome the hebrew slaves in egypt who built the pyramids this whole history is built on the backs of slaves and thats really the thing you cant look at me for restitution - you cant look at me for retribution - because i am not responsible for my fathers sins - any more than you are responsible for yours and even if i were my father wasnt here when you were slaves most white people emigrated to this country in the late eighteen hundreds and early nineteen hundreds with ellis island and all that and even in the time of slavery only a very small percentage of the population actually owned slaves - so to say that white people today are somehow responsible is ridiculous because almost none of the white people that owned or supported slavery have descendants who are around today - plus the fact

that ultimately that position is self defeating because
you are saying that you dont want to be held
accountable for the crimes of others if you are a good
and law abiding black person who wants to be educated
and looking for a job or who is educated and working
and you are saying dont judge me by the actions of
those other black people who are killing people or
stealing or on welfare or on drugs just because i am
black i have nothing to do with that and you cant
penalize me just because i am black for those actions -
that is what prejudice is - so you cant turn around and
say that i am responsible for something that some other
white persons great great grandfather did to your great
great grandmother a hundred and fifty years ago - come
on

what is really ironic is that all of these blacks want to
go back to africa by joining the nation of islam which is
how they became enslaved in the first place - thats how
slavery black on black slavery was institutionalized in
africa after the invasion of the nation of islam and
without that slave system already in place the europeans
who brought the slaves to america and the west indies
never could have done it because they would have all
died of disease smallpox and other disease and it was
their own people that traded their own black people to
america in exchange for rum - so if they want to be
pissed off at someone they should be pissed off at their
own ancestors

there was some collusion sure i wont dispute that but
the kind of slavery that was in america was so much
more brutal than anything that came before and it wasnt
just slavery itself like indentured servitude as a concept
but that culturally they were stripped from their families
and their language and their environment and their god
and then what happened to them in america was so
brutal because in africa it was more of just a fuedal
system or a caste system and in a lot of tribes you are

really generalizing because in a lot of tribes it was very
you had some that were egalitarian and free and all
kinds of different scenarios and you are making
generalizations that doesnt apply in hundreds of cases
but the slavery they did have was more of fuedal or a
caste system and then when they came over to america
there was really that bright line distinction between
black and white and torture and brutality and families
stripped apart and auctioned and raped and bound with
chains and whipped and had their toes chopped off so
they couldnt run away and lynched and burned and
castrated and just that constant fear and violence and
brutality and continued really until the nineteen sixties
we were living in the dark ages

but now they have blacks who fly on planes and
drive mercedes and pretty soon it wont matter cuz we
will all be mulattos and it will be beautiful because we
will judge people by who they are and not what they do
and there wont be too much interpretation into things
and too much or too much labelling after the fact
because all that lives is holy but lets not forget where
we came from shall we - lets not abandon our desires
and our lusts - lets not forsake our passions too much
and our motions and our song and our athletes and our
dance slam dunks and lets not forsake the sky up there
we love so much our dowries and our stories and our
psalms lets not all become robots shall we

sometimes its not as important that you understand
things as it is that you feel "cant stop it - cant beat it -
the original taste of coca cola classic - cant stop it - cant
beat the real thing" one have a bushel and one have a
peck - one have the cornfield round his neck - whats the
matter with the mill - done broke down - whats the
matter with the mill - done broke down - cant get no
grindin tell me whats the matter with the mill - but if
you judge people by who they are and not what they do
thats the thing and thats the problem with criminal law

because it operates based on what people do and the whole point is to protect people from society - who cares what they do - this is not vengeance this is not retribution this is not punishment - thats no way to run a government - the reason we have jail is to protect people and if you have some guy that makes one mistake and kills his wife in a heat of passion but isnt a threat to society then there is no reason to lock him up but if you get your hands on some guy who is just pushing cocaine but heez got a life of crime and heez in a gang and carrying guns its only matter of time until he kills someone so lock him up and throw away the key - but you cant just let people get away with killing their wife and not do anything - why not - i mean if you kill your wife because she cheats on you or you want the insurance money or you want to get married and run away with your secretary you are not a threat to society - the only person you were a threat to is your wife and sheez dead - so its too late - thats the problem - youre looking at actions in the past but the whole point of the law is to prevent action in the future - but you cant just go around arresting people who you think are likely to commit crimes in the future - i know thats the problem - not a problem in the sense of an insufficiency or an error which needs to be corrected but a problem in the sense of an inherent problem - an internal inconsistency - which cant really be remedied

but back to what you were saying before if you tell people that they can kill their wives to get the life insurance money or run off with their secretary then a lot of them will - they have to have that fear that they will be punished - yeah but why - i mean they are in a position to judge their own husband or their own wife - and that stuff is just gonna happen and its really not a societal problem - its personal - so you can just let people kill each other as long as its personal - i dont know - obviously it doesnt sound right - you dont want people running around killing their wives and their husbands but if you look at each individual case the damage has already been done so whats the point - its kinda like the button - it doesnt make any sense to press the button and yet you have to have your finger on the button as a threat to avoid having to use the button in the first place - i mean its a deterrent but its like a threat to do something that makes absolutely no sense for you to do - i mean if we are gonna die why blow up you - it doesnt make any sense but we have to be prepared to do it or at least pretend like we are prepared to prevent russia from doing it to keep us from having to make the choice in the first place - but reagan would do it - yeah he would do it out of spite

thats really the thing of it is spite - and resentment is connected to the issue of standing - if there is anything the government is doing just out of resentment or spite then that just shouldnt happen - like inheritance tax is the perfect example - its completely ridiculous to have an inheritance tax because you are taxed twice on exactly the same money and the only reason we have it is because of spite - because people resent the fact that other people are born with money - well that gives you no right to take it away from people you have no standing just like you have no standing to tell people they cant have abortions or that they cant be gay or to punish people just for the sake of punishment even though it doesnt do any good - we have all these homeless people and all of these abandoned homes so just let the people go into the homes but god forbid that anyone gets anything that they dont deserve - people are so spiteful - theyre so resentful - they would rather spend a million dollars out of their own pocket to prevent someone else from getting ten bucks that they dont think they deserve - people hate lawyers so they want to punish their clients - thats so absurd - people are so resentful of the fact that lawyers are gonna make money that they will completely screw these poor innocent people that have been completely fucked by the government or by companies - and then when they get hurt or they get injured and they go to a lawyer and the lawyer says im sorry theres nothing i can do then people want to know where there constitutional rights are - wheres their due process wheres their right to trial by jury wheres their access to the courts - everyone says its about economics but its really got nothing to do with economics its all about spite

god i want to go back thats all i want i just want to be in third grade again with robert and my parents and destin and mardi gras and jazz fest and football and chemicals and cops and robbers and throwing stuff at cars i wish my parents and great gram and uncle g and the air and the water and no pollution and more ozone more oxygen more nitrogen less carbon dioxide more produce more algae more forest more rain forest more grass more livestock more endangered species more fresh water more iron more granite more sand more soil more oil more coal and i was that person among those people with that past that present that future and those things that music art literature photography av film computer toys games clothes sports stuff collectors items and miscellaneous paraphernalia i wish i had those friendships and relationships with robert and annie and c and kendall and julie lynn and an affair with judy hamilton no would i want to have an affair with her yes no i would send her the letter and she would know but she would keep it secret and it would be just between us and destin and mardi gras and jazz fest and football and soccer and rugby and sailing and scuba diving and band pep band jazz band and s a r and alpha chi and the band trip the float y o washington the sophomore bazaar and party endymion and bacchus and beach parties and christmas party medieval banquets pledge banquets sink nights and bleets pig sticks crawfish boils swimming tubing atlantic city the beach destin mardi gras jazz fest thanksgiving passover pool pong barbques bequests and bleets

god i miss annie i want to go back oh quiet bride of ravenous of undisturbed oh undisturbed bri oh disturbed bride of quietude oh

i want to go back but even as we speak something is unfolding - something is unfolding before us in china even as we speak in america in the oceans in the wind the emerald forests of the sky are free as things unfolding down to me before us even as we speak reagan weeps into his pillow trying to collect his broken baggage shambled crumbs of what was once and lost like broken fragments of a dream

lets kill the fucker and dance on his grave - reagan - heez a nazi fuck - lets kill the fucker and dance on his grave - falwell - heez a nazi fuck - lets kill the fucker and dance on his grave - helms - heez a nazi fuck - lets kill the fucker and dance on his grave - bork - heez a nazi fuck - lets kill the fucker and dance on his grave - farakan - heez a nazi fuck - lets kill the fucker and dance on his grave - north - heez a nazi fuck - lets kill the fucker and dance on his grave - lets pound that broken coffin deep into the earth and let those rusty bones regenerate into the soil and grow into something fertile - alabaster forests black with deep rich soil and olive roots beneath the walnut trees and apricots and basil leaves

no they gotta change things they gotta change everything they gotta throw all those fuckers out of there and get some more intelligent people those goddamn democrats are just as bad or worse than republicans i hate them all - see but we dont even need to have a republican government anymore we could have a real democracy with the telephone lines and the lines of communication we have now we could just elect people to propose laws and then we could all vote on them - and everything is one by one you cant piggyback one piece of shit bill on the back of a good bill to get it through - and everything has to be fair - fair is more important than effective - that is the first thing that the government has to do is be fair - thats its first prerogative imperative thats like the first categorical imperative of government is that it treat everyone the same - rich poor black white christian muslim buddhist atheist jew everyone gets treated the same - the second categorical imperative is that the government should not hurt anybody - even before actively doing something for people it first has a duty not to hurt anyone - and if they do they should pay for it - even more than private citizens and corporations the government has a duty not to do harm - then you do good - thats the third imperative is effectiveness - and to do things well and the first thing they gotta change is the taxes - you cannot use tax breaks for social engineering - because you just cant - and because you do it to redistribute the wealth and do all this shit for poor people and then you do it to give tax breaks and credits to all of these rich people and corporations and the middle class just gets fucked - the middle class just bears such a heavy burden - you cant do that - the government is setting up and promoting a war between the classes - because the middle class just bears such an inordinate burden - and where you have taxes that is the closest - most fundamental - most basic universal relationship between you and your government - and if that isnt fair - or if its too complex - or bureaucratic - or whatever - then everything just multiplies from there - if you cant put the entire tax code on one piece of paper then its no good - not tiny print not a huge piece of paper an eight and a half by eleven piece of paper twelve font times new roman these are the brackets these are the exemptions - bam - thats it - if it cant fit on one page throw it away they just have to say these are the brackets you have three percent everyone pays something and everyone pays something even if you are on welfare you have to give some back - thats stupid - no its not - even if its only symbolic no one can be excluded its the most basic fundamental responsibility even if its only symbolic - and so you have like three seven thirteen seventeen twenty three and twenty seven percent maybe thirty but no more than thirty three - and thats it - no loopholes no credits no exemptions period - well you have to have a few exemptions - yeah you have to have a few you have to have charitable contributions and you have to have education expenses and health care for you and your family - necessary health care - not boob jobs but legitimate health care - and thats it - no exemptions for car companies or drilling companies or sailboats or people that happen to be friends with this senator or that congressman - or whatever - what about a national sales tax - oh my god that is completely unfair - why - if you have rich people they spend more money - they are gonna be buying mercedes and you are gonna be buying chevrolets - yeah they spend more money on goods but they spend more of their money on other things that are not goods - a poor person spends all of his money on goods - a middle class person spends almost all of his money on goods but a rich person spends a lot of money on services on consultants and lawyers and accountants and other nontaxable services and they invest a lot of money - and they save a lot of money - its the consumption function - so they might be paying more taxes in real terms but comparatively they will be paying much less - because for poor people it will be a hundred percent - they wont pay a hundred percent in taxes but they will be taxed on a hundred percent where the upper class will be taxed on like sixty or seventy percent - that was the biggest crock of shit when the republicans passed the tax code saying it was simpler because there were less brackets - its no simpler - its no simpler to figure out eleven percent of your income then it is to figure out seventeen percent - and even a flat tax would be okay its really not fair but it seems fair and its almost more important that things look fair than that they really are because you dont want people to be resentful - so i could accept a flat tax but they should still only allow deductions for those three things charitable education and medical and nothing else - because the government basically is charity - thats what the government is - a bunch of people pooling their money to provide collective services and if people are doing it voluntarily anyway then there is no reason why they should have to be taxed on the same money compulsively - because essentially they will be taxed on the same money twice - thats the same thing with education and the same is basically true of health payments between welfare and social security and medicare and medicaid the charity hospital system blue cross and blue shield and if youre not subsidizing health care then its probably something that should be nationally subsidized - at least for necessary medical care

thats the real problem is that the middle class is shrinking so much and that is when you have unrest every revolution in the history of the world has started with the middle class we think its the poor the poor against the rich but it always starts in the middle class because they have the money they have the education they have the organization and every revolution begins when you have just what you have in america right now with the rich getting richer the poor getting poorer and a shrinking of the middle class because they feel their feet falling out from under them and some of them are moving up but the ones that are left get nervous because they dont want to lose everything so you got that - and then you got the complete sacrifice of all the poor and the blacks and the hispanics and the gays and the environment and the homeless and the violence and the drugs and the gangs and the aids - and its if the right eye causes you to sin pluck it out but thats not what he meant thats not what jesus was talking about - because you cant make analogies to the body plato was always doing that thats why and its wrong because the body doesnt work like society because the body is not made up of a group of independent autonomous beings - i mean there are cells but they cant live apart from the body - a part of the body is nothing without the whole - the appendix the spleen it doesnt have any value except its value with respect to the operation of the body but it has no intrinsic value or life of its own - its not its own ends - the society is in fact is what is irrelevant its irrelevant without the individual - it has no life except for the life of the individuals that belong to it - its just a tool of individuals to improve the quality of their lives - its like the spleen it just helps us to process the blood but its not the same you cant be a doctor on society you cant perform surgery on society you cant sacrifice part of society because you will just be killing yourself - its suicide - its got no value i mean things can be more than the sum of their parts but you cant say we are gonna cut out people to accommodate society which is just a tool of those people which is supposed to improve their own lives - and we have got to get rid of sacrifice - we have got to rid ourselves and exorcise ourselves of the whole idea of sacrifice - we shouldnt make sacrifice holy - isaac and jesus and lambs and all of this sacrifice is so deeply imbedded so that we think its noble we think its holy but god doesnt want sacrifice - god hates sacrifice - if there is anything that offends god its sacrifice - why would god make a lamb if he only wanted us to kill it - why would god make a forest if he only wanted us to destroy it - why

would god make an ocean if he only wanted us to kill it
- god hates sacrifice - god creates things or lets things
be created or lets things develop and evolve because
they are beautiful because he loves them and he wants
us to appreciate them he doesnt want us to sacrifice
them - or maybe he just puts them there for our
enjoyment - yeah maybe we can use them to eat and to
make things as raw materials to create great things and
to live but only what we need - you think he wants us to
kill things so we can make a belt - if he wanted us to
use fur then why did he create cotton - if animals are
supposed to just be food then why do we need them
because plants make better food we can feed everyone
in the world with the grain just in the midwest - the
grain in the midwest can feed everyone in the world a
thousand calories a day but we subsidize the farming to
make the prices stay high and the biggest thing is that
we use it for beef and cattle livestock chickens and beef
it takes like a hundred or a thousand or some exorbitant
amount of grain to produce one pound of quality beef -
we feed more grain to our animals than we do to
ourselves - but youre not a vegetarian - hell no - i love
steak - and i want to keep on eating steak but i think
that that choice is available because the people that are
starving are so distant from me - if i were presented
with the choice of do i eat this steak and this person
starves to death or do i eat this cream of wheat and this
person can not only survive but be relatively healthy i
would obviously choose to eat the cream of wheat but
the problem is distribution - the problem is that he isnt
right there in front of me - and its not to some extent a
real choice because i know the reality is that if i eat
steak its not going to make a damn bit a difference if i
dont eat the steak it will get rotten and they will throw it
away and it wont have any larger global institutional
effect - but if everyone were a vegetarian - cumulative

effects its like what robert wrote hard to change because only cumulative effects are noticeable

we should have steak for everyone to eat like three or four times a year and the rest of the time eat grains but instead we have people like me consuming steak and hamburger and tacos and everything else a few times every week and that just takes away too much at the bottom its like a zero sum game but its so complex - its so distant - that no one is presented with that specific choice - it would take such a concerted effort everyone would have to change if i just stop eating steak thats not going to do anything - so i just eat steak because i love it and its not going to do enough good by just me quitting to make it worthwhile to give it up thats the problem - its too complex - its too big - its too distant - and it takes too many people to make a difference - only the cumulative effects are different like what robert wrote to me hate pollution starvation are always overlooked by society because only their cumulative effects are visible and its impossible to see that one person can make a difference one person can make a difference but only by moving others to act - thats the thing thats the thing that martin luther king does he couldnt do it by himself but he could - such courage he had such character a poise and moral fiber that he compelled others to act together in concert and thats what brought about the change but one man did make a difference because you needed someone with that quality but it would have happened anyway truth is on the march nothing can stop it its whether the geniuses like darwin and einstein and freud maybe they are geniuses or maybe they are just seeing something thats obvious or soon to become obvious and they are just the first ones that happen to see it i want to see something like that what is left to discover like that thats the thing and i dont know what it is and if i did then i would have already discovered it but its going to be someone else

because what are the odds i mean there are millions of
people so what are the odds that it would be me it
seems to happen kind of fortuitously anyway - the guy
that figures out how to make salt water into fresh water
that is going to be the most important person he might
not be a genius in a metaphysical sense like einstein or
darwin or einsteins wife but he will be the most
important for our daily lives like edison or ford i wish i
could go back and invent the railroad and write the
constitution like jefferson and de vinci and melville and
frank lloyd wright concrete and steel and steel i wanna
be your hero - mighty youngblood wishes he was
famous - mister moses just wants someone to believe
you believe in miracles - i believe in you if you believe
in me

you know what i think about martin luther king -
what - that it wasnt really the organization or anything
like that - it was the person that he was he had so much
courage and genius and intelligence and strength and
character and poise and grace that when confronted
with that all of those racists and bigots they could try to
lie to themselves but deep down inside they couldnt lie
to themselves any longer because in the face of martin
luther king he proved to them on some level that they
werent superior - they could lie sure and they could call
him a nigger and a coon and throw bricks and water and
even take a shot at him but when they looked deep in
the mirror and looked at him they knew that it was all
over because the force of that could not come from an
inferior race - anyway what was i thinking

the next plane

but the what is the next plane that is the question -
but its not something you can make happen - it just has
to come to you you cant really plot it out or think about
it - what if there is no next level - what if we are at the
highest level in a quantum sense there is always
progress in a technical sense but what if there are no

more breakthroughs real legitimate breakthroughs that change things irrevocably so that they can never be put back together again not just physically but metaphysically - in the way people think - in the way people view the world - anyway i dont know

she is a pie - who is that - i love her - how can you love someone just based on the way they look - in the beginning there is nothing else to go by - that is the only way that you can judge someone is by the way they look not just they way they appear factually but the way they seem essentially metaphysically - what are you gonna choose by how smart someone is - you gonna take i q tests and fall in love with people with high i qs or how good of an athlete because that is just as arbitrary - whether you are smart is just as arbitrary as how you look - yeah but you need to stick to the eighty five percent rule - thats true

everyone thinks that how smart you are is your essence but its just as arbitrary thats not why we like each other we like people because there is something about them something that they are something that is special - to us or special to us at least - the bells that the children heard were inside them - and if its because of looks we dont even know why we couldnt help it even if we did maybe it would make life easier but its just truth and you are an object of sexuality - i dont know why - maybe because of your looks or something else the way you talk or the way you hold yourself or the way you move - but its something - and its arbitrary - and that is the truth its not good truth or bad truth it is just the truth is beauty beauty is truth - that is all ye need know in life and all ye need to know because when you look into that painting they are going to the funeral and they are never getting there and its sad its you cant break it apart or you will destroy him you have to let him die because if you cut him open you will destroy him but it doesnt work that way does it - cuz

you arent cutting into the essence you are just cutting
into the byproduct - god i dont know - i am lost at sea
out there at sea and its stephen dedalus and he is out
there in the sea and he swims and swims but there are
these currents and waves and if he swims hard enough
if he paddles and paddles like theres no tomorrow then
maybe he can just manage to stay in exactly the same
place - and he is trying to get out beyond where they are
breaking the white foam and the little peaks that spring
up seeming spontaneous from the top and not at all like
the big swells from below and then you are lying on
your bed that night and you can still feel the waves i
love that - thats a good day

"if it doesnt come from you shouldnt it come from
gerber" gerber now thats a name that instills confidence
schmuckers of baby food gerber what does that sound
like it sounds like a baby spitting up gerbers gerbils
rodents or something like rats oo gerber does anyone
breastfeed anymore i love breast feeding its so sexual
not sexual but sensual not while its going on but the
thought of breastfeeding like the knowledge of it is
sexual to think about its sexual to think about but not
necessarily to look at "geo" gee oh owe sounds like a
dying cat gee oh owe what is a geo a geo is a rock i
want to name my car after a rock hmn go get him sam
sams gonna get this guy "how can you account for the
killings" yeah yeah you tell him how "no one has been
killed" a likely story - yeah well man thats the breaks -
you can "can you say that when we have hundreds of
thousands of feet of" bodies "footage" what oh footage
"violence and death" yeah "that is the false creation of
some new technologies" what - come on - but that is a
great idea for some movie or something the government
or something fabricates the news all over america to
induce not induce pro voke provoke a reaction of the
citizens maybe just an attitude a psychology like what if
you wanted to start a war or something with iran they

could show clips of these hollywood clips of these unsolicited attacks like maybe blow up a passenger plane an empty one and make up a flight number and have crying people filmed in the airport grieving family members and airline officials and no one would ever know - i didnt know anyone on the flight did you - no - no one would know - you mean propaganda - yeah propaganda i guess thats what propaganda is but its we could perpetrate so much better propaganda so much more convincing like war of the worlds or something bigger - they probably do that - no way - the only reason they cant do it is that there are so many stations someone would figure it out - not necessarily because they all get their clips from the same source as long as its not on going they couldnt do a war but they could do a one time event - one person would have a purported eyewitness video and that would get put out on every station there would be nothing to contradict it because all of our knowledge is second hand we dont know anything for sure - everything we know comes from tv and movies and radios and books and teachers and films we dont know anything first hand of our own personal knowledge - they could tell us anything and everyone would believe it as long as it looked convincing and there was no one there to break the story

they could do it - they could do anything helter skelter god im tired helter skelter in the midnight sun baby jesus taken on the run everybody better get your gun cuz the fun has just begun

man standing by the highway by the highway in a ditch - lookin down kinda puzzled pokin that dog with a switch - something something something down on highway thrity one - like if he stood there long enough the dog get up and run - wont you tell us - tell us what does it mean - still at the end of every hard earned day people find some reason to believe - bum pa dah - bum

pa dah - bum pa dah - well mary lou loves johnny a
love mean and true - said ill work for you every day
bring my money home to you - one day up and left her
and ever since a that - waits down at the end of that dirt
road for young johnny to comeback - still at the end of
every heard earned day people find some reason to
believe - watches the river roll on - so effortlessly -
wondrin - where can his baby be - still at the end of
every hard earned day people find some reason to
believe bum pa dum - bum pa dum - bum pa dum - bum
pah dum find some reason to believe what was i
thinking

im tired

goodnight guys - im going to sleep

"goodnight"

"goodnight"

see you in the morning - oh god im tired - ive got to
have some music or something or i am never gonna get
to sleep louis armstrong or miles maybe i could put on
porgy and bess or no holiday no i dont want that
orchestration crap jimi no ill never fall asleep to jimi
and dylan thelonius louis blueberry hill - you know
when my parents were still alive we were at the jazz
fest and fats domino was playing and my parents were
there and i remember getting up on this ice chest on this
cart this grocery cart that my dad and uncle g used to
steal every year for the festival and i climbed up there
and all i could see were people all around "oh the shark
has - pretty teeth dear - and he shows them pearly
whites" i had never heard of fats domino before "out of
sight" and but there were people everywhere "scarlet
pillows" and it was like this magical feeling - i never
felt that way before - and like my parents were dancing
together - and it was i think i may be romanticizing or
making it up as i look back on it but it seems now that
that was the first time i ever saw my parents together -
like as a couple - and not in relation to me - and he was

singing blueberry hill "is that someone mack the knife" and when we left we could still hear it in the parking lot and outside the gate walking to the car it was like the greatest thing ive ever seen - ill never forget that day

"in a tugboat - by the rivereahye - a cement bag - dropping down - and the cements full - of weight dear - thats cuz mack heez back in town - yeah - louis miller - disappeared yeah - at the joint of ah miss gish - and mack heat spends - like a sailor - did our boy do somethin rash - soupey todrin - johnny divo - rodney langdin - sweet lucy brown - oh the line forms on the right dear - now that mack heez" its mack tonight - dinner

the rising moon now over my eye now casts the shadows down upon the plane and this third life now knows its silky mane - i kiss the virgin daffodils - and rape the silent nuns who lock their doors to their own selves in fright and their petals blown across the land till dust and blood powder mix all together until they win and rise again and we will tear it down - but do you shun all teachings of god - no i love him

"i found my thrill - on blueberry hill - on blueberry hill - where i found you - my heart stood still" theres been an accident son - beth - lynn - come here please - this is probably the worst thing youll ever hear - its the worst thing ive ever had to say - kids - im very sorry - theres been an accident - your parents are dead

"on blueberry hill - when i found you - the moon stood still - on blueberry hill - and it wasnt until my dream came true - the wind and willow played loves sweet melodies - and all of those vows we made were never to be - though we did part - you vow to me still - oh you were my thrill - on blueberry hill" i wish it was then and i was that person and we were those people among those people with that past present future and those things - and my parents and great gram and bernard and pawpaw and uncle g - and i wish that

things were all - on blueberry hill - when i found you -
ba do do do zang - babadode beep papa zang - bababa
yee yeahhhh....

AN EPILOGUE:

IN MEMORIAM

May 27, 1991

"Goodnight" we say, and strike the pillow to our bed.
The Love Boat leaves its port - the tv droning, windy blinds
And crickets calling. The flies are wrestling with the air, and then
Upon my nose and brow. The Captain calls to Julie - I hear the tv
Now again it rises in the dream I'm having: We are on this boat
And we are eating cole slaw sandwiches, and Wolfie's
Telling us about this deli down by Chester's Rim,
(In New York), "Timmy" someone is saying "Tim".

"Yes" say I, as we brush at the flies. "Wolfie passed away"
Pete's crying, "Wolfie passed away...
He was coming back from this cabin and he had an accident
Oh God! I cant believe this is happening." And Peter left.
The clock was striking 12:00 and 12:00 on Wolfie's VCR

And I'm thinking that it's his - and what that means.

Knots Landing has begun: They're talking about this theft

That occurred in Dallas and I'm wondering if I can heft

The VCR through the window to stop that 12:00 and 12:00.

But I cant move. My teeth are inside my fingers, with a tear,

And a tear, my shoulders shaking; flies about my head.

There should be a fire, I am thinking, there should be

A shower to stop this cold; there should be a song.

'Will the Circle Be Unbroken' And candles. And Hope.

He loved Hope. He smiled and once admitted to me

That he loved her. My eyes close, and I go to free

My fingers, but I cant move. I cannot move and I open

My eyes so that I can look at Knots Landing on tv

Because I really just want to think about the theft and J.R.

- 12:00 and 12:00 still bothers me, but I cant move

My cold and shaking arms - They are calling the police.

J.R. is gonna come from Dallas to settle affairs. There

Are a lot of pies on the show - Let them come and prove

That it's true. Their cries float up to me, but they dont prove

That this is really true, to me. I see again the 12:00 and 12:00,

The EXIT sign, the DO NOT PASS, the pillow and the cane:
The night draws meaning out of everything this day.
He is gone, I say suddenly, why? Why did You ever leave
Us? And this 12:00 and 12:00, and... Can I not cry more than
This? Am I this dead? Are we really this dead? I think
Because I cannot move nor do nor cry nor be as I believe
I should. Oh God! Can You at least help me to grieve.

'Wolfie was a guy' I hear myself saying to the world
Through my tears: 'We had this party for his twenty
First birthday. And people were having trouble
Trying to tell all of these great stories about him.
He wasnt the kind of guy that was doing outrageous
Things, all of the time. He was just a beautiful guy;
As a friend, he was always willing to go out on a limb,
And he always made you feel good just to be around him.'

I cannot move. I think of his mother, and I start to cry...
Why did You leave us? I ask again. Why did You go away?
12:00 and 12:00, the numbers numb my fingers
Frozen yet against the white teeth bone. We need a fire, think I,
We need a shower, we need a song. But I cannot move
This morning. And the shower waits; and I stand and fall

And stand again. Crawling to the thick and heavy
door I wipe my eye
    And fall into the metal, breaking. Cold. And I see
the leaves fly

    Beyond the window where the wasps and winds
Are waking. The birds are swimming down against
The air, now rising, blooming like the grasses
And the ivies and the mosses, now renewed.
But it doesnt work. The clouds are gray and heavy
Through the branches and the sparrows falling
To their nests; the shushing wind falls all around,
reviewing
    Wolfie on the road. It all descends, and brings the
morning true.

    12:00 and 12:00 I see. The EXIT sign, and DO
NOT PASS,
    The pillow and the cane. I try to bring him back:
    The 'Stevie' and the 'Stolie' and the 'Bone'.
    I think about our motorcycle accident, and try
    To remember our tubing trip with Wally, and our
tube.
    The circuit we did with Ben after the stripper
    Came; and Fenway and fires, Skunk Hollow and Del
Tard. My eyes
    Begin to tear, as Boot appears. I think of Wolfie's
mom, and I cry.

    "Are you okay?" I hear; I cannot speak.
    Yeah. I'm just cold. I'm really really cold.
    You know? And I just want to sleep. 'You are
sleeping'
    The voice inside me says. 'You are sleeping. You,
and Ben.
    You cannot move, you're dreaming. See? You're
sleeping'

He says. 'That's what it means to be here.' And I say

(I say to Ben) "What are we gonna do now." And I crawl into my den

Because all I want to do is sleep, so I can dream about Wolfie again.

- Timothy Stone

Dec. 16, 1998

Dear Mr. and Mrs. Kolman,

After the funeral, Ben and I were talking about how hard it was to try to eulogize Mike with an anecdote, or a story, or a quip. I think that the more special someone is, the more daunting the task of explaining precisely why he or she is so special. Part of it is the fact that in selecting one particular achievement or quality, you are, by implication, excluding all of the others; in telling one story, you are leaving out all the rest. And I remember feeling disappointed, cheated almost, when my parents died, at their funeral, because of all of the things that weren't said. The other difficulty is created by the fact that special qualities are special because they defy description. I think we all know, though we cannot, and perhaps should not, describe it, that Mike had a magical quality about him. He was blessed, in some way. He was charmed. Angelic, almost, to the extent that you can describe Mike as "angelic" - but, somehow, in some part, not part of this world.

I remember when our friend was tragically killed at Dartmouth our senior year. And after the funeral, Mike and I went down to the river and shared a bottle of gin. I am not sure that most of the conversation was vulgar, pretentious, pseudo-intellectual, and inane, but we talked for a long time, and I remember that it concluded with Mike saying that there has to be a Heaven of some kind; there has just got to be more to it than "this".

I know that we drifted apart after Dartmouth, but I feel honored and privileged and grateful for the time we spent together, for the things he did for me, (many probably without even knowing), and for being one of his friends.

And I also wanted to point out that, while I let it go at the funeral, it was actually me who dubbed Michael "Bone", (actually Boner, which was later shortened to Bone).

I am sure you know that there are a select few people to whom you look for approval - or blessing, if you will. People whom you really care whether they like or respect you. Well, Mike was one of those people for me.

I know that you feel cheated, and angry, and wronged. But that you also feel a sense of pride. And that pride will stay with you for the rest of your days.

Wherever Mike is, I know that he loves you, and that he is thankful for the years and the joy that you brought to him.

I want to thank you for giving him to us.

And to wish you all the best during these trying times, and through the days that may bring more happiness in the years to come.

It goes without saying that, if you ever need anything, please do not hesitate to call.

Best wishes,

Tim Stone

THE KING

See the proud deer
Drinking from the pond.
The ripples in the water flowing evenly
From his small tongue.
The deer hears a sharp, quick, noise.
He looks up.
He stares ahead and looks all around
Looking, waiting, for danger.
He stands like a king:
Proudest, quickest, wisest, most handsome, most great
The deer runs
Proudly, quickly, wisely, handsome, great.
Five wolves spring from deep in the woods
He was no match for five.
The proudest, the quickest, the wisest, the most handsome, the most great
The King is dead.

TIMOTHY STONE
February '81

THE BEAR

There is some glory on the autumn plain,
Where rolling tumbles like a bumbled ball.
And lighted blades are beaded from the rain.

A splashing through the crystal waters drain
Down through the charcoal rocks that slowly crawl.
There is some wonder on the autumn plain.

A clutching clawing through the black barked vein
Of trees, whose teeming height does form a mall
Of lighted blades yet beaded from the rain.

With tickled stomach, eyes up-to the crane
Who swims down to the grasses with a call.
There is some beauty on the autumn plain.

The wet and bubbled berry juices stain
Dark and furry whiskers combed, and fall
Among the lighted blades yet beaded from the rain.

The night preserves a whisper. A far-off train
Is echoed to the rocky den, a slumbering hall.
There is some holy on the autumn plain,
And in the shaded blades still beaded from the rain.

TIMOTHY STONE

In loving memory of David L. Wolfson, who always made you happy to see him; Allan Jaffe, who left us with such a rich legacy; Bernard Frischhertz, who would have done anything for a friend; Lily Hoffman, who always loved her prince; Harry Herman, Reba Nell Herman, and Earl Kline, who would have spoiled their precious Alexandra Rae; John F. Leyens, who would have been so proud of his children; and Michael D. Kolman, whom I'm sorry never got the chance to experience the inexplicable joys of being a father - he would have loved it so.

ACKNOWLEDGMENTS

I would like to thank everyone who assisted me in the creation of this book, particularly Russell Jaffe, Andrew Leyens, Ben Coleman, Mike Kolman, John Fingert, John Barker, David Anders, Jamie Ellsworth, Bill Chisholm, Isaac and Lilian Kirshbom, MawMaw, Grandma, Mom and Dad, Penny, Elizabeth, and, of course, Karen.

ABOUT THE AUTHOR

Steve Herman was born and raised in New Orleans, Louisiana, where he attended Isidore Newman School. He received a Bachelor of Arts degree from Dartmouth College, where he was awarded Citations of Excellence in the study of Milton and Shakespeare, and won the Eleanor Frost Playwriting Competition with his one-act play, *The Phoenix Sleeps Tonight.* Herman was then named Order of the Coif at Tulane Law School, where he received his Juris Doctor, *Magna Cum Laude,* in 1994. After graduating from Tulane, Herman clerked for Justice Harry T. Lemmon of the Louisiana Supreme Court. He now practices law in New Orleans, with the law firm of Herman, Herman & Katz. His novels, *The Gordian Knot* and *The Sign of Four,* the non-fiction collection of essays, *America and the Law: Challenges for the 21st Century,* first published by Austin & Winfield, and his most recent book, *My Life as a Spy,* are all also available from Gravier House Press.